SNAKE OIL

NEIL EVANS

Snake Oil
Published by Neil Evans
New Zealand

ISBN 978-0-473-65985-1 (Softcover)
ISBN 978-0-473-65986-8 (ePUB)
ISBN 978-0-473-65987-5 (Kindle)

Production & Typesetting:
Castle Publishing Services
www.castlepublishing.co.nz

Cover Design:
Jeff Hagan

A note to the reader: *Snake Oil* is a work of fiction. All names, characters, corporations, institutions and organisations mentioned in this book are the product of the author's imagination. Any resemblance to actual persons, living or dead, is coincidental (with the exception of references to either quotations from books or which are attributed to the author or speaker as the case may be). Although some real people and places are mentioned, all are used fictitiously without any intent to describe the actual conduct of these people or any conduct that may incur in, or at, such places.

Snake Oil salesman: *Someone who sells, promotes, or is a general proponent of some valueless or fraudulent cure, remedy or solution.*

ACKNOWLEDGEMENTS

I want to express my sincere thanks to a number of people who assisted me with this, my third novel.

Thanks to those who looked at the first draft. They include: Mike Evans, Mazhar Kefali, Valerie Evans, Warren Patterson, Ray Patterson, and George Bryant.

Thanks Chris Hayden for your encouragement and very helpful suggestions.

Thanks everyone for your advice and insights.

Thanks also to my editor Janette Busch.

Great cover design thanks to Jeff Hagan.

Cover images: Zulmaury Saavedra, Gabriel, Zac Durant, Ramon Kagie, Mark Panratte: Unsplash.

I appreciate 'my people' at Gaze Burt who allowed me to use their names as law firm partners namely Jane Postow, Marie Mitchell, Jan Crews and Katrina Cheeseman-Skinner.

Thank you to my colleague Jan Crews, the Head of the Grammar and Punctuation Police, for her valuable assistance. (Any misplaced commas are due to my own revisions.)

Finally, thanks to Castle Publishing for their technical assistance and support.

CONTENTS

PROLOGUE

The anointed prophet looked around his environment.

He was in a small room, dark and simple, with a toilet in one corner and a hard slab along one wall with a very thin mattress, which identified the structure as a bed. There were bars across the one small window.

He wasn't dreaming. This was real. He was in Auckland Central Remand Prison.

He sat for a minute and wondered what it was that God had done that he was in this position. He knew it would only be temporary. He had preached the gospel. He was God's man for the people of Hamilton. He was the pastor of a mega church and yet, for some inexplicable reason, here he was behind bars.

Perhaps it was an opportunity for the power of God to be released. He recalled a verse in the Bible that told him that those who lived godly lives would be persecuted. In his eyes, he was as godly as the next person.

It was time to put his training into practice as he recalled the time he had spent in Memphis with his great mentor, the Reverend Carl Quincy Adams.

Yes, he wouldn't be bound by his circumstances and, as he had preached to so many people in the past, he would preach to himself. It was time for him to declare that he was free, that the imprisonment was merely temporary and that God would surely move. After all he was a child of God, so God was bound to act as he declared.

"I speak and declare freedom over my life. I will not be bound, nor will I be in chains. I am free and I command these walls to come down."

He sat on the bed satisfied that God would indeed do what he had bid. After all, wasn't the Apostle Paul delivered from prison by a powerful earthquake?

Like Jonah sitting down watching what he hoped would be the destruction of Nineveh, he waited to see what would happen, as a man full of faith and confidence.

Where did it all begin?

CHAPTER 1

While Lorna Smith groaned in agony as the contractions increased, she managed to say to her husband, who was nervously standing alongside the bed in the delivery room of Hamilton Hospital, "I have a good feeling about this child. I believe he will have a prophetic anointing. We have to name him Joseph after the prophet."

Lorna and Steve, her husband, attended the Church of Jesus Christ of the Latter-day Saints at the temple in Hamilton, but despite the strict church requirements they were not always regular adherents. Steve struggled with the theology and managed to keep some of his vices secret from the other members. In particular, he was cursed with a love of coffee, whether it was an espresso, a flat white or a mocha. He had mostly succeeded in hiding this addiction, although his wife had caught him out a couple of times and reprimanded him severely. Since then, he'd managed a number of different ways to conceal this sin. His best practice was to grab a coffee on his way to work at a café hidden down an alleyway. Knowing most of the congregation, and where they worked, he knew the chances of anyone seeing him would be remote.

His other vice was that he liked a weekly poker night with some of the boys from work. His excuse to Lorna was that Tuesday was a day he had to work late and this was better than bringing work home. Occasionally, when he had some good winnings, he would magnanimously give some of the cash to Lorna and tell her the boss had recognised his hard work with a small bonus. Lorna was a trusting soul. When there were shortages from his inevitable losses, he managed to fob her off, telling her he'd put too much into the church offering or the car had cost more to repair than it had.

Joseph was to be their fourth child, being blessed with three older sisters. Steve was excited that they would finally have a son. The girls were 'girlie' girls and didn't enjoy camping, fishing or other outdoor activities despite Steve's encouragement to head them towards these pursuits.

Steve and Lorna had married when Lorna was 19 and Steve 21. Joseph would be born while Steve was still a young man, at 29.

The contractions were coming quickly now and Lorna moaned deeply before she gave a sustained heavy push. The midwife, Sandy Thomas, who was a recent graduate, was distracted, looking at the heart monitor and Lorna's blood pressure reading, not realising the baby was coming so quickly. She hadn't seen such a quick labour during her short time in her profession.

Suddenly, Joseph Smith made his dramatic appearance into the world and, as he would later say, his birth was nothing short of miraculous. The truth was that Lorna's final push expelled the baby so fast he slipped off the delivery room's bed and was heading for an ignominious drop onto the black and white tiled floor below. Whether he would have dangled off the edge while being held by the umbilical cord was a moot point, as the placenta had detached at the same time.

Steve became the unexpected hero of the day. Seeing what was unfolding, and not really believing it, but nonetheless acting instinctively, he dived to the end of the bed making a one-handed catch that would have been the envy of any professional cricketer. Being a second string wicketkeeper for the first eleven at Hamilton Boys' in his youth had finally proven useful. He almost yelled out 'howzat' but fortunately stifled his enthusiasm just in time.

At the head of the bed Lorna let out a scream, whether from delivering the baby or realising he had slipped off the bed was undetermined. She knew what had happened and was horrified that the birth of the prophet might be immediately be followed by the death of the prophet. Having seen Steve dive to the floor out of the corner of her eye, she could only hope her baby would be miraculously saved.

A few seconds later Steve held his catch up and presented the beautiful new baby to his relieved but near hysterical mother. The young midwife was similarly relieved and wondered how she would account for this incident on her birthing report.

Once Lorna composed herself, she exclaimed, "I knew it, this child is special and already the devil has got it in for him."

Steve had no such thoughts but was just grateful he had made the catch. Despite being a backsliding Mormon Steve didn't think too much about either the devil or God. So, he put the events of the last few minutes down to his natural quick reactions and his five years of after-school training in the cricket nets.

Matters soon returned to normal in the delivery suite and the rather nervous Sandy Thomas asked Steve and Lorna whether they intended to make a 'fuss'. Steve saw the immediate opportunity to gain some pay off but, when he saw Lorna glance at him, he knew this was neither the time nor place, and agreed that nothing untoward had happened. If anything did happen there would be no further action that would be taken.

Despite being a slack attender at church Steve had learned some biblical principles so, on this occasion, he spouted off to the midwife that he believed, having regard to all the circumstances, he should exercise patience and overlook the offence.

Sandy was so relieved; she wondered how she could make it up but Lorna nipped that in the bud and simply said, "You could come to his first birthday celebration in a year's time as we Latter-day Saints don't practise infant baptism."

Little Joseph, none the wiser of the events of his birth was thoroughly normal and, after two days in the hospital, was sent packing to his home in Temple View, Hamilton.

CHAPTER 2

The young Joseph Smith (Joe to his father, but always Joseph to his mother) had a singularly unremarkable first year of life, managing to be entirely average in all the critical development milestones, such as height, weight, sight and hearing. His parents immunised him against all the childhood diseases. Lorna was a practical woman as well as a spiritual one and realised there was no sense in listening to the crazy message of the antivaxers.

Despite Steve's middle name being Cornwallis (Steve's mother had a wicked sense of humour and named her third son after General Charles Cornwallis, who surrendered to George Washington in the revolutionary war), there was no way Steve or Lorna would make a 'negative confession' thereby in their minds dooming their son to a life of failure. They had to speak and embrace positive words because they believed there was power in the tongue to bring about what was spoken. Therefore any suggestion of Cornwallis as a middle name was assigned to the rubbish bin where it belonged.

Steve hadn't bothered to learn history and it was only at a quiz night a few years before Joseph was born that he'd learned about the heritage of his middle name. His mother only laughed when he confronted her. He decided he wouldn't change his name by deed poll and would succeed despite his name. In fact, it turned out that General Cornwallis had, in fact, been quite successful, having served as a civil and military Governor of Ireland where he helped bring about the Act of Union that created the Kingdom of Great Britain and the Kingdom of Ireland.

Steve and Lorna decided no middle name was necessary, so he

remained Joseph Smith. There had been some debate as to whether a more 'Christian' middle name would have been appropriate. Lorna had heard about the group at Gloriavale where the leader had used the name 'Hopeful Christian' but Steve firmly vetoed this. He said young Joseph would end up being picked on at school and, if he really did have a 'prophetic anointing', then this didn't need any further embellishment but would be fully revealed in God's time.

Joseph's first birthday came around all too quickly, and the young midwife, Sandy Thomas, found herself at the modest three-bedroom house of the Smith family on Saturday 28 March. She wondered how the first year had treated the little 'miracle' baby whose birth circumstances would not be talked about.

She knocked on the door and it was opened by a young girl aged about eight. "Welcome to the party," she said, as she invited Sandy in.

The house was packed with young and old mainly conservative looking people who were dressed modestly and, in Sandy's view, had old-fashioned haircuts.

As the party got under way the only drinks on offer were herbal teas and fizzy drinks. She remembered now that the Smith family was Mormon, so it had been appropriate that the family had named the baby Joseph.

Steve made a speech. "Thank you all for coming. Today is a special day as we celebrate our 'miracle' baby becoming one year old. I just hope he will be a special baby and like how the Bible described the early life of Jesus: 'He became strong and was filled with wisdom and the grace of God was on him'. Lorna and I value your support and encouragement as we seek to bring him up in the ways of God. Well, as a man of few words, enjoy the party and thanks for coming."

"It seems to me that Steve Smith could start with himself first and get some wisdom. After all he is not all that regular at our meetings. Not much of an example to his son if you ask me," said one elder to another and overheard by Sandy.

Sandy made her way to Lorna as, apart from Steve, she was the only person in the room she knew.

Making small talk she inquired of Lorna how little Joseph was doing.

"Oh, he's surely a remarkable child. Ever since his miraculous birth he has been doing so well. Here, I am sure you would like a cuddle."

As she handed the recently-woken baby to Sandy, Joseph took one look at her, started crying, then immediately threw up all over her.

"My goodness, I don't know what has got into him. He's usually so agreeable, babbling on in his baby talk all the time. I am sure he will make a great preacher someday."

Sandy quickly handed back the baby and decided to be brave and go and talk to someone else. She hoped the rest of the crowd were not all religious nuts like Lorna Smith. On her way through the crowd to the bathroom she was intercepted by Steve who slyly said that he would escort her to the bathroom where she could refresh herself.

Steve led her through the throng and to the one small bathroom in the place taking her in and locking the door behind him.

"You don't want to be annoyed by people while you are cleaning up that mess. Here let me help you." With that, he quickly took a facecloth and began to wipe her neck.

Fortunately, Sandy was not the sort of girl who could be taken advantage of. She grabbed his hand firmly and said, "Don't you try anything or I will scream so loud you won't know what has hit you."

Steve was quite surprised as he'd found opportunities in the past to 'play around' a little and, after all, he was only after a bit of fun.

"Sorry, I don't know what you mean; I was just trying to help clean my son's vomit off you."

"Yeah, right. I think I am quite capable of cleaning the mess up myself. Now, we are even. I won't say anything to your church people about this little incident and I trust you will continue to not say anything about the circumstances surrounding Joseph's birth. Now why don't you leave and let me clean myself up."

This was not the result he'd hoped for but Steve knew he was cornered and readily backed off thinking, you win some and lose some.

Sandy cleaned up, went back to the party, and tried to enjoy herself as if nothing had happened.

She got talking to a young woman who seemed interested in her family but, on further digging, Sandy thought she was only going to push forward an agenda of genealogy and baptism for the dead, which to her seemed quite weird. She held her tongue about the incident that had almost occurred and figured if she was going to say something it was not to the over-earnest young woman.

CHAPTER 3

Several years after Joe's birth another baby was born, this time in the North Shore Hospital maternity ward. There was no drama, and the birth was a natural one without complications.

The proud parents named their third daughter, Yvette, who was fortunate to be brought up in a middle class family where there was no lack of food, clothing or other necessities.

Indeed, she was given plenty of clothes, which were handed down from her older sisters. So, from an early age, young Yvette determined that when she was older, she would be her own boss and able to buy her own clothes whenever she wanted.

While the family were comfortable, they were not able to have overseas holidays every year as was the custom of some of their neighbours in the affluent suburb of Mairangi Bay.

Again, this motivated the young Yvette, so in due course, she would strive to be successful to grab a slice of all life's trimmings. As it turned out, she was blessed with a keen intelligence coupled with good looks. She would do well at school as she was very determined to succeed at everything she'd tried.

Her parents were nominal Catholics and she was brought up in that faith. However, by the time a decision for high school was made Yvette's parents considered a state school a preferable option as education was more important than religion. In their eyes she had been sufficiently indoctrinated during her primary school years.

As Yvette was growing up, she was very attractive and was soon gathering attention from all manner of boys. The parents decided that an all-girls secondary school was necessary so she was duly enrolled at Westlake Girls' High School in Milford, a short bus trip from her home in Mairangi Bay.

She enjoyed her school years and excelled at drama, receiving a commendation for her performance as Lady Macbeth in the Scottish play.

After leaving school she enrolled in law school at the University of Auckland. It was only after her father's promotion in a large insurance company that the family moved to Hamilton where she was able to transfer to the Faculty of Law at Waikato University.

CHAPTER 4

Back in Hamilton, Steve Smith struggled to provide for his family and never got ahead financially. Initially, he was working as a life insurance salesman and often made good profitable sales, which provided him with a comfortable income. However, one downside to selling life insurance was that if another salesman later persuaded the client to swap to a different insurance company, then Steve would find himself owing money to the other company as a claw back. Most of the first year's premium went to the salesman and this became a problem if the money had not been saved and needed to be repaid.

Steve tried other sales jobs but, again, didn't do so well, only staying a few years in each job, blaming management or the lack of opportunities for moving on.

Despite the setbacks he was determined to see young Joseph succeed. He was a hands-on dad who took Joseph on camping trips on the back lawn and, as he got older, they travelled to different regional parks in Auckland where there were plenty of good beaches with camping grounds. Wenderholm and Sullivans Bay at Mahurangi West were favourites.

Time sped by and Joe grew into a tall, dark haired, good looking young man, confident and outgoing, with a smile that could melt the hearts of little old ladies. His father readily saw the talent in Joe and that he would become a better salesperson than he could ever be.

Steve, was in fact quite surprised at Joe's latent entrepreneurial skills. As a 10-year-old he had started selling the pine cones he'd collected. They made great fire starters as Hamilton was renowned for its cold winter mornings. It didn't take long before Joe realised that he could make much more money if he paid his friends to collect the pine cones, then he only needed to act as the salesman.

With his practised cherubic smile, and knowing some of his mother's friends were soft touches, he had no trouble in selling what his five friends could find for him. He soon collected a reasonable amount of money, surprising his father with how much he'd saved.

"I'm going to have a Porsche 911 before I am 20," he explained to his father one day after selling out the whole supply of pinecones.

"Well, you'll have to sell more than pinecones to pay for that," his dad encouraged.

"What else could you sell?"

Young Joe's next venture was to collect and arrange other collectors for empty bottles after rugby games on a Saturday. It was not nearly as profitable, as Joe's friends were well aware of the refund available per soft drink bottle so most of them were unwilling to be conscripted to that particular venture. However, sometimes he had a double payday as he noticed that when bottles were handed in for a refund the empties were inevitably stored outside at the back of the shop. If no one was looking he could appropriate a bagful then wander off to the next local shop along the road and cash them in again.

Picking field mushrooms and blackberries in season were also profitable activities but the Porsche was still a long way off.

He even set himself to work hard on the local golf course as a caddy, for which he was paid a princely sum of two dollars or, if lucky, five dollars for the 18-hole round. This income was also supplemented by finding golf balls and selling them. Sometimes he would see where one of the four players had hit the ball into the rough and would help look for the 'lost' ball. More often than not he would find it and pocket it. Eventually the golfer would give it up as lost and play another ball. It was easy to find golf balls if you knew where to look.

For his eleventh birthday his family bought him a magic set and he soon became skilled at various card tricks and other sleight-of-hand magic, enthralling his little group of friends who thought he was quite talented. He even learned how to produce a rabbit from a top hat. His sister, Debbie, had to get used to her pet rabbit being borrowed on Saturdays when Joe was sometimes invited to little kids' parties to do magic tricks. He would earn between $10 and $20 for an hour of tricks, which he felt was a very good reward for his time and effort. He was also developing his show business technique of enthusing the crowd and winding them up.

"Gather round folks and see the razzle and dazzle. Come and be amazed as a rabbit appears from nowhere. Watch as the magic appears before your very eyes. I present to you the one and only Joseph Smith all the way from Temple View Hamilton."

The hype and the razzamatazz was a necessary part of his act as the crowd of kids had to be momentarily distracted while he worked his magic.

As he grew older other opportunities presented themselves and Joe was always keen to put his ever-increasing skills to the test.

His mother encouraged him to do well at school but he never rose above the median, doing just enough to pass the necessary exams. Joseph repeatedly told his mother that he was wasting his time at school as there were no business classes that could teach him anything useful. Despite his protestations Joseph remained at school until the end, and, not surprisingly, was voted 'most likely to become a millionaire' by his classmates.

His teen years had seen some turmoil in the Smith family. Steve's indiscretions, being both sexual and a flagrant disregard of church ordinances, playing poker and drinking coffee, being the more easily proved offences, became a turning point in this family. Rather than face the angst of 'church discipline' Steve walked out of the Church of Jesus Christ of Latter-day Saints and the children followed. Lorna was dismayed but she remained steadfast and refused to separate from Steve gaining comfort from the well-meaning folks at her church.

It was difficult to counter the argument, "If Dad doesn't have to go to church, how come we have to?" Lorna, however, remained faithful and kept attending on her own for a while. It was difficult and she would have preferred that Steve 'man up' and face the music of his indiscretions, but Steve was too proud and stubborn, simply annoyed that he had been found out.

Over the months that followed Steve was constantly blaming God for his misfortune and naturally enough, this rubbed off on Joe who was secretly quite pleased to have left the life he'd felt was a sham behind him. He'd been introduced to alcohol at various school parties and could see this would be a problem if he remained in the church. Joe was wise enough to keep this little vice a secret from his mother who still constantly reminded him that he would one day soon become a great prophet with a new 'anointing' that would surely see him achieve great service in the kingdom of God.

'Whatever,' Joseph thought to himself.

He loved his mother dearly and certainly didn't want to disappoint her despite her constant reminding him of his future 'anointed' status. It had got to the stage growing up that his sisters routinely called him 'the prophet'.

"What would the prophet like for breakfast today? Does the prophet want some help with his homework? Did the prophet make any miraculous catches at cricket today?"

It all became rather tedious and annoying but being good natured Joe soon learned to ignore them.

CHAPTER 5

University was not for Joseph as he was still many years away from obtaining the elusive Porsche 911 and couldn't see how some wasted years would help fulfil that ambition. He also factored in that having a student debt would quickly send him backwards financially.

Having recognised Joe's entrepreneurial ability many years ago, Steve managed to persuade an old friend, Sam Young, to take him on as a used car salesman.

Like a dog with a bone, Joe couldn't believe his good fortune and lapped up knowledge and skills so quickly that within three weeks the boss recognised that he had some serious talent on his hands, irrespective of Joe's youth. He seemed to be a natural salesman.

With the gift of the gab and his smile with perfect teeth Joe was soon selling more cars than his boss. The two of them were both very competitive and the monthly sales charts generally showed a close result with Joe beating his boss narrowly on many occasions.

They had a good rapport with each other and Sam Young believed Joe was going to go far so it was not long before he took Joe into his office to make a proposition.

"Joe, I've been thinking. How would you like to run the yard on your own? I reckon I could open a yard on the other side of town and between us we could sell twice as many cars."

"Okay, Sam, sounds good, but what about payment for the extra responsibility?"

"Yeah, right. There is basically no extra responsibility. You have been staying late and locking up. You even man Sundays when I go fishing so I am sure I don't know what you are talking about," said his boss dismissively.

"I know you haven't achieved the Porsche yet but how does 40% of the gross profit on each vehicle sound? You could make serious dollars on that. You know how easy it is to buy a $1000 trade-in vehicle, spend $500 tidying it up to warrant of fitness standard and then flick it off for $4500. There is $1200 for you right there."

"I don't know," replied Joe.

"There is also the non-profitable stuff I have to do. That will eat into my time and I will have to work longer hours to get everything done."

Sam knew exactly what Joe was doing and was quite pleased to see his negotiation skills at work. He had, of course, been prepared for this so he went right back to him and 'reluctantly' agreed at 45%.

"50% and it's a deal," replied Joe.

"You're a hard man, but I like you and, yes, let's give a trial for twelve months and, if it works out, 50% is agreed."

This was of course what Sam was prepared to pay all along and Joe was well aware of the strategy but nevertheless the game or charade had to be played out to its inevitable conclusion.

"Oh, there is one more thing," Joe retorted.

"What's that?"

"At the end of the 12 months if my sales are higher than yours, then sell me the business. No money up front and you get 10% of gross profit on each vehicle for as long as I own the business."

Sam had been in the business a long time and by quickly doing the calculations realised that if this kid kept up the kind of sales he had been achieving, Joe would provide Sam with a decent retirement income just with the 10% and he wouldn't need to worry about the overheads of the lease, advertising and the like.

"No way, my friend. You'd be getting a profitable business with no payment up front. I could easily get $250,000 for this little yard if I were to sell it. However, I like your balls so if we make it 20% you have got yourself a deal."

Even at 20% Joe recognised this would still be a great opportunity and after a quick comeback they shook hands at 15%.

CHAPTER 6

Joe had a new lease of life and was desperate to succeed.

He had the opportunity of a lifetime at such a young age and was determined to make some serious money. It was all in his hands how much he could make.

He was at the yard early each morning making sure the cars looked their best. He refined his skills at covering over little dings and disguising rust. He was often found on the premises late at night working on cars and finishing the paper work.

To get rich quickly, Joe decided a few short cuts were in order. One summer morning, Joe thought God must have been smiling down on him because an elderly gentleman in a very tidy 1972 Mercedes 250C W114 came into the yard wanting a more modern, smaller car to replace the older one.

Joe introduced himself to the man and quickly discovered the car had been imported new and had relatively little mileage for its age. Joe immediately recognised the car as a sought-after and valuable collector's model and hoped the old man didn't realise this. Joe had a very careful look at the car and suggested he take the car for a short drive around the block and back again to see how it was running as older cars sometimes had issues. The customer made no objection and Joe pointed him in the direction of where his more modern cars were parked before picking up his small backpack and driving up the road. What a superb car.

Carefully bringing the car to a stop in a small side street Joe looked around circumspectly, and seeing no one, he opened the fuel cap and proceeded to remove a small bottle of 2 stroke oil from his backpack and poured some into the tank.

On the return drive back to the yard Joe noticed the desired effect of blue smoke exiting the exhaust, and the motor running roughly.

"Oh dear," remarked Joe on his return.

"Looks like the motor is suffering as it's blowing a bit of smoke," he said, as he got back into the car and revved it up.

"It seemed good to me before I came out," retorted the old man.

"Well, that's the thing with these older German cars, you never know when they might start to cause trouble and they end up costing quite a bit to fix as the parts become harder to find."

Finally, the old man was persuaded, and Joe offered him what he considered a very reasonable price and, in effect, swapped his car for a tidy automatic Toyota that was only two years old, with Joe pocketing a very tidy profit.

This modus operandi became quite common for him, and there were other 'tricks of the trade' to increase the value of the various trade-ins that came his way.

One common trick was to find a European car where the odometer only went to 99,999 km before flicking back to zero. Unsuspecting customers really had no idea of the true mileage of the car and, even if the car had done 240,000 km. Joe could readily sell it as having done only 40,000 km, especially if it was a one-owner car and Joe could manufacture an interesting back story. To help with the deceit Joe would make sure the upholstery was tidy, replacing the rubber on the brake and accelerator pedals and ensuring the handle of the handbrake was replaced with a new one. New tyres were added to equate with the new mileage. Seat belts were another giveaway so these had to be replaced to complete the illusion.

Such cars were not always easy to find but when he did find them he made use of the small garage he had on site and, with the older cars, was able to attend to 'odometer corrections' to increase the value of the cars. The models with digital odometers were a little more difficult but he had a colleague who was a hacker and, for the appropriate fee, could readily achieve the desired result of making an old car new again.

With this and other dishonest means Joe was able to substantially increase his profit margins and see the business flourish. However, he couldn't be in all places at once, selling and prepping cars for sale as well as dealing with all the paper work.

He was making a lot of money but, on the other hand, he would make more if he was not bogged down with the various administrative tasks. It was simple enough to conclude that doing administrative work was not the most profitable use of his time. Paying someone else to do it would free up more time to source vehicles, have them prepped and sell them.

It was, therefore, quite fortuitous that Yvette Carlisle walked into his office one chilly early autumn morning. Joe thought he had seen a vision. Yvette walked confidently on her high heels, undid her black woollen coat to reveal a body hugging bright red dress and smiled coyly at Joe. She had long dark hair, almost black, and piercing green eyes. For a minute Joe was almost hypnotised as he took in this mirage of beauty.

"Good morning, ma'am, Joe Smith. How can I help you?" he said as he stretched out his hand to shake hers.

"I am here to buy a car. A friend of mine said you would look after me," she said with a twinkle in her eye and a seductive smile.

"Well, what kind of car did you have in mind? A convertible, a sports car or something a bit more practical?"

"I kinda like red as a colour," she replied as she took her coat off. She turned around, bending over with her back to Joe as she placed the coat over a chair."

Joe wasn't sure, but he could have sworn he saw a little twitch of her backside as Yvette was turning slowly back to face him.

"I have got this great little Mini Cooper S in red that was just recently traded that you might like. Let's have a look at it. It's not quite ready as it has a few paint scratches I'd have to get tidied up but we should go for a test ride and see what you think."

Moving out of the small office, Joe quickly locked it and put up a temporarily closed sign indicating 'back in ten minutes' and escorted Yvette down to the rear of the lot where the Mini Cooper was parked.

"Oh, it's lovely," she exclaimed.

"She's not just lovely on the outside but has great performance. She's got 168 brake horsepower and will get you to 100 kph in just under seven seconds. If you are daring enough, you might get her up to 200 kph. Are you looking for that kind of performance?"

"Most of the time I like it slow and steady but occasionally a quick and hard acceleration is good."

Joe's heart started to beat a little faster and he looked at Yvette as he opened the door. He would have to be careful with this little minx or she would take the car for free the way she was playing up.

"Do you live locally or are you just passing through?" Joe asked.

"I've moved down from Auckland to Hamilton just last month and am enrolled at Waikato University in their law programme."

"Well, since you probably don't know your way around town, how about I drive you out and about and then you can take her home."

"Sounds good to me," she replied buckling herself in as Joe eased the Mini out on to the main road.

"Do you like the sound?" he said, as he quickly revved through the gears before dropping back to second gear as he entered a 25 kph corner, then quickly accelerated out.

"Wow, I am loving this car," gasped Yvette as Joe pulled over into a quiet cul-de-sac to get out of the driver's seat and let her drive back to the yard.

"Excellent," thought Joe, as he could see a nice tidy profit coming his way.

Yvette proved a competent driver as they returned to the yard and Joe began his sales spiel.

"A second-hand beauty like this would normally cost you $15,000, but hey, I like you and I think you and this car will be great together. You will be the envy of all your friends when they see you turn up in this little beauty. I could give it to you for $13,500 which is a real bargain. You won't find another one as good as this anywhere in town and I will throw in the tidy-up of the little scratches at no additional charge. I'll also get a new warrant of fitness, and it will have at least six months registration to go. What do you think?"

"I don't know, it seems a lot of money. Perhaps some other arrangement could work?" Yvette replied with some cheekiness in her voice.

Joe didn't want to jump to any conclusion that could be mistaken, so he immediately thought of his need for a new administrative assistant and thought it would be nice to have the flirtatious Yvette hanging around a little longer.

"How about you come and work for me and you could pay the car off in your wages each week? I need someone to do the office work for about ten to fifteen hours per week. Can you manage that in between your studies?"

"Yes, I think so. What are you paying?"

"Let's say $25 per hour and we can call it $15 per hour cash. The other $10 can be tax free and can be deducted off the car. Of course, I will need a 30% deposit or a trade-in equivalent."

Yvette readily agreed and her little Mazda Familia was given a trade-in value of $3000. As per his usual modus operandi the trade price was under its real worth and would still be a profitable 'flick' at $5500. Joe decided rather prudently that it would best sold on Sam's lot as he didn't want Yvette to be outraged at the rather quick money that would be made if she saw the sign on the car when she reported for work.

After the paperwork was all done Joe said, "Can you start tomorrow morning and I will show you the ropes? Nine o'clock okay?"

"I can do eleven," she replied, making an excuse for her nine o'clock class on employment law.

Yvette arrived at work the next morning at 10:50 am wearing a more conservative outfit of skinny jeans and a turquoise turtleneck sweater both of which showcased her perfect figure. She wore dark mascara and had vermillion-coloured lips. Joe's heart skipped a few beats as he couldn't believe his good fortune to be working with such an angel.

Joe's business was fairly straightforward. He was the only salesperson and the yard held about 30 cars mostly in the affordable bracket of $3000 to $20,000. He explained to Yvette that the bulk of clients needed finance and he showed her how to organise credit checks followed by the requirements for filling in motor vehicle finance application forms. As he was doing this, and reflecting on the rather high interest rates that accompanied such lending, he wondered whether in due course he could add money lending to his business interest.

Next, he demonstrated his preferred method of answering the phone, and impressed on Yvette that, no matter if they didn't have the specific car the customer wanted, she should always try and get the potential buyer to come to the premises where Joe could work his magic.

Joe also impressed upon Yvette that even if the customer asked for a specific make and model they didn't have, he could easily get it in. While Joe had not got into importing used Japanese cars he had contacts who were doing this.

After explaining the rudimentary bookkeeping system and how to prepare bank deposits, it was lunch time and Joe suggested that Yvette hold the fort while he went off to buy some lunch for them both at the local 'Chinese'.

The small and very busy takeaway was only 200 metres from the yard and as he walked Joe couldn't stop thinking about the beautiful Yvette. Surely it was 'miraculous' that she had suddenly walked into his life. She was smart, good looking, flirtatious and pleasant to be around. Would she stick around? Joe certainly hoped so. If she stayed Joe could see the Porsche arriving in the not-too-distant future.

With chow mein for two in hand he walked back to the yard. There was Yvette with a customer who seemed very interested in her as she leaned closely in front of him, lingering briefly before opening the door of a moderately priced sedan.

"I think you will find this little number perfect for your teenage daughter. It's automatic, not too powerful, with power steering, economic on the gas and, of course, backed by 'Honest Joe's' three-month no questions asked guarantee."

Joe watched as she appeared to have entranced the man and he figured she probably had this effect on all the men she met. Whatever she did had certainly worked for him.

Five minutes later she was back in the office writing up her first sale. She had declined to haggle and had sold the car at full ticket price. Joe hadn't told her there was always wriggle room as the ticket price was routinely inflated. He decided in his own interests not to enlighten her on the aspects of pricing and would keep that secret to himself.

Following the sale, Joe couldn't help but express his appreciation and complimented her on her skills.

"Nice touch, by the way. I never knew I had a three-month no questions asked guarantee. It's probably not a bad idea as most of our cars are pretty good."

Yvette just smiled and Joe wondered whether she might soon outgrow the role of administrative assistant and graduate to sales.

Over the next few months Yvette settled into her role with ease and soon became part of the sales team whenever Joe was busy with another customer. She had no hesitation in asking Joe for additional pay when a sale was made and Joe, who was anxious to retain her, readily agreed, not even bothering to play the negotiation game.

The only non-negotiable was that the bonus would be deducted from the debt on the Mini Cooper, with tax evaded again.

As well as having this very satisfactory business arrangement Joe and Yvette had a strong sexual attraction towards each other. Joe ignored his father's advice, who had previously counselled Joe to get his bread and meat at different shops.

"It will only lead to trouble, and you'll end up in the Employment Court or worse if you start playing around with the staff. She will be your downfall."

"No, not a chance Dad, Yvette and I have an understanding and you know I wouldn't put a woman ahead of my work," Joe replied emphatically.

"Mmm, he will have to learn from his mistakes," thought Steve.

In due time, Yvette moved in with Joe into his little one-bedroom flat. At age 22, he had not yet purchased a house but was steadily saving for the elusive Porsche.

Occasionally, he would imagine driving his new Porsche along a lonely highway with the beautiful Yvette sitting beside him. Along the coast, with the music turned up and the roar of the engine as gears were shifted down and the car clung to the road through the corners. What could be better?

Joe maintained a list of desirable collectible cars that he passed on to Yvette with their values. He wanted to make sure he wouldn't miss out on the profits from any hapless motorist who might turn up at the yard. If in doubt and he was out with a customer she should immediately phone him as such opportunities didn't come along very often.

Joe didn't tell Yvette about the other tricks he had learned but she was not stupid and did notice some of the cars ended up having different odometer readings than when they were traded in.

CHAPTER 7

Despite the unorthodox arrangement of Joe and Yvette both working and living together this had distinct benefits for them.

They both enjoyed each other's company and the fine things money could buy. Despite Joe's general penchant for saving, he was not averse to occasionally throwing his money around. They would often enjoy frequenting the latest trendy restaurant to open in Hamilton and having a flutter at the casino.

Unlike his father, Joe had a better understanding of the odds, a good memory for cards and numbers, so more often than not, he won some tidy amounts playing poker.

Yvette was ambitious and switched-on. She could see that law could get boring and like Joe was soon hooked on the rush of selling cars even though she was still the administrative assistant.

One evening she suggested to Joe, "I am thinking of dropping out of law school. I really enjoy working in the business with you but how about we open another yard together that I can run? We can make so much more money that way and I believe can effectively double our income."

It was with a sense of anticipation that Joe listened intently as his sweet Yvette laid the proposition before him.

"Good idea, sweetheart," he replied, "but I think your timing is off."

"You know, I have no doubt you will succeed and make a lot of money but we have to look at the long term, to the bigger picture. I believe that together we make an exceptional team. Your brains and your beauty go a long way and I have the street smarts. I think the

Joe and Yvette partnership will need a good lawyer. You are only 18 months away from finishing so why not carry on as we are and as soon as you graduate and get admitted to the bar, I will set you up with a yard. That way if you get sick of selling cars you can always practice law."

"Let me think about it," replied Yvette, "as you are not the one who has to sit through the boring administrative law lectures on Tuesdays and Thursdays."

After a few days' reflection and thinking Yvette had to agree the plan made good sense. She knuckled down at university scoring good grades all the while working with Joe at his ever increasingly profitable business.

The good times continued to flow and it was not long before Yvette had graduated, got admitted to practise law and a decision had to be made.

Not unexpectedly, Yvette wanted to run her own yard and Joe was soon on the lookout for the best spot in town to run a business from. It needed plenty of traffic, and a corner site with two entrances would be ideal. Joe was thinking big. A mere doubling of his space would be insufficient and, as luck would have it, the right place became available. The yard was three times the size of the existing premises, and Joe was already counting on making three times as much money.

"Do you think you can handle a yard this big?" he asked Yvette as they walked around it one Saturday morning.

Yvette was delighted and up for the challenge.

"This will be ideal", she replied.

They discussed the proposed operation and it seemed they would need three or four smart salespeople to staff the yard. However, in Joe's mind he could imagine a yard with three or four beautiful young women in miniskirts as salespeople who would draw the punters in.

"How sexist," Yvette retorted when Joe had explained what he had in mind.

"Still, I like you're thinking. Most car buyers are men and most men enjoy a bit of attention from an attractive young woman, not looking at anyone in particular. However, I would sell more if their wives or girlfriends were not with them."

The ins and outs were discussed and it was not long before they put pen to paper and had leased the new yard.

Honest Joe's Limited now had a second yard and the business would surely be on the up and up. As part of the arrangement Joe suggested that any prep work on the traded cars be done on his lot as he was reluctant for Yvette to learn of, or participate in, any shady practices, especially since she was a freshly minted lawyer. She needed to maintain her good character.

The employment of staff was undertaken with both Joe and Yvette carefully vetting the applicants while being particularly careful not to infringe employment laws or human rights legislation. Despite being careful in their questioning it would be obvious to any independent outside observer that all the staff who managed to obtain a position were stereotypical young and sexy women.

The entrepreneurial couple made sure they gave some training in all aspects of the business and made sure that a reasonable salary could be earned provided sufficient sales were made.

Yvette naturally didn't trust Joe with his new staff. After their initial training together, she decided it was in their best interests if she kept all new staff at her yard. So, she sent only one new staff member to replace herself at the first yard as Joe's new administrative assistant. Somehow, this happened to be a plain ordinary girl with the personality of a wet fish. Yvette was sure Joe would not be entrapped in any extra outside of work activities with Cherie.

Business at Joe's remained steady but showed no increase, whereas the trading figures from the new yard were very encouraging for the first six months. After the initial flurry of enthusiasm, marketing, and sales the deals at Yvette's yard also began to reduce to nothing exceptional, but the profits were still there.

The two directors watched the weekly sales figures and realised they needed to do something or the massive monthly lease payment would soon have them going backwards. Always the optimist, Joe ordered increased advertising. More flags were installed out the front, which surely helped, but selling cars was sometimes just pure luck. Facebook posts of beautiful women selling cars also seemed to help.

However, it soon transpired that this was just a winter slump and come spring sales began to bounce back up. Joe and Yvette soon learned that in business you had to be able to cope with the slumps as well as the good times.

His mother had always told him to put some money away for a rainy day. Joe would rather put it into a Porsche.

CHAPTER 8

As it happened about this time, Lorna Smith, who had never lost her vision of Joe becoming a respected prophet with a new 'anointing' decided that Joe and Yvette needed to stop living in sin and become married.

After putting up with Lorna's nagging and her old-fashioned beliefs Joe and Yvette thought they'd had enough of her prodding and decided it would be a good time to tie the knot and enjoy a honeymoon overseas. It would be their first holiday as a couple. In their time together they had been too busy studying and building up the business and had largely neglected taking time out to enjoy life together.

The next issue was the marriage ceremony. Lorna was bitterly disappointed that a temple wedding could not proceed as Yvette was not a Mormon and Joe was marginal at best.

Lorna didn't want a simple civil ceremony and pestered Yvette to see if she could find and submit to a Christian wedding of some kind at the very least. After some robust discussion, Yvette wisely decided she would do well not to offend her future mother-in-law despite what she believed to be her mental health issues in regard to her son being 'the anointed prophet'. Watching from the sideline, Joe was quite content to let the women figure it out. He would go with the flow and do as he was told, not wanting to cause any schism between his mother and his future wife.

Yvette remembered a friend, Lizzie Harris, whom she thought was a Christian, who might be able to suggest a solution. She would also be a suitable bridesmaid as Yvette didn't want a large wedding or have her sisters as bridesmaids.

Lizzie Harris was Yvette's closest friend and they had met in their first year of secondary school at Westlake Girls' High School on Auckland's North Shore. Lizzie had accompanied her parents when they had moved to Hamilton with Mr Harris, taking up a position with a large dairy exporting company when the girls were in year 11. It had been a few years before they had met up again in Hamilton and renewed their friendship.

Lizzie was tall, with fair skin and wild red hair, which made her an attractive young woman. She had sparkling, blue eyes and an outgoing and vivacious personality.

The family were nominal Christians with Lizzie involved in the Friday night youth group at a local church. She had barely a mediocre understanding of Christian doctrine but enjoyed the social elements of meeting with other youth and hanging out at various events when Christian music groups came to town.

In her first year of university, she had been approached during orientation week and offered the opportunity to attend a free BBQ. Not doing anything else and understanding it to be some kind of 'Christian' group she readily accepted and soon found herself enjoying good food and company from what she perceived were hard core Christians who kept asking her if she had accepted Jesus. She figured, having been brought up in a good and upright family who worked hard at not breaking the Ten Commandments, that she had accepted Jesus long ago.

The church young people, who identified themselves as coming from the 'Hamilton for Jesus' church, readily accepted Lizzie into their group and it wasn't long before she started attending the Sunday evening youth- focused church services where she felt very welcomed and accepted.

Some practices seemed a bit strange and some things seemed quite radical for someone from her background. She was surprised that the band was bashing out loud and upbeat songs with enthusiastic bass, acoustic guitars and a drummer who could have been straight out of a heavy metal or punk band. He was covered in tattoos and had all sorts of piercings in his ears and nose.

The preacher was enthusiastic and the talks seemed to be uplifting with positive advice about reaching your true potential. Occasionally, people were invited to accept Jesus.

Lizzie soon became a regular attendee and, despite her friendship with Yvette, the two of them never seemed to agree on matters of faith and practice. Yvette was a bit cynical and politely declined any invitations to come to church. After high school Yvette had stopped attending the Catholic Church having found its services quite boring and repetitive. She enjoyed the free and easy party scene of the university's social life. She had learned how to manipulate and use men to her advantage whereas Lizzie was more circumspect. She had a boyfriend from church and was well liked by all the church youth. Many of the young men were very keen to ask her out on dates but although moderately keen on Victor, she was happy to hold the others at bay. Lizzie, like her friend, Yvette, showed an ambitious desire to get ahead but, to date, the right opportunities had not yet come her way.

"Hi Lizzie, got some great news for you. I'm getting married."

"Wow, fantastic. Joe is a great guy and you make a wonderful couple. When is the big day?"

"Well, it will not be such a big day as we are planning a fairly quiet intimate affair with just close family and a few friends."

"Terrific. Anything I can do to help out?"

"Glad you asked that. Two requests for you. Can you be my bridesmaid and is there any chance we could get married in a church or something?"

"I'm speechless," remarked Lizzie.

"All those months at university wasting my time trying to convert you without success and now you want a church wedding. This is quite the turnaround."

"Well, yes, it is a bit different from my expectations but Joe's mum is a Mormon and wants a church wedding. We can't have a Mormon wedding because Joe is not regarded as such; being brought up as one doesn't count if you are not a regular attendee. So, in desperation to keep her happy, I thought I would see if you had any ideas. Of course, a Catholic wedding is also off limits so a generic kind of Christian wedding would be an ideal compromise."

"Actually, I think I can help. I recently went to a wedding up in Auckland and the couple got married at McLaurin Chapel in the old Government Gardens which is part of the university. I am sure there are no restrictions on who can be married there and I believe you could bring your own celebrant to conduct the wedding ceremony."

"Excellent. Thanks so much, Lizzie. That sounds perfect, but I don't know any marriage celebrants. Do you?"

"Well," replied Lizzie rather hesitantly, "I do know someone. My youth pastor from church would probably do it. He is very obliging and I'm pretty sure he wouldn't be too troubled that none of you are believers as such."

"Hey, that's not entirely true. While I am a paper-only Catholic, as you know surely Joe would qualify as a believer? He was brought up a Christian."

"Sorry to rain on your parade," Lizzie said, with an expression of some cheekiness, which no doubt was felt through the telephone call, "but we Christians don't regard Mormons as real Christians. They are a cult, as they don't believe in the Trinity, God the Father, God the Son and God the Holy Spirit being three persons, but one God."

"Oh well, perhaps another time but for now it would be great if you could ask your youth pastor if he could marry us."

"Leave it to me," replied Lizzie, "and, once again, congratulations."

Over the next few weeks, with Lorna satisfied, all the necessary arrangements were made and the wedding was all but ready to go. In between the planning for the wedding Joe focused his attention on the honeymoon.

There were two places on his wish list, Rome and Las Vegas. Joe was keen on some of the old movies, Spartacus, Ben Hur and, more recently, Gladiator. History had been his strongest subject at school and the ruthlessness of the Roman conquests had left an impression on him. Many businesses had developed a ruthless mode of operation as they sought to be number one in their field. While selling cars was not for everyone, success did require a degree of pressure.

As for Las Vegas, he wanted to play the slots and a bit of poker. His mother was appalled at this decadent choice of honeymoon venue and tried to persuade the young couple to abandon the Las Vegas option and, instead, visit Salt Lake City the spiritual home of the Church of Jesus Christ of the Latter-day Saints.

Negotiating out of this impossible situation would take some doing. In the end, after some discussion even Joe couldn't beat his mother so the best way forward was to lie.

"Okay, you win. Rome and Salt Lake City it is with Vegas off limits. I hope you are happy."

"Yes dear, you just wait and see, Salt Lake City will be a real revelation to you."

CHAPTER 9

The big day finally arrived and it was on a sunny spring day in Auckland with the oak trees in the Government House Garden, fresh with their newly-opened leaves and the recently mown lawns all contributing to a wonderful venue for the wedding.

McLaurin Chapel was an inspired choice, small and intimate yet participants could be mistaken for being in a cathedral, such was the sound of the organ when played very enthusiastically by a skilled practitioner.

Yvette felt a degree of hypocrisy as a Christian song was played and she felt a little tense after the ceremony as the exuberant youth pastor, getting ahead of himself, wanted to give some guidance and advice to the young couple. During his short sermon speaking about the virtues of marriage and the importance of love and fidelity he paused, he looked quizzically at Joe and said,

"This may seem a bit strange but I believe God has his hand on your life and even though you may not recognise it as such I believe he has anointed you for a great task that lies ahead."

"Oh dear," were the almost audible thoughts of both Joe and Yvette as this would be music to Lorna Smith's ears. As if they hadn't experienced enough of the cursed 'prophetic anointing' thing for years from Lorna and the frequent mocking from Joe's sisters. Who had prepped the pastor was his first thought? He didn't put it past his eldest sister to have had a word in his ear before the service. She may have even given him some cash and asked him to make sure he called Joe 'anointed.'

Hearing this, Joe's sisters could barely hold themselves together, grinning from ear to ear, fearing they could lose it altogether, particularly when Joe looked up and gave them a look, which he obviously hoped would bring them back from the verge of a breakdown.

Immediately after the service Lorna couldn't help herself,

"Joseph, wasn't that wonderful. What a great service. That young man surely confirmed what I have always known – that God has an anointing on your life." She continued in the same vein for the next ten minutes before Joe could extract himself to be available for the photos.

Their photos were taken in front of the ancient oak trees, with the impressive historic government house also providing a grand backdrop. The happy young couple moved to the reception at one of the more upmarket hotels on Auckland's waterfront.

After enjoying a wonderful (and expensive) dinner it was time for speeches. Joe had been pleased his mother had not insisted on speaking, instead, following the tradition that it was the groom's father who would speak if any parent was to be given the honour.

Joe believed he would be safe to let Steve speak, after all, he felt they had both been cut from the same cloth.

Steve stood and faced the small gathering, clearly pleased to be given the opportunity to address his only son and his bride.

"Good evening Mr and Mrs Smith, family and honoured guests. It is a privilege and a pleasure to be here today. Joe has asked me to keep this speech to a minimum, so I will be brief. Joe you are a credit to Lorna and me. We have watched you grow up and already we have seen you succeed in your business and can only see a great future ahead. You have a strong business head and I believe that, in whatever you put your hand to, you will prosper.

"Yvette, welcome to the family. You certainly look beautiful. Marriage requires give and take. Don't let Joe dominate as sometimes you will need to curb his business enthusiasm. In addition, you will need to balance him with wisdom and caution but, at the same time, don't quench his enthusiasm, Even as a kid growing up, most of his seemingly daft ideas were a success, so let him run with them. Enjoy the ride. You don't want to put a tight handbrake on him," he said as he wistfully glanced at Lorna.

"I am reminded by my dear wife to mention that there will be an opportunity in the future, and this may even be sooner than you think, that you will be anointed by God to work for him. Neither of us have any real understanding of what that will look like but, you know your mother has always believed something good will happen. She reminded me again, even at the service this afternoon, that the young celebrant even had an inkling about your future. With these things in mind please enjoy your visit to Salt Lake City and we look forward to hearing all about it.

Congratulations and may you have many happy years together."

After the other speakers – being the best man and Lizzie, as bridesmaid – Joe, without referring to his father's speech, gave a fairly traditional speech and hastily sat back down to enjoy his dessert.

CHAPTER 10

After spending a crazily romantic night at a local hotel, it was off to the airport the next morning for the first leg of their long flight to Rome.

Joe had finally decided to ask Yvette the meaning of the tattoo written in Chinese script on her upper right thigh. He had previously asked her but she had hedged and had not really explained it. She didn't want this to be a barrier so simply explained that it meant 'seize the day'. She explained to Joe that she had always been an optimistic person and rather than have the traditional 'carpe diem' she thought the Chinese script would be more mysterious.

"It is like a life statement: as each day comes make the most of it and look for the opportunities that come your way. You set me up with the car business and in a very short time and then our love bloomed. Don't you agree I have seized the day?"

Joe thought that was quite cool.

Trying to live the dream, they flew business class via Bangkok on Thai Airways. Joe was all but smitten with the beautiful Thai stewardesses, who handed out a fresh orchid and a hot towel to each passenger as soon as they were seated. God had surely blessed the Thai men with very beautiful women.

After a pleasant uneventful 12-hour flight they arrived at 8:00 pm local time at Suvarnabhumi Airport. They immediately noticed the swarm of people from every race and culture buzzing around like flies, rushing to their gates or, like themselves, in a hurry to get to the exit. Fortunately, they were soon whisked away in a limousine to their central city hotel for a two-night stopover before flying to Rome.

The next morning was spent on a river cruise along the bustling and muddy Chao Phraya River. It was hot and sticky and the air seemed to weigh them down and suck the life out of them. Street noise and pollution from delivery trucks and the tuk-tuks added to the oppression. The smell of the river was foul and almost vomit inducing. It would be a difficult place to live in but Joe was immediately delighted at the entrepreneurial behaviour of the locals as at each stop along the journey little canoes laden with produce, flowers, cooked food or fresh fruit would pull up alongside their boat and the haggling would begin.

"You want banana? Special price today only. You lucky first customer? Only 20 baht."

"No thanks, I don't want any bananas."

"How about pineapple? Very delicious. Here, you try free sample."

By the time Yvette and Joe had sampled the fresh fruit they had to admit it was better than any imported pineapples they had purchased back home and felt obliged to purchase. It was also very hot and muggy, so a pineapple would certainly help then hydrate in addition to the water they had taken from the hotel before setting off. Joe had to haggle a little as he recognised this was a cultural norm and besides, being used to the game, he quite enjoyed the process.

He was already missing the cut and thrust of selling cars as he enjoyed the highs that came with a concluded sale, not to mention the profit that came with it. His thoughts turned to thinking about how his staff were managing without them.

"You know, things have been a bit slow lately. How do you think the staff are getting on?" he asked Yvette.

"You worry too much, Joe, they will be doing fine. They probably don't even miss us," Yvette answered, reassuring her beloved.

"Shall I give them a call?"

"No, leave them alone. You have to trust them to get on with what they do. They are quite capable without you micromanaging them."

"Okay, okay," Joe replied putting his hands in the air to surrender, while continuing to entertain his doubts.

After the boat trip they stopped to visit the Temple of the Golden Buddha. Joe had learned the history of the Buddha, how it was for a long time covered with stucco to hide its true identity and value, and had remained an undiscovered antiquity for more than 200 years. It was only when it was dropped during transportation to another site and some stucco chipped off that the underlying gold was seen. When it was finally cleaned up the statue weighed 5.5 tonnes of pure gold. No wonder it drew so many tourists.

Now, how could he get his hands on that much gold? That was the question. Where was the answer and how quickly could he get it? Joe was looking forward to going to Las Vegas. That was surely where the quick money could be found.

CHAPTER 11

Despite its charms, the young couple were keen to leave the chaos, the noise, the pollution and the heat of Bangkok behind and head to Rome. Another 12-hour trip in business class would surely make the journey that much more enjoyable.

"I could get used to this quite readily," grinned Yvette as she sank into a comfy armchair in the Thai Airways business class lounge, drinking champagne and waiting for their boarding call.

"Not too shabby, is it?" Joe retorted as he did the same.

After boarding Joe was happy to engage in some conversation with a handsome, well-dressed man in his mid-40s wearing a new Thai-made silk suit. Joe didn't miss much and observed the white shoes, the gold signet ring, the gold Rolex watch and a gold medallion around the man's neck on what was surely a 24-carat gold chain.

"Bit over the top for me," thought Joe, but nevertheless it was hard to avoid the ostentatious confidence of the big money that was on display. Joe was keen to engage with this stranger.

"Hi, I am Joseph Smith," he said holding out his hand in introduction to this wealthy man.

"Well nice to meet you, sir," responded the silver haired man with a pleasant and polite southern American accent.

"Reverend Carl Quincy Adams, at your service and delighted to meet you. And is this your lovely wife?" he inquired, as he looked across at Yvette who happened to bending over at the time, picking up a magazine she had dropped on the floor.

"Yes," replied Joe, as he introduced Yvette.

Yvette decided almost instantly that the man across the aisle was a sleazebag and simply nodded a greeting then quickly turned back to her magazine.

Joe, on the other hand, was intrigued. "Reverend Carl, what church are you the minister at?"

"Well sir, I am surprised you have not heard of me. I am the senior pastor at the Memphis Church of the Lord's Abundance. It is the largest church in the Southern United States with nearly 40,000 members."

"Wow, I never heard of a church having that many people. How did you get so many?"

"It's quite a long story but I guess you can say God put a special anointing on me, and he has blessed me with good health and prosperity."

"I am really interested in finding out more," said Joe and over the next few hours, the Reverend Carl gave some insight into his rags to riches story.

The conversation concluded at mealtime and Carl finished by saying, "Hey, if you are ever in the United States come for a visit. Here is my card," as he handed an ornate gold leaf-embossed card for Joe to take. This card will get you to the front of the auditorium and you will be amazed at what you see. You will also be my guest at a special lunch after the service. Hope to see you there, brother."

The conversation finished and, in quiet tones, Yvette clearly expressed her displeasure that Joe had ignored her for the last two hours hanging onto every word the obnoxious and narcissistic twat had said.

After their meal Joe and Yvette had a sleep and it wasn't long before an announcement indicated they were starting their descent to Leonardo da Vinci International Airport in Fiumicino.

On the ground, they were soon processed, picked up their luggage and were on their way to an apartment in Rome that they'd rented for a week. Centrally located near Roma Termini, the central train station, they were soon ensconced in the second floor apartment.

First, after they had unpacked, was a short walk for coffee and some people watching. They found a café with tables out on the street on one side of a piazza and sat down to enjoy the afternoon sunshine above the seven hills of the eternal city Rome.

"Isn't this something?" said Joe as he looked around.

"Here we are in one of the great and ancient cities of the world, enjoying a coffee and watching the world go by?"

"It certainly is different from Hamilton," Yvette replied.

"You know, ever since I was a little girl, I wanted to travel somewhere exotic. My neighbours would go to Australia, the Islands and Singapore and we never went anywhere as interesting. This is so exciting and I've waited a long time to do this. Look how well dressed the women are. So stylish."

Changing the subject, she inquired, "Why were you so impressed with that American man on the flight? He seemed like a real con man to me."

"Well, you may be right there, but who knows, there may be money in religion. Just a thought, but we need to remain open to opportunities. The car yards may not be our thing forever, you know. I was just wanting to tap into his expertise and experience to see whether we could learn from his story and maybe get on the fast track to prosperity and that Porsche 911 I still haven't managed to buy."

"Speaking of religion and prosperity, I think we should get in the line early tomorrow for a tour of the Vatican Museum and the Sistine chapel."

Having agreed on the plan for the next day the young couple walked away hand in hand from their coffee stop and a little further on came across the famous Trevi Fountain.

"Oh, I read about this in a guidebook," exclaimed Yvette. "Last year visitors threw $1.5 million into Rome's Trevi Fountain. If we throw in a coin and make a wish then we will come back to Rome. Let's do it."

They, along with the other few hundred tourists, threw their coins in and made a wish.

"Don't tell me what you wished for but just remember and when it comes true then you can remind me, okay?"

Joe was happy to go along with it. If he had revealed his wish to Yvette, she wouldn't have believed him.

The next day it was overcast with rain threatening as they waited in the queue, winding their way up a little hill to the entrance of the Vatican. It seemed the world was full of hustlers as no sooner did the rain start to fall than a man from North Africa appeared with a range of umbrellas he was selling.

"To you sir, only six euro. Quick, before this rain starts to get heavy."

"No thanks," said Joe, "Yesterday someone tried to sell me one for three euro."

That was never going to stop a persistent hustler.

"But, sir, it was not raining yesterday and so the price has to increase."

"No deal," replied Joe.

"If you were making money on three euro yesterday the profit will be the same today."

Joe staunchly refused to budge and the umbrella salesman concluded there were easier targets further down the queue.

Finally, they arrived at the ticket office. Because they had not been sure of their exact movements Joe and Yvette had decided not to book online. They handed over €17 each to be admitted and, as was his habit, Joe quickly did his sums when he realised this one attraction had about 5,000,000 visitors a year. €85,000,000.00 was not a bad earner, although that was top dollar because many would get cheaper ticket prices by buying online.

Along with the other tourists they were amazed at the art works, the sculptures, the rare antiquities but, most of all, the Michelangelo frescoes on the ceiling of the Sistine Chapel. Pictures in brochures could never do justice to a phenomenon they were privileged to see in person. The visit seemed to stir some Catholic pride in Yvette as she took in the beauty of the treasures.

"Didn't us Catholics do well?" she said waving her hand at all the priceless artefacts in the gallery.

Joe laughed. "They never told you at school how all this great wealth was accumulated, did they?"

"I dare say these guides or staff will not tell you either."

Joe was not sure how much money the church had made in the late Middle Ages selling indulgences but he knew the business was profitable. An indulgence was a cunning plan introduced by the Catholic Church as a way to reduce the time of punishment a deceased person had to undergo for their sins so they could finally leave purgatory and get into heaven. Certificates were given and a promise made by the church that the person paying for the indulgence would have so much time deducted from their stay in purgatory. Not surprisingly, how the church could promise such a thing, remained unsaid.

Yvette was aware of that system, as purgatory was a certain doctrine for all Catholics who could never be assured they could go directly into heaven on their death. They had to have sins purged after death and for how long no-one could tell exactly.

There had also been other methods used to accumulate wealth. Wars, property confiscations, the fourth crusade, and the sacking of Constantinople in the early thirteenth century brought the church gold, money and jewels.

To have the power and money was something the Catholic hierarchy seemed to know how to hold on to if their history was anything to go by.

CHAPTER 12

Time went quickly as the young married couple enjoyed food and cups of coffee in the local trattoria, sightseeing on the Palatine Hill, the ancient forum, and being scammed by the costumed Roman soldiers at the Colosseum. Everywhere they went they were reminded of the past that was the glorious Roman Empire.

If it was not the grandeur of ancient Rome, then certainly Catholic Rome was impressive. Having marvelled at the extravagances of the Vatican Museum it was time to inspect the largest church in the world, namely, St Peter's Basilica. Joe was certainly overawed at the size of it; the marble pillars, the frescoes, the gold, the artwork, the statues and the impression that no expense had been spared.

The view from the top overlooked the huge square and, as Joe gazed across the vista, he held Yvette's hand and promised her,

"Someday we will make it. We will have a life of wealth and prosperity. Obviously not on this scale, but let's go for it. We can travel and see the world. We can retire at 40. Surely, wealth and prosperity are what this life is all about. That is obviously what the hierarchy of the Catholic Church must believe with their unashamed display of what money can buy."

Yvette, who was a bit more grounded, replied, "Don't let it go to your head my love, as this power and money took many centuries and wars to achieve. A quiet comfortable life is all I really want."

"Well, not for me. I want to give you the best and I am going to work out how we are going to get there. I am glad you are with me to enjoy the ride."

Their remaining days in Rome were spent mainly in Centro Storico, the historic centre of Rome, where they enjoyed the many art-filled churches, observing works by the great artists, such as Bernini and Caravaggio. Each church had its marvels and riches on display. Santa Maria Maggiore with its mosaics and golden ceilings certainly left a mark on the young couple.

Yvette even managed to persuade Joe that if they were not going to be wealthy, they should at least look the part, so €700 later Yvette had one nice outfit she could proudly wear anywhere and was satisfied in the knowledge it was not a hand-me-down from one of her sisters.

All good things had to come to an end and they were soon on another long-haul flight from Rome to New York City. After a couple of hours at JFK airport they transferred to a local five-hour flight from New York to Salt Lake City, Utah.

Feeling quite tired from their travels they were happy to retire for an early night in what was the relatively small city of Salt Lake City. After the buzz of 10,000,000 people in Bangkok, and 2,800,000 people in Rome, the 200,000 people of Salt Lake City seemed nothing more than a village. Before retiring Joe made a quick inquiry to discover that a flight to Las Vegas would only take an hour and 20 minutes, or about six hours if they decided to hire a car and drive.

The next day Joe decided he had better be faithful to his mother and go on a tour of the famous Salt Lake Temple. Having just come from Rome he was not as enthralled as he might have been if he had travelled to Salt Lake City first. While the six-spire Gothic building was impressive enough it was no match for the splendour of St Peter's Basilica. It was also unfortunate that he and Yvette were not able to visit inside as they didn't hold the requisite temple recommend and there were no public tours.

Consequently, the young couple were obliged to visit the visitor centres and generally wander around the 10-acre Temple Square.

Despite the magnificent natural beauty of its mountains, Utah

– and in particular Salt Lake City – seemed to lack vibrancy and night life. Joe found himself eager to leave and recommended to Yvette that it would be nice to enjoy some luxury in a swanky hotel in Las Vegas for a few days as a contrast to the staid and boring niceness of Salt Lake City. It did not need to be said but of course Lorna would not be informed of this little side trip. Yvette didn't need much persuasion so they decided a road trip would be the cheapest and most agreeable option.

CHAPTER 13

The vintage 1966 white mustang convertible soon began to eat up the miles as the young couple drove the road from Salt Lake City to Las Vegas. Enjoying the drive Joe could see himself doing the same trip one day in his own Porsche 911. With Joe keen to get to the casino tables they only made toilet stops and one lunch stop at a small diner. While waiting to be served their hamburgers and fries Joe and Yvette couldn't help but overhear a conversation from two rather loudly spoken middle aged women sitting at the table beside them.

"Did y'all happen to see the Reverend Carl Adams on TV this morning?" the very bleached blond woman said.

"Well, no, I didn't today but I usually watch his programme."

"He just happened to say that he had a real word from God for someone watching his programme who has experienced sciatica problems. Well that's certainly me. I have had years of discomfort with my back, and he said God wanted to heal those people watching. He went on to say it was a matter of faith and if I was to sow a seed of faith in the natural then God would work in the spiritual. He went on to say that if the person or people who had the sciatica problem would send in $500 with a handkerchief he would pray over the handkerchief and send it back and, if I placed it on my lower back I would be healed."

"What do you think, Barbs?"

"Well, God bless that man. He is a very popular preacher and I believe he has helped many people. I've seen people on his show healed all the time. In the great scheme of things $500 is not too much to pay to have your back healed. You have already spent a large amount on chiropractors and naturopaths so I say send the money."

"I believe I will. Let's watch and see God heal. You know I have faith for this, right?"

"Why of course you've always been a good Christian woman – except of course for those two occasions I know of when you slept with those men on our holidays in Mexico. But, you know, no one is perfect, right?"

"Oh Barbs, shame on you for bringing up those minor holiday indiscretions. You know I'm a good, honest woman. Well, at least most of the time," she laughed.

The conversation drifted on and the meals arrived. After eating and drinking the foul-tasting filter coffee that the Americans like to pass off as the real thing the young couple were back in the Mustang and on the road.

"I have an idea," Yvette said. "This Mustang is really good. Why don't we see if we can import some of these old collectors' models and that will pay for the trip and give us some money left over. I'm sure even ones that need doing up would sell well. I mean, the good ones are hard to come by back home, aren't they? I know every day old Mustangs are a dime a dozen but if we get the right ones we will easily pay for our trip and have money left over."

"Good thinking, sweetheart, but I reckon I have a better idea. You heard those women in the diner, right?"

"Couldn't help it, they were certainly loud enough."

"Indeed, but I think that that guy the Reverend Carl Adams is on to it. We need to watch his programme. I reckon he's got a good scam for raking in the money. Maybe we could diversify out of cars and get into religion. There could be a lot more money in it. What do you think?" he asked.

"Mm, maybe. I guess it is not such a big leap from used car salesman to running a 'church'. You do have the gift of the gab and might just be able to pull it off. We'll have to do a bit of research and come up with a business plan."

Both of them mulled their respective ideas over and the discussion continued as they journeyed into Las Vegas. Arriving late afternoon, they checked into Caesars Palace on the famous neon-soaked strip. The location was ideal for Joe and Yvette as they settled into their room and checked out various things on their 'to do' list.

Dinner and a show, then Joe hit the roulette table before settling into a late night of poker. His luck on the roulette tables was poor so he soon quit. He was able to read people well and had a good eye for identifying the 'tells.' He was not surprised after moving to a poker table that he was up on his initial stake. In fact he quite expected to be ahead. Unlike most gamblers, he knew when to walk away and take his profit, which he duly did before heading back to his room at 1:00 am. Yvette was fast asleep and, still buzzing from the adrenaline rush of his substantial winnings, Joe sought to calm down a little so switched on the TV.

He flicked channels until he came across a show with a televangelist in full swing. This was not the Reverend Carl Quincy Adams but a man of similar ilk – brash, persuasive, silky-tongued and giving a very polished performance.

Again, he spotted the common denominators; the lust for money, the promise of health and prosperity and the seeming ignorance and gullibility of his audience as they willingly placed cash in the buckets that were passed around.

Joe was gobsmacked when he flicked channels to another similar charlatan who had the balls to tell his faithful people that the Lear Jet he owned was not fast enough and people were perishing because he couldn't get to minister to some of the more exotic corners of the world in time. A much larger and faster jet would readily be justified to promote extending the kingdom of God. Another offering was taken and pledges were called for. Who were these people who were so readily deceived? The real question was, would such a scam work with New Zealanders, especially with the sensible folk from Hamilton? If it did, Joe could certainly see himself making a truckload of money but if it fell flat then, what then?

He flicked to another channel where he had to tell himself that what he saw could not in reality be true. Here was a preacher who told the crowd that God instructed him to knee a man in the gut to cure colon cancer. God also told him to hit people so they could experience God's power. There was even a flashback to a 'grandma slapping healing' where somehow God had told him to slap an elderly woman in the face and she would be healed.

Another preacher used his white jacket with mesmerising effect as he waved it at people and, seemingly in an hypnotic trance, people fell over as the 'magic' cloak was whipped at them. Could it get madder than that?

Indeed it could, as another preacher had people falling over the floor laughing crazily like hyenas. Some barked like dogs and Joe seriously wondered what sort of circus he had wandered into.

Before eventually falling asleep in the chair Joe promised himself that while in America this little opportunity needed a lot more research.

The next day he broached the idea of a quick trip to Memphis to attend Carl Adams' church on the Sunday morning.

Yvette initially squashed the suggestion saying she didn't want to fly back on their tracks before the long flight home and couldn't they find a similar church in Las Vegas or even Los Angeles on the way home?

While disappointed Joe could see the wisdom in her comment although he was unsure how to go about finding a 'scam church'. Posing this thought to Yvette she agreed that it might be somewhat difficult. It would not be easy to simply google 'scam church' and turn up. They could waste a great deal of time visiting lots of churches. With her finely tuned feminine intuition she felt certain that the sleazy Carl Adams would be bound to have a 'scam church'.

Thankful for his wife's turnaround and insight Joe hurried down to the lobby to find a travel agent who could book them a return flight to Memphis leaving the next day (Saturday) returning to Las Vegas on Monday.

CHAPTER 14

The first thing they noticed on arrival at Memphis airport was the pleasant spring time weather in contrast to the dry heat of the Nevada Desert. It was refreshing as Joe reflected that just a few days ago they had been enduring the stifling heat of Bangkok with its putrid smell of rotting rubbish. Las Vegas was hot but not smelly and now a city where temperatures were similar to a spring day in Hamilton.

In contrast with Las Vegas the city seemed to have a much larger African American population. Joe observed the wide variety in neighbourhoods from the very wealthy to the very poor as the taxi took them from the airport to downtown.

Yvette was delighted when they arrived at the grand old Peabody Hotel. Sure it was expensive but as it was just for two nights it was easily justified as a honeymoon treat.

As they entered the lobby Joe couldn't believe what he was looking at. "Well, I've seen everything now," he exclaimed as he pointed out to Yvette the ducks that were swimming around the fountain in the lobby.

They soon discovered Tennessee was a whole world away from the sin and sexual deviancy all too apparent in Las Vegas. It was an eye opener as the people appeared to be quite conservative, but at the same time, relaxed and not nearly as energetic as the people in Vegas. Even their speech was slower.

Their hotel was a short walk from the Memphis Church of the Lord's Abundance and for the first time in his life Joe was looking forward to going to church the next morning.

On Sunday morning they were ready for church. Stepping out of the hotel and on to the street they were pleased they could walk in the cooler weather. They walked slowly and were excited to arrive at the very large auditorium at 9:50 am in plenty of time for the 10:00 am start. The air-conditioned building was enormous, comfortable and hugely impressive. It was far larger than any auditorium he had ever been in. They gazed at the opulent surroundings. No expense had been spared. True to his word the gold pass opened the right doors, as they were politely ushered to some fancy seats near the front. They had provided their names and country of residence to the usher who explained they would be given a special welcome as a gold card holder.

The atmosphere was one of buzz and excitement about what would happen, with people chatting to one another and preparing for the start, as a very large instrumental group and choir came on stage.

First impressions were that the operation was very polished. The instrumentalists and choir were a very professional and talented group. The choir were dressed in satin-like purple gowns and swayed with the music. After a few opening numbers it was quite clear to Joe and Yvette that the vast audience were enjoying this performance.

Then there was a pause in the proceedings and the lights were dimmed. With a mixture of fanfare and drum roll, and wearing a white suit, white shoes and splendid gold bow tie, the 'Reverend' Carl Adams appeared on stage under a blazing spotlight and with dry ice wafting low over the stage. This seemed to signal the start of the circus.

"I am here to tell you God loves you," proclaimed the Reverend in a booming voice.

"Amen," shouted the enthusiastic crowd.

"What is God's purpose for your life?" the preacher asked enthusiastically.

"To prosper us and to do us good," was the chanted response with equal enthusiasm.

This marked the opening of the Carl Adams show, as Joe later put it to Yvette. After some more introductory salvos to warm up the crowd Carl announced, "We have some special guests all the way from Hamilton, New Zealand. Let's welcome Joe and Yvette Smith. Stand up and wave to God's people."

Rather embarrassed, Joe and Yvette stood to their feet and waved, to thunderous applause, then sat down. Attendees from other countries were given a similar treatment before the show continued.

The congregation then began singing with the orchestra and choir. The lights and the dry ice swirling around were all intended to whip the crowd up before what Joe figured was the main part of the service – the offering. What surprised him was that there were two offerings. As far as he could recall afterwards the first was for the general running of the vast organisation and this was followed by a talk before a special offering was announced.

"You know folks, God has put it in my heart after appearing to me one night in a vision and he said, 'Carl, you are doing a mighty fine work for me in this city but I want you to think more globally so the kingdom of God can be extended much further than Memphis'. The church needs a jet."

"But God," I replied, "A Gulfstream G200 will cost at least $6,000,000.00 even for a second hand one."

"You know, I heard God reply, 'My people are faithful and want to be blessed so they will provide this for you. All you need to do is ask in my name'."

"So, folks, I am here this morning wanting to be obedient to God to do his will. I know you want to do the same. If you want to be blessed and prosper then you need to sow a seed of faith. I am asking you to open your wallets and sow into the kingdom of God. Some of you came not prepared to give today but the ushers will also hand out pledge cards as the baskets are passed around."

"Thank you and may God richly bless you as you give."

"Wow, can you believe this?" Joe whispered to Yvette. "Look at what's happening. People are giving."

After the offering was taken up a sermon about what seemed to be having your best life now was preached and then Carl moved onto something quite different from anything either he or Yvette had seen before.

"There are some dear folks here today whom God wants to heal. I believe there are some with back problems and in particular the lower back. Raise your hands if that is you."

A number of hands were raised then Carl looked at someone seated a few rows in front of Joe and Yvette and proclaimed, "You, sir, yes you in the blue shirt in the fifth row, come up here."

The middle aged balding man with a stooped walk came forward and walked slowly up on the stage.

"What is your name?" the reverend asked.

"George Brown," was the reply.

"Well George, I believe there is a real anointing on you at the present time. Are you ready to be healed?"

At that phrase, Joe's brain began to tick. All the times he had heard that phrase 'anointing'. Next minute, Carl proceeded to get all excited and he proclaimed healing over the man.

He shouted at the man, "Go free!" and it seemed like he gave him a big shove and the man ended up flat on his back on the floor. At least he didn't knee him in the gut or slap him around.

"This will be interesting," thought Joe as he watched carefully to see what would happen next.

The man seemed to give a jerk and then he suddenly sprung up. Carl immediately stepped in and asked, "Tell us what happened, George?"

"Sir, I believe God has wonderfully healed me. My back feels fine and I feel 20 years younger."

"Praise the Lord," exclaimed Carl. "Now go back to your home and tell of the wonderful works God has done through his servant, Carl Adams."

George walked smartly off the stage and waved to the crowd who cheered and hollered as he walked back to his seat.

"Isn't God good?" Carl shouted, which resulted in a chorus of loud 'amens' from all over the auditorium.

The service wrapped up with more singing and then a final prayer before the crowd was dismissed.

An usher approached Joe and Yvette and asked them if they wanted to come to a light lunch put on by the church for gold class guests, to which they readily agreed, eager to find out more about this bizarre kind of church the likes of which they had never experienced before. Only in America? Or could it be exported?

Escorted into a large dining room there was a hotel quality buffet spread out for the guests and Joe and Yvette were encouraged to pile up their plates and make the most of it. The people seemed nice and normal and were interested to listen when Joe told them he was just a used car salesman from New Zealand on his honeymoon.

After a satisfying lunch of good ol' southern fried chicken and other specialties Joe and Yvette were trying to head for the door when the great man himself came up to them and thanked them for coming to church.

Taking the opportunity Joe immediately went on the offensive,

"You know Reverend Carl, that was a very interesting service. I think something like this would go down really well in Hamilton. What do you think?"

"That's an excellent point you raise and in fact you have hit the nail on the head. My team and I have been looking at expanding internationally; hence, my reason to visit Thailand and Singapore, where we met on that flight not so long ago. I think a franchise situation could work quite well. How about we meet tomorrow and see if we can figure something out?"

"Well, sir, Yvette and I have our flights already booked to return to Vegas tomorrow so we really can't afford to break them."

"Oh, don't you worry about that, the church will pick up the tab and fly you back business class on Tuesday. How does that sound?"

"Okay, sounds good to us. Let's meet tomorrow."

"Breakfast at Brother Juniper's at 8:00 am? Does that work for you?"

The details sorted, Joe and Yvette were able to leave and returned to their hotel for a debrief meeting.

"I am stunned," said Yvette, not really believing what she had experienced that morning.

"To be sure that was one slick operation and that guy who claimed to be healed must have been an actor planted in the audience. I wonder how much they had to pay him? You know, Yvette, seeing how much money they were taking in, we could be on to something big here and, being in the right place at the right time, this could be our moment. I know you think Carl is a sleazebag and he probably is but let's see what kind of a deal we can put together tomorrow."

Yvette was still unsure of what they were getting themselves into and it was with some trepidation that they entered the very popular Brother Juniper's for their business breakfast. They could not miss the Reverend Carl dressed in a flamboyant paisley ensemble as he beckoned them over to a booth near the back of the restaurant.

"Well, how y'all this morning?" he exclaimed. "What a great day to be alive."

Joe wasn't sure whether Carl's constant positive attitude was just a well-rehearsed front or whether he was a genuinely optimistic person. Maybe time would tell. After Joe ordered the cinnamon roll pancakes and Yvette, the garden and lamb omelette, they soon got down to business. Joe passed on the coffee and thought tea might be more drinkable.

Carl began by giving them the ballpark figures of the history of the church, the weekly attendances and, more importantly for Joe, the average weekly offering.

Joe was staggered at the figures.

"But you must have quite high overheads with your staff and auditorium running costs?" he inquired.

Carl brushed that aside and indicated the church was paying him a salary in excess of $1,000,000.00 per year.

Joe and Yvette gasped in unison, "But you are a church. How do you get away with it?"

"Quite simple really. The church would not exist without my talents and my board recognise that any great business needs an entrepreneurial leader who can take us forward. Actually, the fact that I pay my board quite well keeps them in line. It's my church so I figure I can pay myself what I like."

The conversation carried on in that vein for some time and then Carl came to the point.

"Have you guys got what it takes? Could you set up and run the Hamilton branch of the Church of the Lord's Abundance? I am willing to take a punt on you guys. I like what I see in you two", he commented as he gave a sly wink to Yvette.

"What do you say?"

"Well, we are greatly impressed with your confidence in us and I certainly take that as a compliment. Now, I must admit, I know how to sell cars but I have no training in preaching and although I am very willing, this project would be quite outside my comfort zone."

"I surely understand," replied Carl, "but together I think we can make this work. I will provide the initial seed capital of say US$20,000.00 to help get you set up for the first few months, hall hire, advertising and the like. I will also send you an order of service each week, some songs to whip up the crowd, a sermon, and off you go. Get ready for the ride. As I am taking a big risk on you guys and putting up some funds, I think it would be fair for me to take a franchise fee of 25% of the gross offerings."

Joe immediately went to his car dealing persona and said, "Whoa, hold on just a minute. I have never heard of such a large franchise figure for any business. That would be just unsustainable. I wouldn't expect to make any money on that basis. I suggest a graduated scale working up to 25% after we reach certain milestones. While the operation is small, we start at 10%, gradually increasing to 15%, 20% and then 25% once we reach certain milestones and targets."

"Mm, what you say makes sense. I can see we are going to do very well together. I will get my lawyers to email you a franchise agreement next week for you to look at and we'll take it from there."

"One other thing. I will give you my special training for a week. It will be a small international course as I have a number of visitors coming from overseas who are also keen to be part of the Lord's Abundance church worldwide. I will need you back in Memphis for training on 1 November. Hope you can make it."

"Yes, count me in," Joe quickly responded.

They shook hands and, after enjoying a second coffee, Carl pulled out his wallet and flicked out $1000 in cash, which he handed to Joe saying that that should cover the additional accommodation and the airfares back to Las Vegas.

Thanking him for his kindness Joe asked one more question before leaving the restaurant.

"If you don't mind me asking Carl, how did the offering for your Gulfstream go on Sunday?"

"Surprisingly well, actually. We are already at $4,000,000 so I expect we will get the balance in the next month or so. At $4,000,000 that is only an average of $100 per person so I am expecting much more to come in. Don't be surprised if I jet in and get the opening of the Hamilton Church of the Lord's Abundance underway for you. I'll be in touch." And with that, they went their separate ways.

CHAPTER 15

On the trip to the airport, sitting in the lounge, and later on the plane, Joe was buzzing and couldn't stop himself counting the money he expected to make with this new venture. He was already calling himself God's new anointed prophet to Hamilton.

"Let's not get too excited," said Yvette. "I will want to have a good look at that franchise agreement. I don't trust that slimy bastard for one minute and I expect his little document will have all the fish hooks that his dodgy lawyers can think of. Let's keep ourselves grounded and not get too carried away. Don't you even think for a minute that there will be any Christian ethics from that man."

"Well, it sounds pretty good to me. No start-up costs for us so, if it falls flat, we just go back to the car business and keep pushing it," said Joe.

Yvette was quick to reply, "I don't know Joe. Won't it seem a bit strange for a minister to also be running a car yard? Maybe I should run both yards and if we put them in my name, or a company owned by a trust or similar, no one will know who the real owners are and we can continue."

"You have a point, darling, but I think trusts can be a bit complicated and look a bit shady. I think we can be transparent and just put them into your name."

"Well, I don't know. We should just take things slowly from a business perspective and see how things go," was Yvette's reply.

Their honeymoon drew to a close but not before Joe had picked up some small change from the poker table. On the road trip out of Las Vegas back through the desert towards Los Angeles, they were able to pick up two Mustangs for an excellent price, one a convertible and the other a classic 1966 Shelby Mustang GT350. After making all the necessary arrangements, they were satisfied they would be able to pick them up from the Port of Auckland in about six to eight weeks' time. The profit on the Shelby alone would cover the entire honeymoon costs so Joe was naturally super excited about his deal of a lifetime.

On the way back to Hamilton the young couple considered their future options and Yvette, perhaps the more cautious and business minded of the couple, as well as being the brains, soon put down a business plan as best she could.

"It will obviously have to be modified as we get more information but I can see a couple of decisions that will need to be made quite quickly. For a start, how big a hall do we sign up for? Do we start small or just get the biggest venue in town and go out in 'faith' as I believe the term is and see how we go?"

"Oh, let's not worry too much yet. I reckon Carl will have his ideas, because don't forget he has a vested interest and will want to see us succeed."

"I am sure he will also provide a full plan with the upcoming training."

True to his word within two weeks of being home in Hamilton Joe received an email with a 32-page franchise agreement as an attachment, which he promptly passed over to Yvette to peruse and comment on. She printed it off and then spent the next two hours making comments about each clause.

"There are some pretty heavy issues to address in here and, with my limited experience, I really think we need advice from a top franchise lawyer to look through this and guide us to a good outcome."

"I wouldn't worry too much about it my love, as I think Carl wants us to succeed as I told you before," replied Joe.

"Don't be a sucker. You've read about those movie deals where someone is supposed to get a percentage of the profits and even though the film makes millions the studios manage to trick the star or director out of their rightful entitlement. No, I insist we pass this over to Postow, Mitchell, Crews and Cheeseman-Skinner, who I understand are the best franchise lawyers in the city."

"Okay, you win, babe. Talk to them and set up a meeting after they've had the opportunity to consider it."

CHAPTER 16

The following week Yvette met with Mrs Postow, a leading specialist in franchising law. Numbered among her clients were some of the major fast food chains, lawn mowing franchises, cleaning conglomerates and a host of others.

"This is a strange thing Mrs Smith, if you don't mind me saying so. I am on the vestry of St Paul's Anglican Church. In all my years of legal practice and franchising law experience going back to the mid-1990s I have never seen a church or religious system in a franchise agreement. This will be a legal first for New Zealand."

"I know you are bound by client confidentiality and privilege Mrs Postow, so I know that anything I say will not leave this office. You should know that my husband and I are simply looking at this from a business and money-making opportunity. I want you to also look at the structure. I am guessing we will need a Charitable Trust but at the same time the trust must be able to pay a decent salary to my husband and me as workers in the new 'church' we are setting up," replied Yvette.

"You will need to be very careful that your church or should I say more accurately, business, does not breach the Fair Trading Act by engaging in misleading and deceptive conduct in trade."

"That is a given," replied Yvette.

"At this stage, I just want you to go through the draft agreement on a business basis and give me a summary of the issues and fish hooks that we need to address."

Intrigued by the opportunity and the challenge Mrs Postow was up to the task and agreed that she would look at it in detail and report back in a few weeks. After signing the terms of business Yvette was on her way home where she discussed the ins and outs with Joe.

"I think I blew Mrs Postow away by immediately telling her this was business deal so she must consider it as such. She is also going to ensure we are protected from the IRD and the Charities Commission, so Mr Moneybags doesn't rip us off. I am looking forward to seeing her response. By the way she said we were making legal history with this transaction."

Joe laughed, "I knew you were up to the task and I'm confident that when we start we won't be taken for a ride. By the way, old Carl sent me some links to some of his 'sermons'. He has a real cheek the way he always seems to preach on topics encouraging his people to give money. I hope the good folk of Hamilton are ready for this kind of church."

"Well, time will tell. The main thing is, are you confident you can pull this off?" Yvette inquired.

"Are you kidding? I am the anointed prophet and the people will be looking forward to handing over their money."

"However, I think we need to be cautious in our business set up," said Yvette.

"I think there is a fair bit of risk and if the church idea turns to custard, then we need to make sure we don't go bankrupt," she continued.

"So, what are you suggesting, Mrs Lawyer," replied Joe.

"It would be a good idea if we split the assets and I take full ownership of the two car yards as you suggested, while you take the church, its assets and its income or, at least, what is not officially in the charitable trust that will end up running the place. After all, if it all goes to plan, there will be a great deal of tax-free money. Your income will well exceed mine but, if it fails, then we still have the yards to fall back on. The creditors will not be able to claim against the car yard assets because they will be out of your name. You can then sign guarantees and leases without fear of personal comeback if the church goes south."

"Yes, you have a point but let's see how we go to start with as I think you might be being a bit conservative. We've gotta have faith, sister," exclaimed Joe, getting into the swing of the new jargon he was learning.

"Okay, but I think we need to revisit this three months into the new set up just to protect ourselves."

A truce was reached and the conversation was shelved for a little while.

Joe now concentrated on listening to some of Carl's sermons, checking through the instruction manual provided with the franchise agreement and checking out his 'to do' list of all the requirements he needed to have in place before the grand opening.

CHAPTER 17

The first of November came around very quickly and Joe found himself back in Memphis booked into a large hotel for a week with the training being undertaken in one of the hotel's corporate lounges. Joe was not sure what to expect but the agenda seemed to cover all sorts of issues that a church and its leaders might expect.

First was basic presentation, which had a number of different sections: grooming, public speaking, sermon material, mixing and mingling, meeting and greeting and tricks of the trade.

Joe was given special praise as he always liked to be well groomed. Carl explained to the group how a well-groomed handsome man would appeal to women and it was women who tended to be the bulk of attendees at a church. Carl even had preferred hair products, after shave and breath mints that he would make available to the new 'pastors' at 'cost' price. This aspect of 'selling' was not rocket science for Joe as he was very familiar with these add-ons but he welcomed the revision of basic principles.

Next was public speaking. Joe was an outgoing talkative kind of guy but the public speaking sessions were an eye opener as various techniques and key elements were shared. They were all given opportunities to practise and be critiqued. This was an invaluable experience and by the end of the sessions, Joe was very much a believer in his own skills, so he was certainly looking forward to performing in front of a live audience. This wasn't too different from his self-taught magic trick introductions.

Sermon material: Carl informed the group of disciples that he would send out regular sermons and he wanted them to note the themes in advance.

"You won't hear me talk about sin and such like. That is way too negative. People need uplifting. You have to raise their self-esteem so they feel good about themselves. You have to give them hope for health and prosperity. They don't want to hear about doom and gloom. They already have enough of this in their dreary week-day lives. You have to speak blessing. Visualise it, speak it, believe it and you will have it. My sermons will follow these themes and I guarantee people will flock to hear these positive messages. People don't have a lot of free time so you want to make sure that when they come to church on Sunday they have a happy uplifting experience. You will need volunteers to help run the church so you have to keep people enthused and supportive. Give them a vision to be part of. In addition, a sense of humour is important so have a funny story ready and try and keep it relevant to the message. You have to warm up the crowd.

"Prophecy is very important in the church. What is it I hear you ask? It is where you speak telling people what God has spoken to you. Well of course the real benefit is this gives you great opportunity to give authority to your words. After all if God has said something no one can contradict God or say what was spoken was wrong now, can they?"

Mix and Mingle: Over afternoon tea the attendees were invited to mix and mingle and engage in general chit chat. Part of the training involved some skimpily dressed cocktail waitresses who suddenly entered the room and began to offer them food and drinks. This was not all, as they unashamedly began to flirt with all the attendees.

Joe could see this as some kind of test so he made sure he remained polite but engaged. He cast his eyes around the room and, unsure whether it was a set up or not, noticed a couple of the attendees kissing the hostesses quite passionately. He continued to watch and observe until time was called and Carl came back into the room grinning like the proverbial Cheshire cat.

"Ha ha ha," he exclaimed, "that was entertaining observing you through the hidden camera feed."

"What did you learn?"

"Well," said one young man, "God gives us every good thing to enjoy."

This brought a round of laughs but Joe still had no idea where this was going, so he tactfully waited for others to respond.

Another attendee volunteered, "The man of God will face temptations which he must overcome."

"Excellent," replied Carl but still grinning away.

He added, "You are correct, of course, because you will all be observed constantly in a very public environment. There will be many enemies who will jealously want to take you down. If you want something on the side you must be discreet as there will be lots of opportunities, believe you me. Women will practically throw themselves at a successful and prosperous pastor. It's an occupational hazard."

Joe was astounded but on further reflection he shouldn't have been. Of course, if the main purpose was to make money, then naturally any additional side benefits could also be readily enjoyed.

After this entertaining session next on the agenda was the very important first two minutes of meeting and greeting. How do you find out someone's net worth and whether they were worth building a relationship with? How do you achieve that in a minimum length of time? Joe already had some ideas because when selling a car you had to quickly find the person's budget then stretch them higher, but Carl took this to a whole new level. Joe was lapping it up, knowing this was gold, both for the car yards and the new church.

Tricks of the trade: This would be a profitable session on the nitty gritty of miracles. Carl was quite up front. "Sometimes God heals miraculously but most times he doesn't so we have to help him along." He then went through a number of miracles that he said were guaranteed to be successful 100% of the time, and were proven to increase the size of the offering. One helpful tip was to start with the fake leg lengthening trick. This was readily explained. Get the person to lie on a mat and make sure that they are wearing shoes with a firm back and no straps. Next, ensure that they are not lying straight so one leg can be made to look longer than the other, then steadily put pressure on the 'good' leg and make the legs go back to normal. Joe was mesmerised. He'd never known of such blatant conning by a church man. How could a church of all places get involved in such things? Yet, Carl was the proof. Forty thousand people were eating up this stuff every week.

Carl also discussed various gimmicks that could be used. He noted one preacher liked to use his white jacket to wave around and whip people with it. This was the man Joe had seen on television just a few weeks before. Even wearing a gold tie could be seen as a 'trademark' for the preacher if it was worn consistently. Carl even said that some of the preachers liked to see people speaking in tongues, barking like dogs, howling, sobbing, uncontrollably laughing and fainting. The one useful thing he mentioned here, was if this were the road they wanted to take, it could lead to all sorts of trouble as those manifestations were similar to those observed in the practice of kundalini yoga. He didn't recommend that their franchised churches get too deeply into that. However, at the end of the day he said he didn't really care and would leave it to the individual. He didn't discount the potential for more control and, consequently, more money when using these techniques.

Joe's main takeaway from the week's intensive training was that the biggest cons needed a high degree of confidence. He thought he would stay away from the uncontrollable stuff as he felt he would want to keep a tight control on what was going on. He wasn't sure if he was ready for the ride of his life but he was certainly going to give it a go.

Knowing the relatively conservative nature of people from

Hamilton he decided he was not going to start slapping people or kneeing them in the stomach. He would try to develop his own unique trademark.

CHAPTER 18

Back in Hamilton, and following up from Carl's inspired teaching, Joe had to put in place one more thing every successful 'church' needed. This was a competent 'worship' leader who could use the power of music to create the necessary atmosphere to obtain maximum funds at the crucial offering time. The person needed to have both an outgoing personality and at the same time, be an accomplished piano or guitar player.

Joe had a friend, Brydon, who was a talented musician but whose talents were wasted at the local Mormon Temple where he was very much restricted in the style of his musical expression.

Joe promptly arranged a meeting at a local coffee shop where they sat down to discuss the offer of employment. After giving the general plan to start a church, but not discussing the actual business plan, Joe came to the point.

"Brydon, I would like to appoint you as my music director for my new church, which will be called the 'Hamilton Church of the Lord's Abundance'. The role is to be in charge of the music, to select and train musicians, guitarists, drummers and the like and to learn a range of musical styles. I am fortunate in that I am being assisted by a pastor of one of America's largest churches who will supply music sheets and appropriate songs we can use to get started. Of course, we can then add our own local music to the mix as we get things going. What do you say?"

Brydon responded rather sceptically, "Joe, I don't see myself as a hard core Christian. Does that matter?"

"No, not really, at the end of the day all you are doing is leading singing. No problem for you my friend."

The idea of being a full-time music director had some appeal and Brydon was interested but he was also a realist. If he were to quit his job working as a butcher in the local grocery co-op he would need a comparable income.

"Well Joe, I really appreciate the offer and I have a few guys that I jam with outside of the church, but to leave my current job I would need $45,000 a year."

"Mm, that's quite a bit. How about we agree on that figure and, after the first year, if we are going well and there is enough in the offerings to keep us going, we agree to up the salary to $60,000. How does that sound?"

"You sure the new church will get enough in the offering bowl to pay this kind of money," queried Brydon.

"Brother, I am confident. I am Joseph Smith, the newly anointed prophet for the Hamilton Church of the Lord's Abundance. If I declare it and believe it, it will surely happen. It is God's will for this new church to prosper. But, hey, if you don't want to be part of it let me know now. There are others lining up to be part of Hamilton's biggest church. Oh, and did I mention that in time the services will be broadcast on national television and you will of course be a significant figure on the show. Think of your profile and the fame that will come. Are you ready for the ride of your life?"

"Wow, I like your confidence. Okay, sign me up."

With that, Brydon had cast his lot with the 'anointed' prophet.

One of the other tasks on his to do list was to get his mother's support. He was wary because she had been a committed Mormon all her life and to start a new church, which could readily be seen as being in competition, might be a hard sell. However, Joe was also aware that the last few years had been very difficult for her because Steve had left the church and she felt she was the pariah. It was with some degree of concern that he drove around to his parents' place to have the discussion. Better to win mum over first as dad would not be the key player.

"Mum, you know very well how I have not really treated this whole 'anointed' prophet/teacher thing very respectfully growing up and even at the wedding when some mention was made of it again. In fact, I have been really cynical about the whole idea, dismissing it as an impossibility. I'm sorry about all that and the grief I have probably caused you. However, I have had cause on my honeymoon to reflect on my life and where it is going. Yvette and I attended a very large church in the United States when we were there. I also had occasion, as I told you, to visit Utah as well as the largest church in the world, St Peter's in Rome. As a result, I want to become a preacher and I have some wonderful news for you. I am going to set up my own church here in Hamilton."

"But that's wonderful news son," beamed his mother.

"But, you can't just set up a Mormon church. There is all sorts of red tape. You haven't even done the two years voluntary work overseas."

"You're correct Mum, but it will be a regular Christian church," replied Joe.

"On the other hand, have you considered what that entails? You haven't had any training and I don't think you know the Bible all that well. As far as I know you don't even pray."

"Plenty of ministers have had their training in the school of life and hard knocks, and I believe I don't need formal training. Anyway, I have already had a week of extensive training. As you know, I can sell cars so I reckon I can sell religion. I don't think it will be too difficult. After all you always said I had the gift of the gab."

"Don't be crass Joseph," said his mother with some horror at Joseph stating he could 'sell' religion.

"You don't sell religion. It is a special thing and not something like a used car."

"I'm sorry Mum but you know what I mean. I want to be a force for good in this town and help people find God. Now I know it will be different from the Mormon practices but some things will be the same. There will be plenty of singing and just like you I now believe God has anointed me so I will be able to preach. I am already looking through selected passages in the New Testament."

"I guess we will just have to wait and see. You will understand that although I will be behind everything you do it might take me a little bit of time to extricate myself from the temple before I join your church."

"Yes, completely understood, thank you, but you know I couldn't do this without your support and backing."

After discussing his plans and meeting most of his mother's concerns and answering her questions Joseph was satisfied that was one more thing he could cross off the list but more importantly, he knew he could count on his mother to bring along her friends, especially to the grand opening.

The next step in his multiple tasks was to find the largest building in Hamilton that was available for rent. He was aghast at the cost of hiring some of the venues. The Claudelands Events Centre and the Mystery Creek Events Centre were too large but remained a future possibility. In the end he settled on a large community hall that was very solidly booked during the week but was always available Sundays. It was large enough to hold 1000 people and had a suitable kitchen and other facilities. In addition, there was plenty of storage space for sound equipment, musical instruments and other items needed every Sunday. He was able to book if for every Sunday for a year and, as a church, the rent was fixed at a minimal level. Already he was ahead in his budget calculations.

Joe was getting quite excited with the anticipation of getting his new venture up and running but many small and large jobs remained. He let Yvette deal with the lawyers and after some to-ing and fro-ing with Carl, his lawyers, and their own, an agreement they could live with was signed.

Carl felt it very important that he come and lead the opening service. It would be a good excuse to try out the new Gulfstream. Of course, selling the trip to his own people was an easy matter, exhorting them to give for the need of the gospel to be preached in the outer most parts of the earth, even in distant New Zealand.

There was still a lot to do. Joe kept himself busy learning the new jargon, practising his 'preaching' trying his best to sound humble but persuasive, and having regular meetings with Brydon, his music director, to see how he was getting along with the various songs that Carl had been sending.

Joe had been given some marketing advice from Carl but some of it was just too American to work so he had his car yard marketing gurus look at it and make some changes. He wondered whether it was worth having some initial television advertisements but thought that could wait until the church was flush. What he needed, and was advised to do by his marketing people, was to have something spectacular happen at the first meeting. A special 'miracle' was required. He had to start big.

This was going to require some clever thinking and acting. He pondered the problem for a few days and he thought the removal of a very large growth might just swing it. The person to be healed could not be a local Hamiltonian so he had to dig around in his list of old buddies to see who he could persuade to accept a few dollars to come on stage and be 'healed'.

He knew a school friend who was always a bit shady in his dealings and would be a ready player, so he arranged to meet Tom Cruikshank in Auckland a few days later.

Meeting in a suburban café in Pukekohe for lunch Tom was intrigued by the phone call he'd received earlier in the week about an opportunity to make a quick buck.

"Joe," he said, "long time no see, what have you been up to since leaving school?"

"Oh, a bit of this and a bit of that but now I want to let you in on a little secret. I am starting a church."

"Whoa, that's a bit left field. I never knew you were religious."

"Well, I've changed and now God has led me to start a church in Hamilton and I just know it will be the biggest and greatest. It will be terrific. The best church in Hamilton and people will flock to it. I will put Hamilton and Joseph Smith on the map. I am God's chosen man."

Tom's immediate response was "what a dick" but decided to keep those thoughts to himself.

"Sounds like you are getting ahead of yourself, young fella. How do you plan to bring in the numbers?"

"Well, this is where it gets interesting. I know God is going to heal people and you know how people want to be free of their sicknesses and ills, but just in case He chooses not to heal some people this is where I need a real show stopper. I need your help. However, before I give you all the details are you interested in making $300 cash for less than a morning's work?"

"You bet, but what's the catch?"

"Just read this," replied Joe as he whipped out a one-page pre-prepared non-disclosure/confidentiality agreement from his briefcase. Yvette had helpfully prepared this the day before.

"You will have to sign this before I can tell you anymore."

"Okay, I'm intrigued," and with a flourish Tom quickly signed the document and pushed the paper back across the table.

"Give me the goods," he continued.

"It is as simple as I can say it. I want to get a makeup guy to put a very realistic growth on your throat. I want you to come forward when I call you and say a few words from a script I will give you. I will then pray a few words, place a large scarf around your neck and then pull off the growth. You will then testify using words from the script and from then on people will start coming to the church. There may even be some opportunity for some more 'miracles' but obviously we will need to change your features, such as having your hair dyed, growing a beard, wearing glasses and the like."

"I don't believe it. I've never heard of these kinds of fake miracles before. That's crazy man. People will not fall for it. I am as good a con man as the best of them but this is a whole new level."

"Let me put you straight, Tom. Remember in the 80s on television there were all these stories about Mexican and Filipino faith healers who removed lumps from people's bodies without surgery. All fake, but thousands of people believed in them. The key thing here is that although the miracle will be a fake, only known to you and me, it will give people hope and a positive outlook. With a change in attitude, they will even see their own health improve, which is what I want it to do. Think of it this way. You will be helping people have 'faith' that they too can be healed."

"Well, when you put it like that, I can't really see anything wrong with it so, yes, count me in."

"Okay then, brother, you will hear from me again in the next few weeks just before the opening. Can you give me your address so I can send you the script? I don't want to use email in case you get hacked. Unbelievers out there won't understand and I'm sure when I become popular there will be people who will be out to knock me down."

After concluding their business Joe drove off in his fairly new Commodore Calais, confident that he was getting all the boxes ticked and nothing would prevent an amazing start to his new life as the 'anointed prophet Joseph Smith'. There was just one thing. What sort of car would best suit his image? He wasn't sure what sort of car Carl drove but he made a mental note to find out soon. Perhaps an 'anointed prophet' should have that Porsche?

CHAPTER 19

Finally, everything was ready. The venue had been hired. The advertising in the local paper had been done and flyers had been dropped into letterboxes. Two faces appeared on the flyer – the famous Carl Quincy Adams and the not so famous, Joseph Smith.

Joe had called on his network of friends and acquaintances to fill some roles in the grand opening. The after-church catering had been sorted. The carpark attendants had been briefed. The ushers were hovering about the foyer. The musicians were prepped and ready to go. Lighting and smoke machines had been hired and installed. Carl had arrived and there had been some publicity on radio and even on the local news as it was not every day a private jet arrived in Hamilton. Carl was in his element giving interviews and he was very effusive in his praise for his 'sidekick' the Reverend Joseph Smith.

Joe was teased a little about his name but was able to turn things around when he said,

"You know, Joseph Smith founded a very large movement. I believe God has called me to set up a church here in Hamilton. Who knows, like my namesake it too may quite easily grow to be a worldwide phenomenon."

It was with a real sense of excitement that Joe and his team of greeters met people at the auditorium. The greeters had been quickly roped in and were none other than the lovely sales team from the car yards, it being a necessary and exceptional occasion for which it had been decided to shut the yards for the day.

The advertising and publicity had worked and people streamed into the building. There was a buzz of excitement in the air.

Joe stood and as confident as a circus promoter, he addressed the crowd.

"Thank you for coming to church today. Who is excited about what God is going to do today? Who wants to be blessed? Who is looking for a 100-fold blessing?"

After 10 minutes or so of revving up the crowd Joe introduced the Reverend Carl Quincy Adams all the way from America.

"I am privileged to know this fine pastor. He leads one of the largest churches in America. I am humbled he has come all the way to New Zealand and taken time from his busy ministry to meet us and give our first sermon as we open up this new fellowship of God's people today."

Joe waxed lyrically for a few minutes longer and with a hearty hug gave the floor to the Reverend Carl.

He was quite the picture, white suit, white shoes and a flamboyant multi-coloured tie. He launched into his well-rehearsed speech seasoned with honey and flattery.

"What a real privilege for me to come to New Zealand. What a beautiful country. Hamilton is a wonderful city. I can hardly believe I am here. I have heard so much about New Zealand and its people and after longing for many years to come, now here I am being a small bit player on this memorable day in the history of this great city. Make a note Hamilton, today is the day God will move here in this hall. At this hour during the opening of this wonderful church you will see God move. You have a great pastor in Joseph, my brother. I am impressed that you have before you such a man of God. My, you guys look terrific. You look ready to receive the blessing of God. I feel in my spirit that some exciting things are going to happen this morning. Hamilton are you ready?"

Carl then began to speak for the next ten minutes or so about what a great church he'd founded and how the people were so giving and how very much they had been blessed in return.

Joe took over, introduced Brydon, and then the music team flawlessly led the congregation in some singing. The lighting guy, who had also been hired, made sure the spectacle was one to remember. He provided the right mood changes, a bit of strobe here and there, then he darkened the stage before a solid white light shone side-on to Joe before he was to hand over to Carl to preach.

So far so good, it was all going ahead according to the agreed script as Joe walked to the front of the stage.

"You know, just during our time of singing God laid it on my heart that there is a young man here in this congregation who God wants to heal. Young man, God gave me a picture of a growth that has been plaguing you for a number of years and doctors have been unable to heal you. You are like the woman who came to Jesus and had faith to believe that if she came to just touch the hem of his garment she would be healed. I believe the growth may be on the upper part of your body, possibly your neck. Come forward and let me pray for you that God may heal you. Have you got faith this morning?"

Joe waited. Nothing happened so he spoke again.

"Don't be shy. This is your morning. Give God a chance to do his work. Come on, come forward. I know there is someone here. Get out of your seat and come forth. There is a miracle waiting for you."

Another minute passed. The congregation looked around in anticipation and then a young man with a grey woollen scarf wrapped around his neck edged his way out of a seat about half way towards the back of the auditorium and made his way forward in a slow shuffle. He came up the stairs to the stage and Joe reached his hand out to shake hands as he brought him on to the stage.

"Sir, what is your name?" Joe inquired.

"Tom," the young man responded.

"Well Tom, what do you want God to do for you?" asked Joe.

"I want my growth on my neck to be healed," he said.

"Can I see it?"

Tom peeled back his scarf to reveal a very large lump sticking out from the side of his neck. It was clearly visible to the congregation on the big screen that was at the back of the stage.

There were a few gasps as it was not a pretty sight, especially to those sitting at the front.

"Tom, I think God is going to do a wonderful thing for you today. He wants to heal you. Are you ready to be healed?"

"Yes, sir," he replied enthusiastically.

"First, there is a story in the book of Acts of how the Apostle Paul prayed over a handkerchief and then it was placed on a person who was healed. I didn't bring a handkerchief to church this morning but I don't think it matters. Do you mind if we use your scarf in place of the handkerchief?"

"Whatever you want, I just want to be healed."

Joe helped Tom wrap his scarf around his head and then placed both hands on the scarf directly above the growth.

He then said to the congregation, "Jesus didn't do long prayers for healing but they were very simple and to the point so I will follow his example."

"I say to you devil, get your hands off this young man. Tom, may you know God's blessing. I speak a word of freedom over your life. Be healed."

The makeup artist had done a pretty good job, almost too good. To the crowd it looked like Joe was wrestling with Tom as he was grabbing his neck and shaking him about. Suddenly with a loud "hallelujah" Joe seized the whole scarf from around Tom's neck and hurled it to the back of the stage as far as it would go revealing young Tom with a 'healed' neck.

"Praise the Lord," Tom shouted, and "thank you Pastor Joe," as the congregation erupted in a cacophony of shouts.

After that event there was more singing and then Carl took to the stage in preparation for the most important part of the service, the offering. He stressed how God was doing a new thing and to be part of it now was the time to sow abundantly so in due time there would be an abundant harvest to reap. Of course, Carl was a well-practised expert at extracting money from wallets and it certainly seemed this would be a bonanza first service.

He concluded by saying, "It is God's will for you to live in prosperity instead of poverty. He wants us to have plenty of money to fulfil the destiny he has for us. Give and it will be given unto you."

After the offering bags were taken up and placed at the front of the stage Carl stepped forward to give one of his more popular sermons, focusing, of course, on God's desire to bless abundantly.

Finally, after 90 minutes the service was over and people moved into another room for a very nice catered lunch. This was not the usual bring a plate of sausage rolls or a chicken casserole but rather a local café had been recruited to bring some cold meats, salads and some nice desserts. They had even set up a state of the art coffee machine.

People could be heard saying, "Wow, if this is what we can expect of church I am definitely coming next week. That was terrific. Best church service ever."

The vibe and atmosphere were enjoyed by all, and after the last person left Carl and Joe sat down together for a quick debrief.

"I reckon, you did pretty good for a greenhorn. You've got the makings of a fine preacher."

Who knew if Carl was just using flattery or was genuine in his praise. Joe didn't care but the conversation soon turned to the main event.

"How much did we make partner?" asked Carl.

"It was just over $20,000," replied Joe.

"How much over? Let's be a bit more exact here."

"$20,064.30 is the exact figure I believe."

"Not bad for an opening but as word spreads, I expect you to be getting a lot more than that. Congratulations."

Carl didn't wait around and a few hours later he was back in the Gulfstream heading home to Memphis.

"I hope I don't have to come to this dreary town again," he was overheard remarking to his pilot as they made their preparations to leave.

"The quicker we leave the better."

While Joe was elated with the first offering he was already think-ing ahead and his best business principle that cash was king. Perhaps it would be relatively easy to not count the offering as carefully as had been done this morning. After all the smaller amount that was declared the less that greedy old Carl would get his hands on.

While giving online and through automatic payments were likely to be the most usual way of collecting money this, unfortu-nately, was readily able to be audited. The cash offerings, which he wanted to promote, could easily be skimmed.

CHAPTER 20

Rosemary Plimmer was a close friend of Lizzie Harris. Although not as tall or as good looking as Lizzie, she still possessed a captivating beauty with her clear hazel eyes, full smile and beautiful teeth.

She decided she needed to catch up with Lizzie and phoned her one evening. They arranged to meet the following Saturday afternoon at Hamilton Gardens. The sun was shining warmly as they wandered around taking in their splendour.

"Lizzie, I know you have been attending the 'Hamilton for Jesus' Church but have you ever been to the Hamilton Church of the Lord's Abundance? I went a couple of times as my own church is a bit strict and the music is dull and outdated. It seemed to be really buzzing. I really value your opinion."

"Rosemary, to tell you the truth even though I was bridesmaid for Yvette Smith, the senior pastor's wife, I still haven't attended despite a number of invitations. I was overseas during its big opening but I've heard it has already grown quite large."

"Can I suggest we go together next Sunday and see what it is all about? Will you come with me?" said Rosemary.

"Yes, what harm can that be? We can check it out together and compare notes. Tell you what, I will phone Yvette and she can save a couple of seats for us. We can then meet up afterwards and share our thoughts."

The following Sunday the two young women drove into the carpark at the community centre and were immediately struck by the warm greeting from the handsome young men who were at the door and shook hands with them. One of them even commented on what beautiful red hair Lizzie had. While Lizzie was soaking up the attention Rosemary was more interested in the very attractive young women from the same team who were focusing on greeting the young men who came in. Lizzie noticed their impeccable make-up, and their stylish clothing which she thought somewhat over the top for a Sunday morning church service.

Nevertheless, they made their way forward and saw Yvette milling around the front of the hall chatting to people, so they edged their way towards her, moving past an enthusiastic group of people engaged in happy conversation. There was an air of excitement as the musicians played upbeat pre-service music. Lizzie overheard an excited woman saying, "I wonder what miracles we will see today and isn't Pastor Joe such a dreamboat."

Catching Yvette's eye Lizzie introduced her to Rosemary and then the 'anointed' prophet himself came over to say hello.

He gave Lizzie a very warm hug and a kiss on the cheek.

"Lizzie, where have you been? Haven't seen much of you since the wedding. We must catch up soon, "he said, giving her a sly wink at the same time.

"Who is your lovely friend?"

Lizzie introduced Rosemary, who was starting to blush after hearing Joe's comment. Then, after some small talk, Joe excused himself and said he had to get the service underway. He then moved to one of the front seats in the auditorium and sat back as Brydon skilfully amped up the music and got the congregation singing with gusto.

Lizzie didn't know the song but it was a catchy tune and the crowd was enjoying it. On the other hand, while enjoying the song, Rosemary noticed that there seemed to be a few lines of choruses that were repeated over and over, which she felt was a bit too much. She also observed the words were more people-focused than God-focused. She didn't want to be overly critical so joined in as best she could and soon the two young women were busy singing along with the others.

After a bracket of about three songs Brydon introduced Joe.

"Here comes Pastor Joseph to the stage so let's give him a warm welcome."

The congregation clapped unanimously and some of the youth whistled and cheered extravagantly.

"Very pleased to be with you again this morning in the house of God. Are we ready to sow a seed of faith this morning and see what God will do? I for one am looking forward to all that God has for us. You know, I love that parable of the farmer who went out to his field to sow his crop. Some of the crop yielded 30 times, some 60 times and some 100 times more than what was planted. As it is in the natural so it is in the spiritual. God wants us to sow the seed of faith and look forward to the increase. Here in the Church of the Lord's Abundance I want to see 100-fold increase and I am sure you do to. With that in mind let us give generously this morning for the work of God and sow that seed of faith."

As the offering bags were being passed around Rosemary watched people dropping in $20 notes and $50 notes. It seemed like the people were very generous as the bags were collected and placed at the front at the feet of the prophet.

Joe added, "Always come prepared with cash in your pocket, but for those of you who don't like carrying cash around make sure you stop at the Eftpos machine on the way out. We also have an online option for giving but have cash available because there will be additional opportunities to be blessed at every service."

He prayed, "Thank you Lord that this is indeed the Church of the Lord's Abundance and you want your people to prosper and live abundant lives. May you multiply these seeds and bless the people as they have given. May they receive a 100-fold return. Amen."

Again, this seemed a prayer that was not God-focused and quite different from the prayers Rosemary had heard at Mercy Fellowship. No mention of the funds being used for the glory of God and the extension of his kingdom or anything like that. Oh well, she had to keep an open mind about this church. Didn't the Bible teach, "Judge not lest you be judged?"

The service continued with more enthusiastic singing and then there was a short sermon from Pastor Joe. The sermon focused on living your best life now and being blessed by God. It was clear to Rosemary from the sermon that being blessed by God meant enjoying good health and a prosperous lifestyle.

Rosemary observed there were minimal Bible references and the teaching seemed to be just Joseph's experiences and anecdotes. It was interesting enough but quite a contrast from the scripture-based teaching she had observed at Mercy Fellowship.

After wrapping up the sermon, a final song was sung before the congregation was dismissed.

As they were leaving Joe and Yvette offered to take the young women out to a café lunch to enjoy fellowship together. They decided on the River Kitchen in town. They had a convivial time and Joe enjoyed sitting with the three attractive women garnering stares of envy from the various guys who wandered in for lunch, and the hostility from their wives or girlfriends.

Inevitably, Joe wanted to hear about the girls' experience of church that morning.

Lizzie began, "I enjoyed it, the music was lively, people were enjoying themselves and the motivational talk was excellent."

Rosemary countered, "I enjoyed it but it was quite different from what church has been like for me in the past. I agree the music was lively. However, although your sermon was positive it didn't seem to mention God often and I notice you didn't seem to use the Bible much."

Joe quickly and smoothly responded, "You know in these latter days God is raising up a vibrant new body. The old ways will fade away as he is doing a new thing. You can't put new wine into old wineskins. You can't put God in a box. He is far bigger than that. I am finding that God often speaks to me in dreams and visions. As I listen, I preach and teach on those things to give everyone encouragement. You know, in the days we are living in people are anxious and concerned. I give them a message they need to hear that God wants to bless them with good health and prosperity and that is why they leave so uplifted in their hearts."

"Can't argue with that I guess," said Lizzie.

Rosemary kept her own counsel thinking that somehow an important point or message was being overlooked.

As they enjoyed a very pleasant meal and wine together Rosemary couldn't help but observe a couple of things. Joe was being quite flirtatious with Lizzie but the other more puzzling thing was that Yvette either didn't notice or didn't seem to care. Lizzie was certainly enjoying the attention, but this was something Rosemary would discuss with her as they left the café and headed back in Lizzie's car to her flat.

"He's a bit of a flirt, don't you think?" Rosemary said as they got into the car.

"Yeah, I guess he is, but just a bit of fun and after all he is married so I don't think he was coming on to me," Lizzie responded.

"Well, you just be careful. A guy like that will certainly attract the attention of the ladies. He is certainly the classic tall, dark and handsome, well dressed, speaks well, and is a bit of a mover and shaker. If you met him in the street, you certainly wouldn't pick him as a preacher, more likely a film star, basketball player or someone of that ilk."

"Yvette and I have known each other for a few years now. Surely, she must be aware of this? What woman wouldn't be and yet she says nothing. I'm sure a lot of guys flirt with her too so it is probably brushed off by both of them as harmless fun," said Lizzie.

"Look, no problem, let's just see what happens. I expect it was just a one-off thing. Do you want to attend church again next week with me?"

"Yeah, okay, I am still curious as to what is going on. It is so different to what I know of church."

The two women then agreed to meet and travel to church the following week.

The church service on the next Sunday happened to coincide with a time that Joe planned another miracle. Joe decided to speak again on his favourite topic, which was God providing abundantly, and began to teach about Jesus' first miracle at Cana in Galilee. In Joe's mind it was all about abundance and how God would supply even better than the original wine to those who believed.

"Who believes God can turn water into wine today?" he exclaimed.

There were not many amens so he said it again, "Who believes God can turn water into wine?"

"Yvette, fetch me some water please. I am feeling thirsty."

On cue, Yvette brought a glass and a pitcher of water and sat them down on a little side stand. No-one could observe that in the bottom of the glass was a small amount of white powder. To all intents and purposes, the glass looked completely empty. Joe made a show of pouring the water from a little height so people could see he really was pouring water into the glass and suddenly before everyone's eyes the water mysteriously changed colour and appeared to have become wine.

This was a trick Joe had practised many times in his childhood at his magic parties but even he was surprised at its impact on the crowd. Now he had them in the palm of his hand and Joe nonchalantly carried on with his sermon almost as though nothing had happened.

"Do you expect miracles to happen?"

"Why not?"

"God is the same yesterday, today and forever. Sow a seed and believe for that harvest. Let's take up the offering."

After the service Joe was pleased that the offering had increased by about 35% more than before and he decided to review the matter with Yvette at their Monday morning 'directors' meeting.

The next morning Yvette mentioned how well the 'miracle' was received but she couldn't help warning Joe that he had better not go too far with some of his tricks as surely at some point he would be exposed as a fraud.

"No worries, my dear. People will believe even more outrageous things if they want to. Who was it that said if you are going to tell a lie the bigger the better?"

Yvette responded, "Might have been Josef Stalin who I think said, 'the death of one man is a tragedy. The death of millions is a statistic'. I don't know about that but just be careful and don't pull out a miracle every week."

"Yes, keep them hungry is good advice and keep them expectant. After all they do come for entertainment."

"Moving on, how do you think Brydon is going with the music?"

"Actually, he is very polished and his team are enthusiastic. I think as an encouragement we should give them $1000 to arrange their own celebration and enjoy a night out together. It would be a good team building exercise for them."

Joe decided this was a good idea. After all, people should not be taken for granted and he needed to keep an enthusiastic team going. Anything that would improve the bottom line was worthwhile and to be encouraged. While Brydon as team leader was on a salary, the other talented musicians were volunteers, so they would be pleased to be recognised in this way.

CHAPTER 21

The next day Joe and Yvette sat down with a cup of coffee on the terrace of their rented house and reviewed their business enterprises.

The car yards were doing fine after a bit of a slump the previous year. A new advertising campaign seemed to be working and a better incentive for their staff was producing results. They were profitable but not spectacular as the current staff were not as gifted at sales as Joe and Yvette had been.

Now that the church was up and running smoothly Yvette decided it might be better if she gave more attention to the yards and had less involvement in the church. She was a little troubled by the outright deception she had seen and still didn't like being associated with the American 'sleazebag'.

"I think it would be better if we can lift the game with the car sales and I think I am better utilised there than in the church. I can motivate the staff and lead by example. Perhaps we can even use the church newsletter for me to advertise the car sales?"

"Good idea, honey," responded Joe, but I will need an executive assistant as the church continues to grow.

"In just nine months the church is doing so well and with the money we are making with the yards and, now with the church, I think we need to make the decision to move out of this place and into a home of our own. We need to look at some houses and I think the best place in Hamilton for us is in Harrowfield. I mean, if I am going to preach abundance, it had better look like we are enjoying our own abundance."

"I am good with that, let's start looking," said Yvette.

Yvette continued, "You know Joe I have always been distrustful of Carl despite him getting us off to a good start. I think for risk avoidance we go ahead and enter into a relationship property agreement whereby I have the car yards in my name. I'll relinquish my role on the charitable trust that runs the church and no longer draw a salary from the church. Perhaps you can appoint our accountant or someone else to that role in my place. Then whatever income flows from the yards I can keep in my name and you keep the income from the church in your name."

"Are you sure?" Joe retorted.

"The church is making far more than the yards, and is on a consistently higher trajectory so that doesn't seem a fair split. It hasn't even reached its full potential. I mean I can see in the future we can set up separate franchise territories, which could happen quite easily and would multiply the profits."

"It is actually just a paper transaction," Yvette responded smoothly, "as we can still share what we make in our communal pot. It is only if something were to go wrong."

"Okay, sounds good to me. Let's diary it but, first, let's go and look for a house. Actually, we can sort this at the same time with the eventual house purchase."

Over the next few weeks, they scoured the papers, real estate brochures and looked at a number of houses. Finally, when they were about to give up, their agent, Charlie Baxter, phoned to say there was a house that would suit them extremely well and it was just coming on to the market. A widow had decided her house was too big. It needed a bit of minor work and she just wanted a smaller brand new place in a local retirement village that she had set her heart on.

When Joe and Yvette heard what street it was in they were delighted to find it was Kotahi Avenue in Beerescourt. This was not Harrowfield, but even better in Charlie's opinion. It was therefore, with some excitement, that the agent met them at the property and introduced them to Mrs Smythe-Prendergast, the owner. She was immediately struck by Yvette's beauty and charm. Joe bided his time, allowing his wife to work her magic to soften up the old lady. It was just the house they wanted but at $1,200,000 it was a steep ask. Something needed to happen.

Yvette explained to Mrs Smythe-Prendergast that they were a young married couple starting out. They did operate two car yards but car sales were not going so well at the moment and the lease payments were high. Although the house was priced way more than they could afford they just felt that God wanted to bless them.

It was time for Joe to step in. "I believe that just as God has blessed you with this wonderful home it is now our turn as I am sure he wants you to pass this blessing on to us. Do you attend church Mrs Smythe-Prendergast?"

"Well yes, I do. I have been a member of the Church of Jesus Christ of Latter-day Saints for many years."

"What a coincidence. My family attended for many years as well. In fact, my name is Joseph Smith, named after the great prophet, and now I am continuing the legacy having started my own church a few months ago."

"Oh, you must be Lorna Smith's son. She was always so proud of you telling everyone she knew how you had a special anointing and God was going to mightily use you in his service."

Joe continued, "I am the very one. That special prophecy is coming to pass. Have you heard of the Hamilton Church of the Lord's Abundance? God is really blessing everything we do."

"Actually, I have. I read something in the paper about it just before it started. I wish you well."

"Thank you so much for showing us your lovely home. I will leave it to Charlie to draw up the papers but we are definitely keen to buy. Do you mind if I bring a builder friend around just to do a quick check before we put in our offer?"

"Sure, no problem," the old lady replied.

"You are such a lovely couple I really would like to sell it to you."

"Thank you so much Mrs Smythe-Prendergast, we will be in contact with you for sure in the next few days."

They bid farewell and, on the way out, Yvette remarked that she really must have the house as it was an amazing property in a beautiful cul-de-sac with views over the Waikato River. She could visualise how she could modernise it and bring in some flair and panache to its tired bones.

"Leave it to me, my love. I will get it sorted but I'm certainly not going to pay $1,200,000. After all, it will only cost the old lady $500,000 to get a brand new unit in a retirement village. What does she need the extra money for at her age?"

The following day Andrew from Number One Builders turned up at the site with a very emphatic brief from Joe to find as much fault with the property as possible.

Andrew spent the next couple of hours noting every possible fault he could see and as per his brief, he exaggerated so much that it looked like the house should practically be condemned.

Joe didn't want Charlie to be aware of what he was up to, so with report in hand, he made an appointment to meet with the old lady. For appearance's sake he brought Yvette along knowing what a good impression she had made on the first visit.

After sitting down to a cup of tea Joe was most apologetic.

"I am sorry Mrs Smythe-Prendergast but the house is not as good as I hoped it would be. I've had my builder friend look over it and he has produced a very comprehensive report. I have it here with me. It is 19 pages long but I won't bore you with the details. Let me just show you the main summary of issues that the builder identified."

"Oh dear," replied the somewhat shaken woman.

"I can't possibly sell you this house in its current condition. I don't know what to do. I would not feel right selling you a property that has got so many faults. I just didn't realise."

"Don't despair," said Yvette.

"We are young and we can certainly over the next few years spend some time and money fixing things up. We know you are keen to get into the retirement village so, how about we just reduce the price a little and take it off your hands. After all, now that you know the issues, it will be hard to sell to someone else."

Joe followed up. "I am sorry but I think a fair price would be $950,000 having regard to all the work that needs doing. I think you should just tell Charlie Baxter that you just want to get rid of the place quickly and that you feel God wants you to give it to Joe and Yvette at a good price to be a blessing to them."

"Oh, thank you, what a relief. You are such nice people and I am sorry the house is not as good as you hoped for. Yes, $950,000 sounds very fair having regard to all the problems you identified."

"Excellent, I will have Charlie draw up the papers and we will sign unconditionally for a quick sale. When would you like settlement so that you have enough time to move into the village?"

"How about three weeks?" she responded.

"Sounds fair and reasonable. Thanks so much. Charlie Baxter will come around later this afternoon with our signed offer. Good bye Mrs Smythe-Prendergast. Perhaps we will see you at church soon?"

"Goodbye."

On their way out Joe inquired of Yvette,

"What does the Bible say? A fool and his money are soon parted? That builder's report sure worked a treat and we've got ourselves a real bargain."

A little surprised, Charlie completed the offer as instructed and then went to Kotahi Avenue to see the vendor that evening.

"That price seems well under valuation. These buyers will be getting a real bargain. Are you sure you do not want to countersign at a higher price?"

"Absolutely not," she declared resolutely.

"They are a wonderful young couple and I know they will treasure this house and I want to give them a discounted price."

Once she had made her mind up the Agent was unable to persuade her to up the price so the contract was signed. Charlie was disappointed his commission was not as high as it could have been.

The upside was he didn't have to spend the next few weeks with advertising and open homes. This was a quick deal and he justified it as a bird in the hand being worth two in the bush.

The time passed quickly but there was a bit of a hiccup when the vendor needed to extend the settlement date. Her solicitor had pointed out that she couldn't settle or occupy the villa at the village until 15 working days had elapsed after the licence to occupy had been signed. There was no getting around that law.

"We will have to ask for an extension of time for the settlement date," he informed her.

After receiving the request for the extension from his own lawyer, Joe consulted Yvette as to what would happen if they did not agree.

"We could charge the old lady interest at 14% until settlement date so, as she is asking for a week, 14% on $950,000 is $2550.68 for the week."

"Wow, we should certainly do that," exclaimed Joe.

This was too much for Yvette, who responded, "Joe that's terrible, we got the property for a song and now you want to claim an extra $2500? Look, why don't you simply be gracious and tell the old lady that of course she can have the extension and see what comes of it.?"

"Of course, you're right as usual. Do you think as compensation we could ask if she would let us have her old writing desk? After all she, will have no room in the new place and I suspect it might be worth something."

"All right, I will mention it to the lawyer and ask him to pass it on as not a demand but something the vendor may like to consider."

As a result, the settlement was delayed a week and the young couple soon found themselves living in a very upmarket street in Hamilton. It was not long before Joe wanted to do some major renovations – new kitchen and bathroom and opening up some space between lounge and dining room to make a more spacious and modern living area.

Andrew from Number One Builders and his team were soon on

site and work was soon under way to bring the house up to a more modern standard.

Two months later Joe had the house valued and was very satisfied to see it had climbed to $1,450,000.

"I think we should sell and do the same again," he said.

"Not yet," replied Yvette.

Although they had agreed the house should be placed in her name, she was solely responsible for the loans so that Joe wouldn't be hampered by personal guarantees and their private lives could be separated from church life.

"Let's just live in it for a while and enjoy it."

"Okay, sweetie, but I am conscious we have borrowed a fair bit and I am hoping interest rates will not rise."

"Hey, prophet, where is your faith? I am covering the loan myself from the car yards' income. The church is going well, and you're pulling in a very good wage much more than the car yards. I suggest you put some of that aside so that if there is ever a slump in the car business we can ride it out."

So, it was settled. Kotahi Avenue would be their home for the next little while.

CHAPTER 22

With Yvette returning to the yards in a more hands-on role Joe needed a new executive assistant.

He knew just the right person. He would discuss what a great opportunity this would be for someone with Lizzie Harris' skill set. He was rather looking forward to working with her. It wasn't that he didn't love his wife it was just that he felt he had more love to share around. Joe got right onto the job, phoning her to ask her to join him for lunch at a nearby café, informing her that he had an employment opportunity that he wished to discuss with her.

Lizzie was quick to agree and she arrived at the café to find Joe seated at a booth near the back. All eyes turned as Lizzie, with her long legs, full length white, night-clubbing boots, and a bright fluoro-pink miniskirt showing off her legs to maximum advantage as she sauntered through the room to meet Joe at the back.

"Wow, you look hot," Joe exclaimed, as he got up and gave her an affectionate hug.

"Hey, you're a married man. You're not supposed to say that," Lizzie replied with a cheeky grin as they both sat down in the booth that gave them a small modicum of privacy.

There was a sudden jolt to his mind and Joe left his fantasy and came back to reality. He now had his imagination slightly more under control. He got up to greet Lizzie who, as expected was dressed in modern office attire. She wore long dark slacks, a sensible white blouse, smart jacket, comfortable shoes and a bright Hermès scarf.

In a very business-like manner she got straight to the point,

"So, what's this employment opportunity you have in mind for me?"

"Well, it's like this. Yvette is going to spend more time managing the car yards and I need someone who will help me run the church. Someone who will be working closely with me, someone who is flexible and can work a bit later on the odd times when circumstances demand. I also want someone who can be a bit of a terrier and keep some of the nutters away from me. Basically I need to be freed up to spend more time on big picture church affairs such as vision casting and the like. You will effectively run the office as manager, allowing me the time to prepare for church services, other speaking events, and my future plans to increase the church and its reach. You will also need to deal with any media inquiries as I think there is a bit of jealousy in the community about how well we are doing. Effectively, you would almost be like a general manager. Do you think you can handle that kind of assignment?"

"Sounds quite challenging. To be fair I am getting a little bored with my current role. What is the salary package?"

"I will be more than fair with you and, given the importance of the role, we will start you on $50,000 per annum with five weeks' holiday a year and there will be the odd perks and benefits as well. You would need to be able to accompany me around the country on any speaking invitations I receive and in time there will likely be an overseas component as well."

"I am interested. Send me an employment contract and we will take it from there," she said very business-like but, at the same time trying to hide her delight at what she thought could be a great opportunity for herself.

Joe was equally quick to show his gratitude as he gave a broad grin and said, "When can you start?"

"I need to give four weeks' notice on my current role so that is the earliest I can move."

"Okay, very much looking forward to having you on board."

They shared an enjoyable meal together and Lizzie left the

meeting quite satisfied that she had secured what she hoped would be a very important and worthwhile role with many dimensions to it and a fairly decent salary as well. Guiltily, she even wondered what some of the perks might be.

The four week notice period dragged along but in time Lizzie was soon at her new desk appraising the situation – the computer system and the record keeping. However, when she came to talk about her involvement with the accounts she was met with a firm but definite caution.

"That will not be part of your role. Look to be fair, our accountant guards his territory like a pitbull so best not to rock that boat. Let's just leave that side of the business to him. If you need funds approved for office stationery or whatever, come and see me or send an email to Walter with your requirements. Okay?"

"Sure thing", replied Lizzie, "Just want to make sure I know what is what and what is expected. Do you have any office policies such as Health and Safety, sexual harassment, and other procedures?"

"You won't find any unwanted sexual harassment around here. This is a church not a law firm! We have however, been a bit loose on developing our systems but I am sure with your experience you will have us shipshape in no time. To be fair we have grown large quite quickly."

Lizzie enjoyed her new position. It was busy and, at the same time, challenging. After a few months settling into her new role Lizzie was very motivated.

At the Monday morning staff meeting when they came to the agenda item 'other business' she suggested an opportunity that she thought the church could be involved in.

"How about we start a soup kitchen? There are many poor people in Hamilton and if we leave this kind of work to the government the pattern of poverty will continue. They will spin it to say how well they are doing in reducing poverty but there will be no change. The press are in the government's pocket and will happily spout announcements telling us all how the number of people living in poverty is declining. We all know of course that the opposite is true. Shouldn't we do something?"

Joe tried to knock it on the head, "Well, soup kitchens are all well and good but they will be a significant cost to the business, I mean, the church, and what sort of benefit will they bring apart from feeding a few of Hamilton's poor?"

Lizzie, was a little shocked by this cold hearted response, but nevertheless continued, "I'm pretty sure it will not cost anything. Members can donate the food and I know we have contacts with some of the large food suppliers who will donate some produce. In addition (using the vernacular she had been picking up), we would be sowing a seed into the community and surely God will bring about the increase."

Joe threw out a lifeline of hope to encourage her. Lizzie had only recently been employed and he did not want to sow any discouragement in her direction.

"Okay, we're running out of time. Walter and I will have a discussion about this. In the meantime, please all pray about it and see what we should do. We will put it back on the agenda for next Monday's meeting. Right, that wraps things up now let's get back to work."

Joe wasn't sure what to do about this soup kitchen and he thought he would run it past Carl so that evening he phoned Carl to get his views on the subject.

"Hey, brother, how are you?" greeted Carl as he picked up the phone.

They chatted away before Carl turned the topic to money.

"Things seemed to have levelled off a little with the giving. What's up with that? Do you need more ideas to ramp it up a bit?"

"What about a soup kitchen?" asked Joe.

"Well, I can't see a lot of good in that," was Carl's response.

"The poor and the downtrodden don't have anything to put in the offering bowl so all it does is divert dollars away from Sunday morning offerings into food for the homeless. You know, I wouldn't feel too comfortable about that if the slice I am getting is diminished. It costs a lot of money to keep the church going and I am in the middle of a big building programme with my little place down in Florida."

Joe could imagine the 'little' place to be something like a five bedroom, six bathroom Tuscan villa lookalike, no doubt with marble tiling imported from Italy, a fancy swimming pool and probably a tennis court thrown in as well.

"What about the publicity and the goodwill?" inquired Joe.

"Surely people will see we are not just collecting money off people but we are doing good in the community and that in itself might attract some generous donors to the church?"

"Well, I for one, have not tried it but, hey, it might work in New Zealand. Your folk strike me as a little less gullible than Americans so this might give a little boost. Give it a trial but if it is costing you and me, then nip it in the bud quickly and pull the plug."

Lizzie was delighted to hear at the next week's staff meeting that her idea would be given the green light and she was put in charge of its promotion and fundraising. She took the opportunity on the following Sunday. She played a small promotional video of some of the homeless in Hamilton her team had filmed, and then Lizzie presented the challenge.

"Many of you have sowed into the life of this church and in return you have been blessed. I am asking you to dig a little deeper and now give of your time once a week on a Monday night, and some seed money, to get this new ministry up and running. We want to demonstrate the love of God in this community and bless the people with food. Sign up for how you can contribute by seeing me after the service in the foyer under the 'Soup Kitchen' banner."

Lizzie was suitably encouraged after a number of people came to see her in the foyer, volunteering both their time and money. She certainly hoped this opportunity would succeed and in time Joe would see she had good ideas and could be a strong leader in the church.

CHAPTER 23

Several streets away from the Hamilton Church of the Lord's Abundance there was a small unobtrusive hall down a tree-lined right of way. The only thing giving away that this was a church was a small sign that read Mercy Fellowship and that meetings were held at 10:00 am on Sunday mornings.

If the success of a church was to be measured by numbers attending then this particular fellowship was a complete failure. On the other hand, if one measured success by the maturity and spiritual growth of the church members, and it's no-compromise stance on preaching the gospel faithfully, then this fellowship would be ranked among the leaders.

On this particular Sunday, Pastor Gene Jacobson came to the pulpit and opened the word of God and began to preach from the gospel of Luke. This passage expounded upon the need for believers to take up the cross of Jesus and follow him.

Pastor Gene began his sermon centred around the text and after 45 minutes he finished with a warning concerning those who would twist the scripture for their own gain. He said further that he had been troubled by the existence and teaching of a very large Hamilton church and more would be shared next week.

True to his word, the following week Pastor Gene opened the Bible in the gospel of Matthew and read the passage regarding the temptation of Jesus.

He shared how Jesus had three temptations put to him by the devil.

Pastor Gene centred his comments on the text. He drew

attention to temptation and how the devil would offer promises of prosperity and a nice easy road to draw people away from a true faith in God and in his word. He contrasted the way of the cross with its motif of self-denial as a true Christian would embrace, with the superficial and enticing promises of health and wealth promised by the false church.

He quoted from a book he had been reading by Dr John McArthur – *Ashamed of the Gospel*:

Size does not signify God's blessing. In scripture big budgets, affluent members, and large membership rolls are never portrayed as valid goals. Real success is not prosperity, power, prominence or any of the worldly notions of success. Real success is doing the will of God, regardless of the consequences.

In conclusion, Pastor Gene gave a specific warning: "My friends, do not be deceived. Do not believe Joseph Smith. Like his namesake who founded the Mormon Church on lies and deception, he is leading people astray and is promising wealth and success and neglecting and even twisting the gospel for his own purposes.

"As I mentioned last week, 'What good is it for a man to gain the whole world and yet lose, or forfeit, his very soul?' 'Be on your guard. The devil prowls around like a roaring lion seeking those he may devour.' He is also a wolf in sheep's clothing trying to disguise himself but he only comes to steal and kill and destroy. 'Jesus came that you might have life and life in all its fullness.'"

He concluded by stating that he would be sharing a series of messages on sound biblical interpretation at the Wednesday night Bible Study and he encouraged all his people to study the word of God so they might be thoroughly equipped for every good work.

Rosemary Plimmer listened intently and was somewhat troubled as she left the meeting. She had visited Joseph Smith's church on several Sunday mornings, having enjoyed the rock style music and the ear-pleasing messages from the charismatic pastor. She wondered why she couldn't have the health and wealth promised as surely God would want to bless his people. She would discuss these things with her friend Lizzie but, first, she would attend the Bible Study on the next few Wednesday nights.

CHAPTER 24

Pastor Gene welcomed a small but keen group of his congregation to the Bible Study. They started with cups of tea and instant coffee together with a gingernut cookie each and, having chatted among themselves for 15-20 minutes, Gene brought the meeting to order and the 20 or so people sat down to take notes.

He began by saying that he had been concerned that people were being led astray by the false gospel being peddled across town by Joseph Smith and, no doubt, many others, particularly that brand of American preachers who regularly appeared on television asking for money.

He spent a few minutes introducing the philosophy behind the Word of Faith movement. He told his people they might have heard expressions widely used to describe these cults, such as 'the name it and claim it' or more crudely 'blab it and grab it' movements. He elaborated and in summary said that the study would cover four basic errors of interpretation of scripture that those teachers regularly used in their sermons.

Rosemary was alert, keen to listen and understand as she had some misgivings regarding Joseph's Smith's preaching but couldn't just put her finger on what was wrong. After all, he did quote some scripture; for example, "It is better to give than receive," and verses of that nature.

"Let's get started then," said Gene, having finished his introduction and heading to his first point.

"There are many passages of scripture taken way out of context and then used to promote a doctrine or belief, which is really quite mistaken."

Pastor Gene was keen to teach on some of the key passages that heretics would use to lead people astray.

"Snake Oil salesmen from The Word of Faith movement love thinking they can go preach and call things into existence as if God had given them the power to do this. They think nothing of visualising, speaking it out and expecting it to happen. What arrogance. They believe they are like God and can just declare stuff and it will happen.

"One thing is certain. These people delight in taking the Bible out of context and manipulating its words for their own ends."

He emphasised that speaking and declaring things into existence was only something God could do.

He continued, "In the book of Genesis God calls into existence the things that do not exist. He created the world by speaking a word. It is ludicrous to expect we take on the role of God and can do the same, yet this is consistently emphasised by these false teachers. Is God our servant to do what we want or are we his servants?"

Pastor Gene introduced a second piece of scripture that was widely used in the movement. It was a passage in the prophecy of Isaiah about Jesus. "The word of faith people use only the last part of the verse, '… by his wounds we are healed.'

"They usually declare it over people's lives. Often, they don't even ask God but simply make a declaration of healing. Please take note, I believe in physical healing and I believe scripture teaches that God can and does heal. However, physical healing is not for everyone. The context of Isaiah 53 is all to do with the suffering servant, the Messiah, taking on sin and by his death redeeming us. We are healed spiritually when we are his children, having repented of our sin and having him deal with it.

"If physical healing was for all of us why was the Apostle Paul not healed of his 'thorn in the flesh'? Why do we all die? The last enemy to be defeated is death. In conclusion, don't give up praying for people. However, at the end of the day we are not privy to the purposes of God for each individual. Maybe God will have them enjoy a closer relationship with him through suffering. Please don't just quote the second half of Isaiah 53:5 and expect that this should be the experience of every believer. Full physical health and its acquisition is twisted by these people. There are many fine God-fearing people who will never get healed in this life. They suffer and go through many trials and yet sadly they are rubbished by the word of faith people. You haven't been healed because of your lack of faith or you haven't been healed because of sin in your life are the words these preachers use. These are cruel words to these people, but they get away with it and people flock to the meetings. They sell false hope and demand money as a seed of faith."

He related the story of the exodus and how when Moses brought the people out of Egypt they had to wander around the desert for 40 years. During that time God provided them with food and their clothing never wore out. He encouraged the congregation to recognise that the point of the story was to trust God for food and clothing and life's necessities and not to forget the good things he has done. He reminded them that God was bringing the people of Israel into a good land. They could take over existing houses and crops. It was a land flowing with milk and honey.

"The false teachers do not mention that it's not because of Israel's righteousness that he is bringing them into the land but, instead, he is driving out the current inhabitants because of their wickedness. The message is simply to be humble and thankful, not boast in your own strength.

This Christian life is not about accumulating wealth for yourself."

He continued, "The next one is one of my favourites and is about binding and loosing and the false teachers who love to go around binding and loosing irrespective of what the scripture actually teaches."

He explained further, "As an example let me quote from a recent prayer from Kenneth Copeland who is one of the leaders of the Word of Faith movement. This is verbatim of what he said about Covid-19.

Standing in the office of the prophet of God I execute judgment on you Covid-19. I execute judgment on you Satan, you destroyer, you killer, you get out … I demand judgment on you. I demand, I demand, I demand a vaccination to come immediately…. You are destroyed Covid-19… No more. It is finished. It is finished. It is over and the United States of America is healed and well again.

"You see the point I am making, and this is typical. Many other so-called teachers of the word of God in their prayers love to use words like "I bind you Satan." By the way, I am sure you've noticed that the United States is still living with Covid-19 and it is probably much worse now for them than when Kenneth Copeland supposedly bound Satan and 'healed' the United States. Even when what he does is blatantly unscriptural, he seems to get away with it and deceived people continue to give to him.

"In the Old Testament a false prophet was to be stoned if what he proclaimed did not come to pass. Now I am not saying this should apply today but people need to be very careful about prophesying what God has said or hasn't said when most of the time what they say is a figment of their own vivid imaginations.

"Scripture teaches that the devil prowls around this world like a roaring lion. He cannot be bound but is bound and thrown into the pit before the millennial reign of Christ is ushered in. He is also described as the prince of this world."

Pastor Gene continued, "I hope you will see the vital importance of the knowledge of scripture and the absolute necessity of not being led astray by wolves in sheep's clothing. Given the publicity and the way that the false church is growing I want to keep this series going so you will be thoroughly equipped for every good work."

The meeting concluded and Rosemary was determined to meet her friend Lizzie again to discuss some of these things. She was concerned that having taken up a role as executive assistant Lizzie was being increasingly drawn into the centre of the spider's web cast by the Church of the Lord's Abundance.

CHAPTER 25

By chance one Sunday morning, Moana Haunui was walking along the road near the community centre and observed a large number of people parking their cars and walking into the centre where Sunday services were being held. She had never seen so many cars parked for whatever meeting was going on in there. As it was a Sunday, she surmised it was a church meeting so, plucking up courage, she wandered closer to have a look.

Curiosity got the better of her and as she entered the hall having been first welcomed effusively. She then tried her best to just quietly and unobtrusively sit near the back to observe the goings on. By this stage in the journey of the church the performance was slick from the opening musical brackets, to the smoke machines, the lighting and, of course, the offering.

Moana was somewhat staggered to say the least when she caught a glimpse of the amount of cash in the basket as it passed her by. She was only used to dropping in a few coins in any church offerings on the odd occasion she had been to church but these people were something else. Their dedication to giving seemed very well trained.

Moana seemed to have an eye and an ear for criminal opportunity. She sensed that the pastor was not all what he was pretending to be and wondered whether there might be a business opportunity for her and, in particular, her brother.

She had been brought up in a gang family, surviving on her own wiles and charm. This had sometimes led her into challenging and dangerous situations but to her credit she had always managed to escape and make money at the same time. It was also fortunate she had no court convictions recorded, more the result of good luck rather than anything else. This gave her confidence and her street smarts helped her read the environment she found herself drawn to. She had an intuition that had seldom let her down.

On her visit that Sunday she was pleased to see the church was advertising a Monday evening soup kitchen. She had some whanau who could use a bit of help so she noted the time and place, determined to bring a few of them to the venue the next evening.

Moana was pleasantly surprised when she arrived at 6:00 pm downtown on a chilly Hamilton evening to find some trestle tables set up, an army of volunteers buttering white bread, others dishing up what looked like a really nourishing soup and a further group putting together some small food parcels, which were given out without questions being asked.

There was no preaching, just a banner stating that this was a community service run by volunteers from the Hamilton Church of the Lord's Abundance. There was a small box labelled donations but she saw little placed in it. Sometimes a person would drop in a few coins out of gratitude but others were unable to even do that but expressed their thanks when handed the kai.

She was impressed by the attitude of these people. They didn't preach to them before they enjoyed the kai. It was offered without any strings attached.

From a distance they saw about 80 or 90 people had passed through by 7:00 pm. Together with her brother, who had deliberately dressed down, as had Moana, they waited at the end of the line then had something to eat. After finishing their soup Moana asked to see the nice lady who was in charge and Lizzie was fetched from a small tent where some supplies were still being bagged up.

"What can I do for you?" she inquired.

"I just wanted to introduce myself and my brother and tell you how grateful we are for this kai and tell you what a great job you are doing. We also wanted to meet your boss and introduce him to one of our whanau. He has a bit of money and I think he is quite religious so he might be willing to put a lot of money your way even though he barely gives us enough to survive on. I always believed charity begins at home but he has some different views. Can I make a time to bring him with me to visit your boss?"

"Well, I don't know, he's pretty busy and I have not got his diary with me at the moment," Lizzie responded, believing these were just the type of people Joe wouldn't give even five minutes of attention to. After all, part of her brief in her job description was to keep these people away.

Finally, to get rid of them she handed Moana her business card and said, "Give me a call at the office tomorrow and I will see if he will fit you in," hoping that these bludgers would simply disappear back to the hole they had crawled out of and put their fantasy away. What was their motive she thought? Had Joe scammed a whanau member either through the church or in his earlier life at the car yards?

Surprising Lizzie, at 8:30 am the following day her phone started buzzing and, not recognising the number, she let it go to answerphone. A few minutes later she checked her messages to find Moana had phoned and was asking for a 30-minute meeting to be arranged with Joe.

Against her better judgment Lizzie went to Joe and explained what had happened and that apparently there was quite a rich relative who was interested in the ministry.

Joe had a very good memory, especially for people who had bought cars off him, and he wondered whether the rich family member may have been the well-dressed young Māori man who had purchased a relatively late model Z28 Camaro from him two years ago. His curiosity was piqued so he said to Lizzie, "Okay, slot them in for Thursday at 4:00 pm."

Lizzie was somewhat flabbergasted as she couldn't possibly fathom that Joe had found some kind of compassion in his heart to give these people the time of day. She had naturally thought he would start raving about scroungers and how the food ministry was not doing anything for the bottom line of the church (whether that was true or not Lizzie had no way of knowing). Perhaps she had been unnecessarily judgmental of the prophet.

Moana showed up on Thursday looking a million dollars, quite different from her appearance the previous Monday. She was wearing $3000 or more of boutique clothing and the value of her jewellery was probably close to $10,000. She wore minimal make up and her dark shoulder length hair provided a beautiful frame to her face. Joe, having an eye for the ladies, was somewhat awestruck at her appearance. Her brother wore a snappy dark suit, well-polished shoes, and a fedora-type hat, pulling off a casual look. The bling he was wearing made him look like some kind or professional pimp, rapper or gangster.

As a person who appreciated the obvious display of wealth Joe was immediately changing gear to his best salesman persona, welcoming the couple and asking Lizzie to bring in some freshly brewed coffee and snacks.

After Lizzie had done her thing, she was quietly asked to leave the three alone in the office. There was business to discuss which would centre around matters beneficial to Joe. He was always on the lookout for the best way he and the church could score from this golden opportunity sitting right across from him.

After the mandatory small talk and inquiring after the Z28 Joe was a little bit miffed to hear that after six months, Zeke had traded it in at a different yard and now owned a nice red R8 Holden, which he declared had far better performance and handling. More small talk happened before Zeke decided to see whether Joe was receptive to a business proposition. He had trusted his sister's instincts and, although he was less intuitive, he too sensed the man across the clean and tidy desk could be on the take. She had told him straight-up she believed this 'pastor' was a con man.

"It seems to me that I might have an opportunity to benefit us both and I take it that the Monday night soup kitchen is part of the church and not something separate?"

Not knowing where this was headed Joe began to talk about how community-minded the church was and how they really wanted to lift people out of poverty.

"Here is my proposition," Zeke said, coming straight to the point. "What I would like to do is be very much involved in this great ministry (he knew the buzz words) and support you. How does $4,000 a week sound?"

Joe practically had a heart attack at the thought of so much money. "What's the catch?"

"What a suspicious mind you have, pastor. Here I am wanting to try and support your wonderful food kitchen and then you ask me what is the catch?"

"Apologies for sure, but it is not everyday someone as generous as you comes into church to offer that sort of support."

"Yes, I understand," responded Zeke then, with a twinkle in his eye, he had to admit there was a small catch.

"Of the $4,000 I give you each week I will want $3500 back. It looks better for my books to be seen to be making a $4,000 per week donation to a charity rather than just $500 per week. I, like yourself, just want to avoid too much scrutiny from the IRD. I just want to pay the minimum legal tax I have to and the donations will surely help me out."

"Yes, I completely get it and would be happy to oblige but I'm not sure how I can do that through the church? Any suggestions?"

"Absolutely, that's a very fair question and, having thought about it, I have a fool proof explanation of how this could play out. You know the soup kitchen is in a bit of a dodgy area of town so I will provide a couple of my friends to provide security and then you can simply pay me $3500 per week and call it 'security payments'. I will also provide a couple of guys for security at church on Sunday to help justify the payments."

Seemingly reading Joe's mind he added, and "I'll make sure they will blend in with your mainly white church. Their tattoos will be covered by conservative clothing and they will be quite unobtrusive."

"Mmm, I guess that will work, but it seems like a very high amount for security. Perhaps we could also call it something vague like consultancy fees as well as security services. We will have to have the odd meeting or two, and I will have to convince my accountant that it is all legit before proceeding but I'm sure things will work out."

Joe added one further requirement. "It has to be paid in cash."

"Of course," said Zeke, a little worried that this might not work but, having seen the greed in Pastor Joe's eyes, he didn't expect to be disappointed. He could see a very prosperous future ahead for both of them.

"I think we have ourselves a nice little arrangement," Zeke concluded.

It seemed like an easy $500 per week to make but it didn't seem right to Joe that Carl would get his greedy mitts on a portion of the money. Perhaps a separate charity should be set up for the soup kitchen independently from the main church activities? He would talk to Yvette and see what she thought before having their lawyers prepare a new charity. He would also need advice to ascertain how he could skim the $500 per week from the charity. Perhaps his own consultancy charges might work?

After considering the opportunity further it seemed to Joe that despite the money coming in via cash it would still have to pass through the books as Zeke wanted 'clean' money for the 'security' payment. In due course the charity was set up, the soup kitchen kept going and was actually successful in the eyes of the community; and the church scored brownie points for their good deeds. Joe was able to provide 'consultancy' to the new entity and the $500 per week was a welcome bonus to his bank account. The Porsche was not too far away.

Ever the one for publicity, Joe decided on an interesting tactic that would play out the following week hopefully injecting a new influx of support and giving.

The next Monday evening the soup kitchen was up and running

as usual when a group of four heavy-set thugs arrived. Initially they attracted no attention as they had walked out of a side street towards the trestle tables. They wore bandanas across their faces and, despite it being early evening, dark glasses. They also wore beanies and, therefore, their faces were completely obscured and they couldn't be identified. They wore dark leather jackets but with no noticeable gang insignia.

The leader declared, "I want this place shut down, you're in our territory and you're interfering with our business. Now get out of here."

Not waiting for a peaceful departure, the group began sweeping food and plates off the tables with baseball bats that they had carried inside their jackets. They then started smashing up the tables and chairs while the volunteers quickly fled in all directions. Likewise, those who were waiting for a meal quickly melted back into the shadows.

Once the destruction was complete the leader of the gang of thugs opened his phone and dialled a number. Thirty seconds later a dark sedan with no plates screamed around the corner to the scene of destruction, picked up the men and promptly disappeared into the night. It was all over in less than three minutes but maximum impact was achieved. A message had been delivered as ordered.

A very distressed and shaken Lizzie was on the phone to Joe almost immediately and asked him to come down to the food kitchen straight away. She explained that there had been a terrible act of violence committed.

"Are you okay?" was Joe's immediate question as he could tell from her tone that Lizzie was upset and almost inconsolable, sobbing, as she related what had happened.

"I'll be there in ten minutes," responded Joe, and after a quick explanation to Yvette, he was out the door and on his way.

Arriving at the scene, he found the volunteers had returned and he quickly assessed the situation. It was indeed a mess with broken furniture and food splattered on the ground in all directions. He reached Lizzie and put his arms around her to comfort her and she clung to him sobbing. Joe didn't know what to do so just kept hugging her until she felt a little better. Joe gathered the crew together and said, "Now is the not the time and place to debrief. We will do that tomorrow evening as I know most of you will be at work and cannot spare the time during the day. I suggest you all go home, have a cup of tea and get an early night. If you need to take a sleeping pill take one, if you have one, as I am sure this has all been quite distressing. Don't worry about tidying up. This can be left."

As the volunteers began to disperse Joe took out his iPhone and began to take photos and videos showing the mess and the pain on the faces of some of the volunteers who had lingered about not quite believing what had happened just a few minutes earlier.

When the last of the volunteers had drifted away Joe invited Lizzie to come with him to a local bar where he knew he could find a quiet spot near the back in which he could comfort her a bit more. He walked with her, arm around her shoulders, across the square and they arrived at the bar and were able to find a suitable booth away from most of the noise.

"You look like you need a stiff drink," he said.

"Well, I don't usually drink, but, yes, thanks, I will have a rum and coke."

Joe went to the bar and ordered the drinks, making Lizzie's a double and they sat down to discuss what had happened.

Lizzie was feeling better, her crying had helped bring her emotions under control and she was able to tell Joe what had happened.

"It all happened so quickly. This guy turns up with some heavies and tells us to shut down the soup kitchen. Before we could even comply, he and his mates start smashing stuff up with baseball bats and busting all our stuff. I mean why? He said something about us being on his turf and being bad for business, but I didn't know what he meant. After all, in the six weeks or so we have been going I haven't noticed any drug deals or anything."

"I really don't know," replied Joe as innocently as he could.

"Did you get any description of the guys?"

"No, it was over in a blink, they were all covered in bandanas, shades and beanies so even if there was any CCTV coverage it would not have picked them up. I don't even know what sort of car they drove away in. It looked like a black car. Quite large, maybe a Holden or Falcon?"

"Where were the two security guys we usually have on?"

"As usual, they had nothing much to do, so when they asked me if they could pop down the road to grab a burger I just said yes, not in a million years thinking they would be needed."

"Oh dear, that was unfortunate. However, I am not going to let any lowlifes wreck our food ministry. We will be back and better. Just watch this space. Of course, I am not expecting you to be frontline, unless you want to but certainly take next week off and let me know."

Lizzie was cheered by Joe's outward show of courage and integrity.

Just what he wanted. It was all falling into plan. After giving Lizzie a bit more time to settle, Joe asked if he could give her a lift back to her flat. Lizzie declined, as she had her car and felt okay to drive.

Joe prevailed, "I don't know Lizzie, I wouldn't want you to be picked up by a cop for being over the limit, after all, a couple of stiff drinks might put you in trouble. It wouldn't be good for your reputation or that of the church. Tell you what I will drop you off. In the morning, I can pick you up and drop you back to get your car or you can jump on a bus."

Lizzie agreed and before long they had completed the short drive to Lizzie's flat and Joe insisted that he come in just to make sure she was okay. As a precaution, he made the most of checking out all the rooms and making sure the back door was firmly locked.

"Are you sure you will be all right?" he asked.

"You don't want me to stay a little longer?"

"No thanks, I'll be fine. I just feel a bit tired so will head to bed shortly."

"Okay, well if you need anything, give me a call."

Joe then put his arms around her and, surprisingly to Lizzie, gave her a passionate kiss on the lips. She was in two minds, somewhat shocked and confused that a pastor would do that but at the same time she guiltily enjoyed the experience. Joe then said goodbye, and quite satisfied with the way the evening had panned out made his way home to Kotahi Place with a wide grin on his face.

Yvette was, of course disturbed to hear of the soup kitchen being trashed and wondered who they could have offended. In her mind it didn't really make sense. She noted that Joe didn't seem to be all that disturbed by the issue.

The next day Joe made sure he sent photos and a report to the local paper. He filed a report with the police satisfied this would go nowhere as descriptions of both the perpetrators and the getaway car were of no use. After receiving his report and seeing the photos in the local paper he decided an interview at the site would be appropriate. Joe would front this, stating that his volunteer crew were still too much in shock to be able to front the media.

For once, the media were sympathetic and the story spread about this brave new church sacrificially giving of their time and money to help the downtrodden of Hamilton. To think that thugs had caused such outrage and here was this charismatic leader who was willing to stand up to them and refuse to shut down the programme.

"I will not give in to violence or threats, the people of Hamilton need this service and it will be open and operational next Monday night. I want to thank the many good people of Hamilton who support our programme. If you would like to give, please text 'food' to 777 or send your donation to 'Feed Hamilton' at Box 12345 Hamilton."

The end result was just as Joe had planned, some sympathy and support but best of all a lot more money would be coming in.

Later in the same week Joe met with Zeke in his office to debrief.

"You cunning dog," was Zeke's first greeting.

"Got yourself some publicity and no doubt a bit more cash to boot."

Joe grinned like the proverbial Cheshire cat and responded, "Funny that, but as the good book says, 'all things work for good'," while declining to add the rest of the verse because he didn't know it.

"I think we can safely say mission accomplished and now I can readily justify the cost of the security and for now we just carry on, business as usual."

"Yes, good job, and the way things are going with my own business I can see the 'donations' increasing. Could you handle $5,000-$6000 per week?"

"Mm, that's starting to get a bit risky but, yes, I could manage that but I think my cut, I mean the church's cut, would have to increase to $800 to compensate."

"Yes, some truth in that no doubt," replied Zeke who was making so much money and, recognising the charity scam was better than being observed and busted at the casino, he reluctantly agreed.

With the food kitchen doing so well it was only a matter of time before Joe could launch into some equally new ventures.

The first year had flown by and it was time to plan the anniversary celebration. Joe was somewhat reluctant to invite Carl back but before any invitation could be discussed Joe had a call from the man himself practically demanding he come and be present at the one-year anniversary and have a business debrief at the same time. This was going to be tricky as he could hardly decline but wanted to make sure the food kitchen scheme could be avoided.

Joe had not told Carl about the success of the food programme but the latter was googling events in Hamilton, New Zealand from time to time and, on one occasion, he'd noticed a large story in the Waikato Times. It was something about a soup kitchen being messed up. He wondered why on earth Joe had got himself into such a mess despite his advice to him that it would not pull in any money. This was definitely off script and had nothing to add to the bottom line. He would make a note to mention that to Joe and reinforce to him the importance of sticking to the letter of the franchise agreement.

CHAPTER 26

Joe could not believe how easy it was to pretend to be a Christian and to fool people into giving money. Really, people were quite gullible and greedy in Joe's opinion, fully deserving to lose their money if they expected health and wealth without having to do anything but give the seed of faith.

Nevertheless, preparations had to be made for the great man's arrival and, as a special encouragement for some more money to be given, Joe advertised long and hard in advance that the Reverend Carl Quincy Adams had a reputation for seeing miracles occurring after handkerchiefs had been prayed over.

There were three types of handkerchiefs provided: the gold class, the silver class, and the bronze class. With the gold there was the promise of longer prayer and intercession than the five minutes allotted to the silver class and the two minutes allotted to the bronze class. In addition, for gold class handkerchiefs appointments could be made with Carl and Joe to both pray with the sufferer together.

In addition, Joe decided that it would be a good idea after one year in operation that they should start a building fund so they could have a permanent site of their own.

Plans were made to have a banquet and to charge $150 per head. At the same time as making money on the dinner Joe and his accountant had decided that an offering as well as a pledge should be taken up.

The normal tithe that Joe and others of the same ilk had preached faithfully was that 10% should be given but Joe thought there was no harm in reaching high and had suggested that a one-off (of course in his mind it would not be a one-off but it would make a good start) sacrificial gift of 5% of people's annual salary for the Lord's work was something for the congregation to aspire to.

Not leaving it at that, he then decided, with the encouragement from Carl, that a television ministry was another way to multiply funds. A much larger audience and with it a much larger money supply could readily be reached. Joe even thought that ten times what he was receiving currently could be achieved.

He had done some research and had seen in the United States that the PTL Club was a television program that had run for 14 seasons and made a lot of money. At the peak of its popularity before the fall of Jim Bakker viewer contributions were said to be $1,000,000 every week. Joe was sure he would be on a winner.

Before the big anniversary celebration Carl and Joe sat down in Joe's office for an annual review and business meeting.

First, Carl impressed upon Joe that in terms of the franchise agreement he would have to see a set of audited accounts and he named the international firm of KPMG as auditors he would recommend, adding that he had checked and that they had a branch in Hamilton.

Joe began to back pedal a little, "Carl, there has to be an exercise of trust among us and that firm will charge significant fees to complete an audit. Look, surely one auditor is as good as another so, if it's okay with you, I will find a local guy in a smaller practice who can do it and that will save us some considerable coin. I think we might even have an auditor here in the church who we could use."

"My opinion, my friend, is that local people are not always that reliable so a larger firm is better. What do you say?"

Joe replied, "I guess that would be okay but since it is so important to you how about you provide us with say $5000 towards the audit fee?"

"No way, Joe, you agreed in our documents that you would have accounts audited by an auditor of our choice and I see no reason to back down on this one."

Joe thought back to the lengthy opinion from Postow, Mitchell, Crews and Cheeseman-Skinner, rueing the day he had not made a fuss about every point that had been raised. He had caved in far too quickly.

"Okay," he replied reluctantly.

"What else is on your mind?"

"Well, I did catch a news article on Google that your church had an incident with your foodbank. Now I know our agreement is silent on foodbanks as typically they lose money rather than make money, but what possessed you to open up a foodbank, despite my advice not to?"

"Two things," said Joe, "First, my personal assistant wanted to do it. She's a lovely young woman and I didn't want to say no. Secondly, she was able to persuade me it would neither make money nor lose money. The whole project is staffed by volunteers and the food supplies are either donated by some large corporates or from members of the church, and she was correct. No money in, no money out. The other thing is that it puts the church in a very favourable light in the community, that we are not just after people's money."

"Yes, I see your reasoning," said Carl.

Joe breathed a sigh of relief knowing that at least this side venture of his was for the meantime safe from the grasping claws of the Reverend Carl Quincy Adams.

The next two topics were the fundraising for their building, and the television fundraising. These were debated at length and Carl agreed there would be no 'take' on the capital costs of buying the television equipment but he would still want his take from the offerings that came as a result of such programmes. Joe agreed, as it seemed quite fair to him and then Carl asked him if he needed a loan to get the equipment and get things up and running. Further discussion ensured and it was agreed. Carl, in his usual business manner, informed Joe his local lawyers would prepare the necessary loan agreement, make recommendations for the equipment needed and then take security over such equipment. Interest was suggested at 8%.

"Seriously?" said Joe, "Do you want to cripple us? Doesn't the Bible say something about not charging your brother interest or something?"

"I don't know about that but all I can say is, if you go to the usual finance companies, they will be charging double digits, probably somewhere between 12-15%. Moreover, the sooner you get started in the television business the sooner you will start to make real money."

Joe was getting a bit annoyed at this stage by Carl's greed and closed things down by saying, "All right, just get the documents done and send them to me."

Things came together as the army of volunteers made the Saturday night fundraising gala a huge success. A seemingly gifted young man had put together an excellent video presentation showing various events in the life of the church, including the well-staged 'miracles' and some of the finer moments of Joe's preaching. The video also included some smiling faces of the city's poor and desperate as they ate a nutritious dinner on a Monday evening in downtown Hamilton. For Carl's benefit some flattering events from his own church's archive (not professionally done, but by a volunteer) were played and it was fair to say the crowd of 950 people went away very happy. This was despite the fact their wallets had been skilfully emptied by the cost of the evening itself, the opportunity to give a freewill offering, and the opportunity to make a pledge – in effect, promising to give money they hadn't yet earned or come into possession of.

The Sunday morning service was a huge success. The choir had new gowns, the lighting and smoke machines were taken to a new level and during one song a young dancer appeared, dropping down from the roof above the stage on a rope to perform a dance, which some said later could be interpreted as somewhat erotic. After her performance she was joined by five other young ladies all dancing with ribbons. The young men were of course enthralled and hoped church could have more of these acts. As if this was not enough on Sunday morning Joe provided yet another opportunity.

"Friends," he said, "we have been truly blessed of God in the 12 months since we first opened the Church of the Lord's Abundance but I have come to believe it is very selfish of me to keep the blessing here in Hamilton. The Lord specifically told me in a vision that we need to start a television ministry so the good news I share can go right around the country, and even around the world. Think of all those people who will be blessed as a result. Now I know this is a big challenge to us, but just as one of our great explorers, Sir Edmund Hilary, reached out and went to the summit of Everest, this is what I am asking of you. We will go up the mountain. We will take this Everest. The scripture says 'Every mountain shall be brought low.'

"Let us each give an Edmund Hilary this morning. A $5 note is not very much but it has the face of Sir Ed on it and as we give, it will remind us of this obstacle we are to overcome. Of course, it will require more than $5 to buy the equipment and get the programme running but it will be a seed of faith. Now, each Sunday, I will be asking that in addition to your usual giving you consider just another $5 to see this ministry take off. God bless you as you give."

With Carl sitting on the stage watching on Joe felt inspired so he stood up again and said, "Praise the Lord, Brother Carl has said his church will match this offering dollar for dollar so if you can give more than $5 that will be special."

The buckets were passed around and it was clear that most people were willing to part with $5 or more.

Carl was inwardly seething but there was nothing he could do about it at that point but he would certainly have it out with Joe afterwards.

At the end of the service after the crowd had gone and the anniversary celebrations had finished, Carl practically popping blood cells, started ranting, "You son of a bitch, don't you dare pull that kind of stunt on me again and I tell you right now, my church will not be matching dollar for dollar. You will get the loan but that is it."

He stormed off and Yvette declared, "Well Joe, sweetheart, don't you think that went well? Isn't he a lovely man?" she said as she grinned smugly.

Becoming serious she continued. "I told you I didn't trust him. He's a ratbag. We should get out of this franchise business if we can. Now that we are up and running, we don't need him."

A week later, Joe received a call from his lawyers saying that the documents for the broadcasting equipment had arrived together with a comprehensive guide book on how to set everything up and the personnel required to run it. The cost and the legal fees were astronomical. Joe quickly passed the whole package over to Yvette for her opinion. He started to feel a knot in his stomach, especially when she asked if he had noticed that Carl required a personal guarantee on the loan from him and Yvette, with the church as the principal borrower.

"This will not do. That man's impossible. Look at the cost. How does he sleep at night? I'm going to tell him to put his television equipment and his legal fees up somewhere the sun does not shine."

Yvette, with her sharp legal mind, interrupted, "Joe, just calm yourself, put the papers down and we'll leave it for a few days or weeks, if need be, then come back to it. Perhaps before we get into this new development, we should get Walter to crunch some numbers again and see what he comes up with. What do you think?"

"Yeah, well, I can't deal with this right now, there is just too much buzzing around my head to see past those horrendous numbers."

Some days later Joe returned to the question of televising his services. He thought it might be better if he could get one of the Christian channels like Shine TV to broadcast for him. He figured they probably didn't make their own content but relied on others to supply it. He next sought advice on whether several store-bought high-end cameras and a mixer could do the trick to produce quality programming. He got bogged down in the technical jargon not really understanding what he would need. Getting good quality non-professional but, still, sharp gear, would mean he wouldn't need to film live. So, with smart editing he could have the product he wanted and either sell that to Shine TV or else put it on his own YouTube channel.

It was, therefore, with great delight he was able to inform the Reverend Adams that he would not be needing to buy equipment or borrow money from him. So much easier to go to a local electronics store and get what he needed on hire purchase, no interest over the first 12 months and by that time the 'Everest' offerings of the additional $5 per person or family per week would more than cover the costs.

As he didn't know much about television or film work, he decided to ask his PA, Lizzie, if she knew of anyone in the industry. Not wanting to pay big money he was hoping for a recent graduate who was up to speed with the technology. This person could recommend the items to purchase and then be in charge of the whole production, the editing and even the marketing aspects with the necessary advertising contracts. Perhaps too much to ask but Lizzie came back immediately with a suggestion.

"My friend, Rosemary Plimmer, who you've met, would be ideal. She knows nothing about the marketing side of things but she is qualified in film production and drama so she is up to date with the technical aspects and I am sure this would be a job she would absolutely love. I think also she'd volunteered her time on the anniversary video as she is a friend of Garth McLaren, who put the video together. She probably did most of it while he took the credit. She is quite a humble person and doesn't seek any limelight. However, one issue which may be a problem is she goes to a very conservative church called Mercy Fellowship. The pastor is straight up and down but very conservative in his views."

"Yeah, I might have heard about him," Joe replied, not wanting to sound too ignorant about what other churches were in the neighbourhood. As far as he was concerned, he had written off that particular church as irrelevant because it was so small and insignificant.

"Lizzie, can you set up a meeting next week with Rosemary and we will chat about how we can push this project forward."

Lizzie duly complied and the following Wednesday Rosemary came to the church office to see what the job was all about.

Before the invitation she had been somewhat concerned. Could she work in an environment such as this church? Pastor Gene, from Mercy Fellowship, had specifically warned against the teaching of Joseph Smith and here she was potentially getting a job offer from him. Well, she would hear him out. After he described the role and what was expected Rosemary became quite excited. It would be an amazing start to a career in television and film work and one where she would carry a great deal of responsibility even as a new graduate.

Joe laid it on thick. "I can see you will be a star in our church. In fact, the Lord told me this morning that I must offer you the job because he has chosen and anointed you for this task. You are his vessel equipped for this good work. He would even say that although you are concerned and worried about it you must take courage for, surely, he will equip you and give you everything you need to be a great success. I speak and declare achievement and freedom over your life."

With that kind of encouragement and manipulation Rosemary soon forgot about the warnings of Pastor Gene and immediately decided that, yes, this was the job for her. Joe explained the usual terms and conditions and the pay, and finished off by saying that there might even be some local and, possibly, overseas trips where she would be expected to come and do the filming.

He finished by saying, "There might also be other perks that would also come with the job."

The meeting concluded with Joe giving Rosemary an enthusiastic hug and a kiss on the cheek.

"Welcome to the team at the Lord's Abundance," were his parting words as Rosemary left his office and went back to see Lizzie and to tell her that she would soon be joining her in the work.

CHAPTER 27

Rosemary turned up to work and sat down with Joe and Lizzie to discuss the needs for the new television ministry.

An inventory of equipment was drawn up with the list from Carl being used as a top of the range blueprint. This was then pared back, with smaller and more compact models that would nevertheless be able to produce high quality imaging.

A budget was organised and it was quite clear that there was currently a big shortfall in what was wanted and what they had. As usual Joe had an idea.

"Why don't we arrange for sponsors of the equipment?" he suggested.

"Someone could sponsor a camera, another a screen, another an editing mixer and so on. There are a number of items and each have different prices to suit the budget. We can even announce who has sponsored what to introduce a bit of friendly competition. What do you think?"

"Good thinking boss," said Lizzie enthusiastically.

"I'm not so sure," chipped in Rosemary.

"Doesn't the Bible say somewhere that giving should be in secret?"

She couldn't remember the reference but she was thinking it was in there somewhere.

"Oh, Rosemary, I'm sure you must be mistaken, people want to know how much they are giving and both of us will need to keep a record so a tax receipt can be given at the end of the financial year. And speaking of tax receipts, we will need to organise this shortly. It also reminds me I will need to do a big push to encourage people to give the third they receive from the government for their charitable giving donations back to the church. With that in mind we could get an overabundance for the equipment we need."

Rosemary remained quiet and felt just a little uneasy, wishing she'd paid more attention to Pastor Gene's sermons. She also thought she had better start reading the Bible more as she didn't like being ignorant. At times, she thought Pastor Joe was just too clever at both avoiding the topic or steering it away to something else.

The train that was to be the television ministry had left the station and started to gather speed particularly after Joe thanked the people the following Sunday for the success of the $5 offerings. He was pleased to see a joyful response as he explained that he would arrange for an engraving on a gold-plated label to go on every piece of equipment with the name of the donor who had planted the seed offering for the new ministry.

He exhorted the good folk of the church to give their tax refunds in order to receive a double blessing. He could almost see the dollar signs as he contemplated the success of this new ministry.

However, Joe also had another plan, which would help keep him in good stead with Zeke and his team. He decided that the very attractive Moana would make a good makeup lady. Now he wanted to make sure he presented himself in the best possible light in front of the television cameras while, at the same time, he had to admit he was somewhat smitten by the sultry good looks of young Moana. He offered her a good contract for the Sunday morning makeup and she agreed to take on the role. It would mean he would have at least 30 minutes with her every Sunday giving him an opportunity to test the waters. In addition Joe had need of her for a mid week message for the new You Tube channel.

After the initial teething problems, the new television ministry was soon up and running and Rosemary had her work cut out in editing and placing the finished product (after Joe had made sure he was happy with it, usually involving a number of edits suggested for Rosemary to tidy up) on the church's web site and YouTube channel.

Inevitably, Pastor Joe and the Church of the Lord's Abundance became even more well known in Hamilton and it was not long before the local producer of 'Eye on Hamilton' decided it was time to prepare an interview about this up-and-coming preacher.

Joe was certainly keen and figured he was sufficiently confident to handle a live interview. Joe arranged for the interview to take place at his office in downtown Hamilton where he could be in control of the staging and in an environment that was familiar to him rather than in the formal TV studio.

The crew turned up one Tuesday morning and preparations were made to film and tape a live interview, which would be for a period of 30 minutes. Some 'patsy' questions had been sent in advance just so Joe could comfortably begin the interview and it was understood that the very well known, Justine Moore, would just ask whatever questions she felt like.

The interview started well, then Joe was surprised with this question from Justine.

"Pastor Joe, I believe you would call the Church of the Lord's Abundance a traditional evangelical church."

"Yes, that would be correct," replied Joe wondering where this was going.

Justine followed on with, "You were brought up as a Mormon is that correct?

"Yes, that is correct."

"Do you believe Mormons are Christians?"

"Well, most people would say that Mormonism is not traditional Christianity, but I believe the church should be as inclusive as possible and to be broad and open, loving God and one another. If someone believes Jesus is the Son of God, then that is good enough for me. Let me go further. I believe Mormons are believers in Christ and Mormons are welcome to attend my church. I don't want to exclude anyone. We are all different but I see them as brothers and sisters in Christ. It is not right to push people away. I want to be the opposite and include people and to give them the benefit of the doubt. I hope that clarifies my view for you Justine."

"Thank you, Pastor, and now another question I am sure many viewers might be interested in. You and your wife live in a very nice house in an upmarket suburb of Hamilton do you not?"

"Yes, we do. God has blessed us as we seek to serve him."

"But aren't Christians supposed to be poor, humble and to suffer for the sake of the gospel?"

"Justine, I think you have misunderstood the will of God for believers. God wants us to rise above poverty, to excel and live our best lives now. A poverty mindset is not the will of God. Don't you realise we Christians are the children of the King? Do you see the children of a king or queen dressed in rags, living in slums, or driving clapped-out Toyota starlets? Of course not. God wants to bless us now in preparation for ruling and reigning in his kingdom."

Joe was just warming up as he continued. "Do you not realise that God's word in Jeremiah tells us it's God's purpose to give to us? He has plans to prosper us and not to harm us, plans to give us a future and hope. Oh, and one further thing you may not be aware of, Jesus himself was very wealthy. Don't forget he was given a large amount of gold at his birth."

Justine was not sure about that answer but getting to the point she asked, "Would you say, as perhaps some of your critics might, that your church has an over emphasis on money?"

"Not at all, Justine. People give because they love God. As a church we also believe in helping our community so we are giving back. You may be aware that a while ago we had some trouble at our Monday night soup kitchen. Others would have caved in to the violence and closed down but we remained open and we feed a great many of Hamilton's poorest with a good meal. You should come and see what we do one night."

Fortunately, the balance of the interview went well and the questions were relatively innocuous, which Joe was able to easily deal with.

At the conclusion of the interview Joe was in two minds about a celebration lunch at his favourite restaurant. He didn't want to ask Justine in case she might ask some curly questions off the record or even on the record, so he was keen to have one of his 'people' accompany him. Rosemary or Moana? Moana was less important in some ways, as she had a less important role but he had to be mindful of his relationship with her brother, Zeke. He liked Rosemary and also wanted to cultivate his relationship with her and get her feedback on the show. Both may have positive feedback to offer so perhaps make a bit of a competition and invite both?

"Ladies, thanks for your support at the interview. I think it would be helpful to me if you could both provide honest feedback. How about we head to a restaurant/bistro for lunch?"

They needed no further encouragement. After all, a paid lunch was always a good idea and Rosemary enjoyed Moana's company now that they were working together so it would help further team bonding.

As they drove downtown conversation was light and humorous with the inevitable flirting from Joe directed at both women. At the restaurant they squeezed into a private booth at the rear away from prying eyes. Rosemary sat opposite Joe who was seated beside Moana.

"The seafood risotto is to die for here," said Joe.

"Well, despite my name I am not a great seafood person," replied Moana, "so I will have the chicken quiche with salad."

"I will give the risotto a try," replied Rosemary confidently.

Joe ordered a bottle of Sauvignon Blanc to accompany the meal.

Rosemary baulked a little, "I don't usually drink," she said.

"Oh, come on, Moana and I can't drink the whole bottle ourselves. Does not the good book tell us to drink a little wine for your stomach's sake?"

Rosemary relented and took a half glass while Joe poured a liberal amount for himself and Moana.

After initial chit chat Joe asked the inevitable, "Well, how did I go?"

Rosemary kicked in first, "Well I thought you waffled a bit, particularly about whether Mormons are real Christians. I've always believed they were a fringe cult."

"Don't be ridiculous, Rosemary, of course God loves them and wants to include them. He loves everyone. They are as Christian as me."

"I thought you looked great," Moana chipped in.

"Mind you I'm sure my makeup helped," she added with a twinkle in her eye.

"Not that I need much," laughed Joe.

Feeling emboldened Joe put his hand on Moana's thigh and gave a little squeeze. Moana was not surprised or embarrassed as she could hardly fail to notice that Joe had the hots for her, as he seemed to with many other women as well. She would have a little fun. She reciprocated by putting her hand on his thigh and slowly moved it up higher to his crotch.

Trying to keep himself together Joe replied, "Well, I'm glad someone thought I performed well."

Rosemary wanted to stay in the good books so felt she needed to contribute something positive.

"I felt you handled the question about your house quite well. I know you keep preaching about God wanting to bless us and make us prosperous but isn't the gospel more about loving God and our neighbour rather than making money and being successful?"

Joe, being rather distracted with Moana's hand moving around where it shouldn't, replied, "Um, err, yes, God does want us to love him and our neighbour but we can have it all, loving God and receiving the blessings he wants to give us. Don't you agree Moana?"

"Yes, you know I just want more," she replied, smiling sweetly.

"We all do, so we will just have to see where we go. Sometimes we have to wait for the right moment. In the meantime, I trust that the interview will draw more people to church and we can continue to grow."

"What do you see as coming next Pastor Joe, in terms of the video channel?" Rosemary asked.

"I think we should keep interest up by at least trying to have a weekly five to ten minute talk. Are you available for extra time, say an hour a week Moana?"

Carrying straight on Joe added, "A midweek talk can keep momentum going and get more people engaged with the ministry. Any longer than that people will get bored. Can you also check about selling advertising in the space as well?

"I need you to monitor each talk and give me a report each week as to which has the most views and see if you can figure out why from any comment sections. Rosemary, please also make sure comments get actioned as soon as possible so that any requests for products can be fulfilled promptly."

CHAPTER 28

Pastor Gene was not one who would waste much time watching television but someone in his congregation had sent him a link to the 'Eye on Hamilton' website, which had the full interview with Joseph Smith.

That man was causing him so much trouble and so many people were following him and his false teaching that he became quite angry. He phoned the television studio to see if he could give a response to the comments Joseph Smith had made.

After suffering on hold for 10 minutes listening to some dreadful music he was finally put through to Justine Moore.

"Justine Moore, how can I assist?"

"Hello Justine, my name is Gene Jacobson and I am the pastor at Mercy Fellowship here in Hamilton. I have just watched your recent show where you interviewed Joseph Smith and I just want to say I would very much like a right of reply as that man is teaching so much falsehood it is giving the true Christian church a bad name."

"Hold on a minute Pastor Gene, I can't get into a debate as to the truth or otherwise of the various comments. That programme was simply to look at what was happening in Hamilton and how this church has grown to become the largest church in Hamilton almost overnight. That was the story rather than the truth or otherwise of what they teach. You will understand I hope, but we can't start a debate on our programme about various doctrines. I'm sorry, you will have to raise the doctrinal issues in some other forum but in the meantime, I am very busy and must go. Thank you for your time."

Justine hung up and the potential debate did not even get to first base.

Pastor Gene was exasperated but was not done yet. He decided to prepare another message that would once again warn his congregation against the like of Joseph Smith. That Sunday he instructed his small congregation to turn to the Apostle Paul's letter to the Galatians.

Pastor Gene set out the background of why he felt he needed to preach on this passage by referencing it back to the interview on the 'Eye on Hamilton" that had shown on the local channel the previous week.

"This man, Joseph Smith, of the so-called Church of the Lord's Abundance has made it clear that he believes Mormons are Christians like anyone else. This is a different gospel and his end will be eternal condemnation unless he repents and comes to a saving faith in the Lord Jesus Christ."

Pastor Gene continued and quickly covered the main differences between Mormon belief and evangelical Christians.

"As many of you may know there is a strong Mormon presence in Hamilton and I dare say you will have some Mormon friends who you thought were God-fearing people living wholesome and godly lives. Let me then share the main points about the differences between traditional Bible-based Christianity and the Mormon belief system."

Pastor Gene then expounded further on the Galatians passage and other similar passages before summarising his points at the end.

Pastor Gene very skilfully exposed and contrasted the different belief structures the Mormons held as opposed to Christianity with the origin of the religion, differences about revelation, a different view of God and of Jesus, and a different view on salvation.

Pastor Gene invited the congregation to spend some time praying for their Mormon friends that they might have their blind eyes opened and they might be receptive to the gospel.

He also reminded his congregation to be wary of false teachers informing them that the Apostle Paul had said "anyone who preached a different gospel should be doomed to eternal destruction."

As he closed the meeting, he asked one of the elders whether he knew what had happened to Rosemary Plimmer as he had not seen her at church for some weeks.

CHAPTER 29

While the church continued to attract the curious and, even the genuine, Joe had to keep trying new gimmicks to keep the congregation both interested and, more to the point, giving. Innovate or stagnate was his motto. His latest scheme, which he had seen on an American television show, was the provision of holy soap.

Rosemary was feeling quite guilty after putting together his latest video for the church's YouTube channel.

In her view the script had been way over the top even for Pastor Joe:

"I am going to wash away all bad luck, sickness, misfortune and evil. Yes, even that evil person you want out of your life. Do you want to reverse all of that and replace it with prosperity, good health, and happy relationships? Of course you do.

"This is what Amanda Brown had to say, 'I received the healing soap from Pastor Joe and within a week my headaches were gone and I received a pay increase at work.'

"This soap has come from the land of Israel and contains olive oil from one of the trees in the Garden of Gethsemane. Those olive trees in the garden have been there since the time of Jesus. The soap has been prayed over and is available now for healing or a money miracle that so many of you need right now. Just phone the 0800 number on the screen, below, and I will rush this soap to you. Now after you have washed poverty from your hands take the largest note you have in your hand and say, 'I dedicate this gift to God's work' and expect a miracle in return.

"Be aware of the law of sowing and reaping. If you sow sparingly, you will reap sparingly but, if you sow generously, you will reap generously.

"God has given me a word just now. I see someone sending in $50 and God will bless them with a large amount of money in the next little while. I see something like a $1000 coming to them. I see someone else in faith sowing by giving $100. Be prepared to be blessed by God."

On another occasion, Joe upped the ante with the holy handkerchiefs that had been prayed over both by him and Pastor Carl Adams from Memphis when he'd visited for the first anniversary of the church.

"I know there are many viewers on this channel who have a little box of savings, perhaps a biscuit jar or, even an old-fashioned piggy bank, sitting in a room in your house. I want you to take the largest note out of there and send it in with the name of the person you want God to bless or for the miracle you are needing and praying for.

"There was one lady whose son was hopelessly addicted to drugs and she sent in a $50 note. Well, we prayed for a very long time over the handkerchief we sent her and within days I got a note back from her saying her son had been delivered from drugs and was reunited with family. Praise God for that. Another person was healed of cancer and a lady who gave $100 had her migraines disappear within a few days."

Another time in the regular giving time at church he would say, "I'm looking for unexplained income. I declare poverty broken over your life. You're going to receive money today. You will be set free. Today is your breakthrough. Money come to me now."

Full of good ideas, one Sunday Joe preached a sermon on ancestral spirits keeping a grip on the lives of good Christian people. The spirits were able to exercise their influence over people via their goods. The items might have previously been owned by someone in the Masonic Lodge. There might have been someone in the family who had dabbled in witchcraft and had owned items of significance.

He told them in no uncertain terms to bring old jewellery and figurines to him and, after praying for the owners, he would remove the curse attached to the people and dispose of the items properly.

There was certainly a happy second-hand dealer in a nearby town who Joe would meet monthly to buy the surplus gold, rings and often valuable Lladro figurines and such like. Naturally, he didn't tell either Carl or the IRD of this extremely profitable side line.

The money kept flowing in but was never enough.

As well as the gimmicks some of Carl's sermons were also good value at increasing the giving.

One of Joe's favourites was a sermon, "Will you rob God?"

This produced very good results because no one wanted to be in the camp of those who would steal from God. They would be under a curse if they did so. The message was straightforward, that all God's people should bring at least 10% of their income into the house of God and failure to do so was robbing God. It was also disrespectful to the prophet of God who spoke on his behalf. The positive spin was of course that if they honoured God with 10% then they wouldn't be able to contain the blessing God would give them because it would be so abundant.

Having seen the success of that particular message it could not stop there because on top of the 10% there had to be free will offerings for special events and occasions in the life of the church. Even Lizzie was aghast at the accountant's suggestion (which idea had been planted by Yvette) to send an email to everyone on their mailing list before Joe's birthday 'suggesting' a surprise offering to honour their beloved 'prophet'. This would be taken up that week and presented to him on Sunday. It succeeded, and a very good bonus was drawn by Joe from the church account that week.

CHAPTER 30

It was not just from the church that one could make easy money.

Given the increase in value of houses in Hamilton and its surrounds Joe realised that there was a potential goldmine to be exploited in that market. He had a plan to supercharge his net worth.

The leafy town of Te Awamutu lies about 34 kilometres from Hamilton and it was this lucky town of about 13,000 inhabitants which was to play host to Joe's next scheme.

He had been introduced to a mortgage broker whom his father had introduced to him. Mike Holmes was an efficient and hungry operator who could readily leverage the Hamilton home(with Yvette's willing consent as owner) to free up money for a good deposit on a rental in Te Awamutu.

He had a colleague Dan Foster, from one of the local real estate companies, who could find him the sort of property he wanted. The search did not take long. The house was a solid brick and tile home that had been rented to a tenant whose rent had not been raised for some time. It was the perfect place and with finance pre-approved, an offer was placed before the vendor. The only condition was the purchaser had to be satisfied with a toxicology test.

The vendor was more than happy to sign as he knew the long-term tenants were a hard-working couple and were not involved in any shady drug business. They had recently given notice to terminate, to take up employment in another city and he did not want to be involved in the rental market any longer, hence the reason for sale.

For Joe's plan to work, he needed a failed toxicology test. He could see two options: a fake report or a real report which showed methamphetamine contamination.

Joe had asked the agent for a second visit. Normally a wise owner would not allow this until after the agreement had become unconditional. Joe explained the situation saying he wanted to measure the lounge and dining room for new carpet. This was readily accepted with no alarm bells ringing.

Carefully, and without the agent noticing, Joe removed a small plastic bag from his pocket. Dipping his finger in, he pulled out some of the product and proceeded to rub the substance on to the bench top, the stove, and other food preparation areas. He also rubbed a little inside some of the cupboards and with that his work was completed.

The remaining product he flushed down the kitchen sink.

"Just making sure the water is still on," he said to Dan.

Joe had been extremely nervous on the half hour trip to Te Awamutu as he did not want to be stopped by a cop to have P discovered in his possession. He would have to express his gratitude to Zeke in some tangible way although he was certain Zeke had made a pretty good mark-up on the sale.

Back in the office he ordered a toxicology report and insisted that the tester give emphasis to the kitchen, lounge and bedrooms. "Those addicts cook the stuff up in the kitchen and then do their thing in the lounge and bedrooms."

"Absolutely," the young woman replied.

"Our technician will go over the whole house thoroughly and you will have a report within seven days."

True to her word a comprehensive report arrived within the stipulated time and Joe wasted no time in e mailing the report to his lawyer.

"This is outrageous," he fumed.

"I want you to show the other lawyer this report and express in no uncertain terms how disappointed I am with this report. I will have to rip the whole kitchen apart. It will cost me thousands. I estimate at least $35,000 to replace the whole kitchen."

Agreeing wholeheartedly Joe's lawyer dispatched a suitably worded email which was received with much incredulity from the vendor's lawyer and his client.

The vendor demanded of his lawyer that he get another test. The vendor took some persuasion as the lawyer himself had used the highly recommended testing company many times before, but to keep the peace agreed to let his client waste some money.

Unsurprisingly the second test came back with the same result and after some haggling the deal became unconditional with a drop in price of $25,000.

The Police became involved and interviewed the departed tenants. For Joe that was unfortunate but he barely gave them a second thought.

$25,000 was all Joe needed for a small renovation and in six weeks' time Andrew and his team from Number One Builders had replaced the kitchen and installed new carpet in the lounge and dining room. A quick paint job in the other rooms meant the house was ready to be sold and with Dan's help a deal was soon signed up and a large profit made.

It was time to repeat the exercise.

CHAPTER 31

Constantly on the lookout to keep the punters coming to church and experiencing 'miracles' so the giving tap would continually stay open Joe heard of an event in a large church in California where gold dust apparently miraculously appeared and drifted down on people during one of their services.

It seemed relatively easy to repeat. There were a number of cheap options because, of course, you wouldn't use real gold dust. He chose a combination of mylar and party store glitter, which he ordered from a supplier with instructions that it had to be ground up into very tiny dust-like particles but still retain some gold colour. He made sure he had the supplier sign a confidentiality agreement as to the supply of such material and he finally managed to get some mica or fool's gold, which he thought was about right because anyone who believed God was going to release gold dust over them were deluded fools.

Again, fearing some scepticism from his own team, he rehired his old mate, Tom Cruickshank, to get into the large air conditioning ducts in the building and sprinkle the formula in various parts of the auditorium on cue at a particular point in his sermon that he'd briefed him on.

Just as he finished speaking about how gold was a symbol of rulership and how Solomon's temple was covered in gold he came to the point where he said, "Somehow I believe we can see more of what God did in the old days even as he reveals himself in new and different ways. Perhaps we may even see this today."

On cue, flakes of 'gold dust' began to drift down. As the lights were off in the auditorium and there was only the one light shining on Pastor Joe people began to see the light bounce off what appeared to be fine flakes of gold.

There were gasps from the congregation as they realised that God was, indeed, giving them a sign. He was showing by the gold dust how much he wanted to prosper them.

"I don't know what this sign means but somehow God is anointing his servant today. Perhaps he is calling some of you to reach out in faith for that miracle you are looking for or a change to your circumstances. He wants to bless you. Amen."

Pastor Joe then called forward those people who he felt needed blessing. He chose some who he knew were quite wealthy.

"Brother Simon Goldstone, Brother Harry Browne and sister Georgina Aldersgate come forward. I have a word from God for you this morning."

They obediently came forward and Pastor Joe asked some of the young men to stand behind them as he prayed for them.

"God is going to touch each of you this morning in a powerful way. He will open more opportunities of blessing in your life but you must remain faithful to God and give to his work."

He then put one hand on the person's head and started repeating, "Blessing of God, blessing of God, blessing of God," and then gave them a quick push; the young men standing behind them caught them and gently laid them down on the floor.

"Praise God," exclaimed Joe.

"Who else is in need of further blessing this morning?"

Not wanting to be inundated with people he took another 10 people and prayed and pushed, telling others that God would meet with them in their own prayer time provided of course they continued to sow seeds of faith by way of special offerings.

People were abuzz at the 'blessing' they had seen that morning and it certainly assisted with the marketing, as the following week more of the curious who were wanting to see signs and wonders walked into church to see what was the next exciting thing to happen there.

After the gold dust Joe tried miracle water. On his YouTube channel he again exhorted those watching to buy his powerful miracle water. He encouraged his viewers to use the water as a faith tool to remind them of God's amazing power to heal. Using fake testimonies, he even interviewed his standby guy, Tom Cruikshank, who testified how his life had been changed by the anointed and powerful miracle water. Another stooge testified how the water had the power to erase his debt.

CHAPTER 32

With the success of the gold dust and the miracle water, some weeks later, the next step some was to introduce a strong smell of lemon, which was done through both the air conditioning and the smoke/fog machines.

"I don't know what that is. Perhaps the Holy Spirit is allowing his fragrance to fill this place. He is here to heal and make you prosperous."

Once again at the end of the service there was a lot of talk and people were saying how blessed they were and what a real presence of God they experienced in the meeting.

In the months since the church had opened Joe had carefully researched psychological means to help a crowd believe and to be emotionally connected to whatever message he had for them. The lighting, the smoke machines, the repetitive choruses being sung and the beat of the music, all helped convince the people that God was truly in their midst and they only had to listen and obey the 'anointed prophet' to be a success in this life. Of course, that was all that mattered as he had no time to be preaching about the next life, let alone the need for repentance and faith in the Lord Jesus Christ.

Joe was lapping it up and each time a different trick was used the value of the offering rose considerably. He decided his next product to offer was special anointing oil (with a distinctive lemon essence smell), which he would launch via his YouTube channel the next week.

Mid-week when he had prepared his message Moana and

Rosemary were present for the shoot and Joe worked his way into his spiel.

"We at the Church of the Lord's Abundance have been hugely blessed of late and a number of our folk have smelled the very presence of God in the meeting. They have experienced a distinct smell of lemon with even a hint of rosemary with it. I have listened to the people and today I have available a special anointing oil with a strong hint of lemon. I believe God has given me a special recipe just like he gave Moses a special recipe for the anointing oil. Use it to pray over people and yourself. Be liberal with it as God loves generosity."

He went on, "This oil has been soaked in prayer and although we haven't got a huge quantity a 50 mL bottle can be yours for just a one-off donation. (Joe had learned that if a figure was put on a product he could, in fact, be shooting himself in the foot and losing out on hundreds if not thousands of dollars.) So, ask yourself, what is it worth to anoint a friend or yourself with this wonderful oil? What price do you put on healing and financial freedom? At this stage I have to limit the supply to one bottle per person so do act quickly and send your donation now."

"That's all this week. Once again, thank you ladies. Can I say, you both do an excellent job and I really appreciate all you do."

Rosemary didn't say much but went away a little sick in the stomach wondering how long she could last in this job. She'd tried to be positive, looking for the good in everyone, but she was getting a little tired of Pastor Joe's antics. He also seemed to have the third potential failing of a pastor. If a pastor was not tripped up by power and money it would be women and Rosemary certainly knew that Joe was always willing to make a move on a woman who was not his wife, be it Lizzie, Moana or herself.

The three of them had been asked to go to the 'Rise of the Mega Church' conference in Auckland in a few weeks' time and so she had better be careful. She thought at least she would be safe in the company of the two other women.

CHAPTER 33

As the church was becoming larger and Joe was becoming wealthier, he wanted more. He even boasted to Yvette that he was earning more than three times what she was making from the car yards and surely the 'prophetic anointing' was on him to make himself wealthy, yet he felt he was nowhere near wealthy enough and he looked forward to the point where he could earn what his mentor was earning.

It was at this point he decided that the Porsche 911 would become a reality. He decided that it might be a bit over the top to get a brand new one so he purchased one with a low odometer reading, three years-old and in gunmetal grey.

He was delighted with this acquisition that he had set his heart on for so many years and here he was now living the dream. Joe was still not satisfied. He had the house, the car and the wife but surely a man in his position should have more.

He was aware that former Mormon church doctrine allowed polygamy. Joe did a bit of study and discovered that his namesake in the 1830s included polygamy as it was practised by Old Testament prophets like Abraham. Smith, the former, taught that a righteous man could help numerous women and children go to heaven by being 'sealed' in plural marriages. Large families multiplied a man's glory in the afterlife. It appears the doctrine was established in 1843 but it was later rejected by about 1890.

Joe was not concerned about this as he knew there were many Mormons who still practised that way of life and, indeed, he had met several in his visit to Salt Lake City on his honeymoon. They even believed that polygamy would be a fact of life in heaven. One breakaway group even maintained that a man must marry at least three wives in order to enter heaven one day.

As he thought back on his honeymoon, he mused that the two main places of worship he visited, the Vatican and Salt Lake City, couldn't be more different, with celibacy for priests in the Roman Catholic Church, and plural wives for the Mormons. He knew which camp he preferred.

Joe was also very much aware that in New Zealand there was occasionally a much-publicised case of bigamy so any doctrine of multiple wives in his book would mean only one legal wife but other willing partners. He would have much to do and plan. Would it be best if he could win Yvette over first with full disclosure or should a second and third wife be kept secret?

After a bit of reflection, he decided he would not dare to ask Yvette. That would be crazy. She was way too smart and, as Carl had taught, he just had to be careful if he wanted to have his cake and eat it too.

He certainly knew who to work on to become his second wife. He'd barely stopped thinking about his second possible wife before his mind drifted to a third and, possibly, a fourth.

CHAPTER 34

One sunny autumn morning after the fog had lifted Yvette was walking around the yard of Honest Joe's when she saw a very nice original 1989 Mazda MX5 sports car slow down and turn into the yard.

A middle aged couple got out and Yvette approached like a ravenous lion stalking an innocent gazelle ready to give her pitch, knowing this couple wouldn't leave without buying a replacement vehicle and lose through the odds on the trade-in. This was a car that would only go up in value and she had to have it. Joe had taught her well and as was her practice whatever she put her mind to she researched thoroughly and then generally achieved it.

Ignoring Yvette as they marched into the car yard the couple turned sharply to see the Nissan Juke parked to the side at the front of the yard. It was this vehicle that they certainly had in mind when they stopped. It was a 2018 model in bright yellow.

"You would certainly get some attention, driving that," exclaimed Yvette as she came and introduced herself to the couple, not mentioning that it had sat on the yard for a while, proving difficult to move.

"Oh, I absolutely love it," was the response of the slender woman, dressed in slacks, shirt and a stylish navy jacket. She had short cropped hair and was wearing Prada sunglasses.

Her partner was more business-like and cut to the chase asking about a trade-in price, whether the Juke could be driven away immediately and generally excited about their good fortune. Naturally, the couple's good fortune was also Yvette's and, having dropped the price just a little and having increased the trade-in price by a minimum amount, both parties were feeling very excited that they had scored a bargain.

As the paperwork was being filled out and the slender woman was putting through the money on her phone, she happened to ask, "Both our mothers want us to get married in a church and we just want to know whether you know anyone who might be able to do this as we have found it hard to find someone. We are fairly new to Hamilton."

Being married to Joe, some of his deviousness had readily rubbed off, so Yvette had no hesitation in referring them to Pastor Gene Jacobson who had a little church called Mercy Fellowship and she explained how they might find it in town.

The happy couple took possession of their shiny yellow car and headed away very pleased that this could be a day out of the box for them.

"This doesn't seem right," said the driver as she drove the car down the unremarkable gravel right-of-way.

"It just looks like an old hall."

"Perhaps it is just the admin centre and there is another building that they use or hire for their Sunday Service," was the reply.

They parked the car and made their way inside, not at all impressed with the building as it seemed very old and utilitarian.

Pastor Jacobson came out of his office and said hello and asked the couple to come in and sit down.

"Tea or coffee?" he asked.

"We will both have tea please, with milk, no sugar thanks."

Gene got up and came back from the kitchen with a tray and three cups of tea. The tea was distributed and Gene got to the point.

"What can I do for you ladies this morning?" he inquired.

"We are looking for someone who will marry us?"

Gene's reaction could not be hidden as his face fell and he paused to let their question sink in wondering how best to answer them.

"First, if you don't mind me asking who suggested you come

here?" He was certain most people in town would know he would never marry a gay couple.

"Oh, it was a lovely young woman at Honest Joe's car yard," one of them said.

Gene was not aware of Yvette and her connection with Joe as the publicity around the Church of the Lord's Abundance was always centred around the prophet himself.

"Her name is Yvette Smith."

"I see," he replied, though in fact he didn't as Smith was a very common name.

"I am sorry but I cannot marry the two of you," Gene replied.

"The Bible condemns homosexual practices so you see as a Christian I can't be complicit in allowing and encouraging this sort of offence."

"But surely, it will be fine. We are both Christian, we just love each other very dearly and doesn't the Bible say we are to love one another and that God loves everyone?"

Gene didn't want to get into a debate but he inquired of them, "Do you mind if I just draw one or two scriptures to your attention and then you can go away and reflect on them. Perhaps after that we can have another talk?"

Gene continued, "Do you remember the Israel Folau controversy?

"All he did was summarise a passage of scripture. What he said was, 'Warning drunks, homosexuals, adulterers, liars, fornicators, thieves, atheists and idolaters. Hell awaits you. Repent. Only Jesus saves.'

"He wasn't picking just on homosexuals but this is of course what the media zeroed in on. He named plenty of other categories of sinners as well. Paul in the book of Romans is very clear that homosexual sin brings about the wrath of God."

Gene continued, "You are correct. God does love you but he wants you to repent of sin, and living in a sexual relationship with each other will bring about God's judgment on you unless you repent. Maybe you know the story of Sodom and Gomorrah in the

Old Testament. Two cities that were destroyed by God with fire because of their wickedness. So, you see, I am sorry but I cannot marry you. I can only pray that God gives you the grace to repent."

One of the women started crying and so her partner said, "We have to go, thanks for nothing," and they left very upset at their encounter with Pastor Gene Jacobson.

"What a horrible self-righteous prig. How dare he say we are not good enough? This won't be the end of it I swear. There will be repercussions."

"Let's go back to the car yard and see if that nice Yvette Smith could find us another minister, this time one who can marry us? I am sure she will know of others."

They returned to the car yard and Yvette had made herself scarce wondering if a poke in the hornet's nest would fire up this couple. She had told her staff that if the two women returned, they were to be told to contact Pastor Joseph at the Church of the Lord's Abundance. Before they returned, she phoned Joe and informed him of what happened. She told him she thought they were a well-off couple and might pay a reasonable fee for a church marriage ceremony.

Having been fobbed off by Yvette's staff the couple soon turned up at Joe's office. As there was no appointment noted in the diary Lizzie was doing her best to say that Pastor Joseph was simply unavailable without an appointment when she heard the door open and Joe appeared.

"Don't worry Lizzie, I am sure these women have something urgent to attend to and as you know I like to make myself available to people in distress," he said having seen the visible signs of tears on the faces of the two women as they were talking to Lizzie.

"Would you like some tea?" he asked.

Despite having just had some tea they replied in the affirmative, "Yes, thank you so much."

Lizzie went off to prepare the tea as Joe interviewed the women to find out their story. After listening and asking some questions for about 40 minutes Joe reassured the women and invited them to church on Sunday where he promised them that they would receive a warm welcome and he would speak to the congregation. Sunday soon came and just before the sermon Joe solemnly came to the platform and commenced his introduction.

"Before this morning's message I have something very important to say to you all today. As you know the, Bible's message is all about love and how we should love one another. There is no room for hate or hate speech. It saddens me to say there is a so-called minister of the gospel in this great city of ours who preaches hate. Before I go further let me introduce Cath and Robyn to you. They are good Christian women whom God loves."

Joe then called the women to the platform and quickly got them to introduce themselves and then he asked them to sit down while he gave his address.

"A certain minister, and I will name him, Gene Jacobson, refused to conduct a marriage ceremony for these Christian women. Instead, he spoke words of hate telling them that they would not inherit the kingdom of God. Well, I am telling you today God loves us all and, as his children, as I have told you many times before, he wants to bless us and prosper us. Now it might seem like I am going out on a limb but last night I had a dream in which a large golden angel came to me and said, 'Joseph, you will not necessarily be popular and you could well receive some backlash from those churches and ministers that don't understand the love of God but I want you to be faithful and to conduct a wedding service for these women.' Well, I tell you when an angel visits you, and what is an angel, but a very messenger of God, you had better listen and obey, so in two weeks' time we are going to have a wedding service and pray God's blessing on this wonderful couple."

The church erupted in spontaneous applause and after it had died down Joe began his short sermon.

Early the next week he spoke to the accountant and mentioned that because of the flak he would undoubtedly take from some of the other churches, it was only fair that he should charge $10,000 to conduct the wedding service. He also discussed the fact that these two women were well off and would no doubt be keen supporters of the church and its ministry.

CHAPTER 35

Despite the fairly overwhelming show of support from the congregation after announcing the up-coming wedding of Robyn and Cath, Joe was very much aware that as far as some in the congregation were concerned, he might have crossed a bridge too far.

He really was stepping well outside the bounds of orthodox Christianity. To put it bluntly, there was a degree of murmuring and dissatisfaction with Joe's announcement. He had overheard some conversations and felt he needed to nip any dissent in the bud before it spread.

Joe checked the materials that Carl had sent him at the start of the venture and, sure enough, in the bundle of sermon materials he found an index of topics to preach on. There must have been some blow-back in Carl's own church because he found a sermon called 'Touch not the Lord's anointed', which seemed to deal with aspects of authority in the local church.

The following Sunday Joe was ready to 'correct' his flock who were surely in 'error'.

"This morning's message comes from the Book of Samuel. There is no need to turn to it in your Bibles." (This was a regular ploy of Pastor Joe, because he didn't want people to gain and understand the context of the verses before and after the one he was going to highlight. That way he could make the verses mean whatever he wanted them to mean rather than how they should be interpreted.) "Before I put the passage up on the screen, a bit of background for those of you who don't know the story about how Saul pursued David, trying to kill him, because he saw David as a threat to his throne. Saul had been pursuing David for a while and now finally David had the opportunity to end it. At night when Saul and his army were all asleep, he crept up with Abishai (one of his lieutenants) to the camp of Saul and despite Abishai's encouragement refused to kill the King. Here is our passage:

> *But David said to Abishai, 'Don't destroy him! Who can lay a hand on the Lord's anointed and be guiltless? As surely as the Lord lives,' he said. 'The Lord Himself will strike him; either his time will come and he will die, or he will go into battle and perish. But the Lord forbid that I should lay a hand on the Lord' anointed.'*

"And again, where David addresses Saul:

> *The Lord delivered you into my hands today, but I would not lay a hand on the Lord's anointed.*

"Even when Saul died in battle there was terrible retribution against the man who had attacked the Lord's anointed.

> *David asked him, 'Why were you not afraid to lift your hand to destroy the Lord's anointed?' Then David called one of his men and said, 'Go, strike him down,' and he died. For David had said to him, 'Your blood be on your own head. Your own mouth testified against you when you said, "I killed the Lord's anointed".'*

"So, you see my friends, it is a very serious thing to attack leadership whether physically in David's case or in the modern era when people write posts, using social media like Facebook. Be careful when you rebel against the authority of your anointed leadership. Even when Saul was trying to kill David, he remained respectful of Saul's anointed authority and did nothing to undermine this.

"Leadership is always difficult and from time-to-time decisions are made that some of you may disagree with. However, none of these decisions are ever made lightly but are soaked in prayer and waiting on God, so you must trust me and my highly skilled leadership team to get things right. In the present case I am very much aware there has been some murmuring about the wedding of Robyn and Cath. I need to tell you specifically that as well as a vision from the golden Angel that I told you about this was backed up and confirmed with a vision from God in which he spoke to me telling me of his great love for all people and that I had to conduct the wedding. Just like Peter who had to change after seeing a vision of prohibited food I too had to change. You will recall God told Peter in the vision to arise and eat what he would decline as an orthodox Jew. Now God is doing a new thing in our midst. If God tells me to do something and, even if I disagree with Him, I dare not disobey. I must trust God and so must you. Maybe I am going out on a limb that is unfamiliar to you but in these days as the anointed prophet of God I am simply doing what God told me to.

"What could be clearer and more concise than these words in the book of I Chronicles?

Do not touch my anointed ones; Do my prophets no harm.

"When you attack God's prophet you attack God. I repeat, social media is not the right way to go about venting. Can I suggest if there are any concerns about anything then these should be addressed in the first instance to my PA, Lizzie, who will certainly bring them to my immediate attention."

Joe continued in like manner and, following the conclusion of the meeting, felt satisfied he had done a very good job in nipping any opposition in the bud.

Yvette, on the other hand was not so sure.

"I think you have poked a wasps' nest with that sermon making it sound as though you can do whatever you like and people must bow down to the party line."

"Not at all my dear, people need to know where they stand and must realise that I, as their leader, need to set boundaries so we have unity. As the church gets larger the whole unity thing needs to be kept and you don't want factions undermining us at every new step. Just wait and see. Things will work out fine," said Joe.

He then added quite seriously, "Don't forget, I am chosen of God and anointed for this task. It has been spoken in the prophecy and now it is coming to pass. I will be the leader of a great church."

"Whatever," said Yvette as she wondered whether Joe had really gone off the deep end and was now believing his own hype. She had never fallen for the whole 'anointed prophet' thing and was genuinely concerned that Joe could be slipping into mental health issues.

CHAPTER 36

True to their threats Robyn and Cath made a written complaint to the Human Rights Commissioner. In it they alleged Pastor Gene Jacobson had infringed their human rights by refusing to marry them. They alleged it was against the law for him to refuse to conduct a legal wedding for them and that he had used hate speech against them to deny them the right to be married.

Gene was in his study when he opened the letter to read of the complaint and investigation the commission wanted to carry out.

He noted the commission had quoted extensively from Section 44 of the Human Rights Act 1993:

It shall be unlawful for any person who supplies goods, facilities or services to the Public or any section of the public;
a) To refuse or fail on demand to provide any other person with those goods, facilities or services by reason of the prohibited grounds of discrimination.

The Commission helpfully added that under Section 21 two of the prohibited grounds of discrimination were sex and marital status.

What seemed ironic to Pastor Gene concerning the complaint was its basis. The two women had quoted the Bible, a book they didn't believe in or take seriously, had referred to a punishment in a hell they didn't accept as a real place, and punishment from a God who to them was probably just a fairy tale, in order to feel affronted. Somehow this turned into hate speech but, to them, it was clearly believed to be just a fable.

This was such a pain to have to deal with. Pastor Gene knew that the word of God stood firm and he could rejoice in it. He was aware the Bible taught that those who wanted to live a godly life would face persecution. Not that he would agree that a complaint was persecution. It could hardly compare to the trials, beatings, imprisonments, stoning, and suffering in shipwrecks that the Apostle Paul endured. It was simply a massive waste of his time, but he would respond to the Commission in due course. Perhaps, if he stewed on it for a week or two, he might calm down enough to respond civilly.

In addition, he wondered whether he could get charged under the new Conversion Practices Prohibition Legislation Act 2022. As he understood the new Act it was now unlawful to change or suppress an individual's sexual orientation, gender identity or gender expression.

He thought back to the words he had said. Could the words "living in a sexual relationship with each other will bring about God's judgment on you unless you repent," be interpreted as falling foul of the legislation?

Whilst not anxious about his own situation he nevertheless despaired at what the world was coming to. After all, prior to 1973 The American Psychiatric Association had listed the condition as a mental illness.

CHAPTER 37

The prosperity gospel of health and money was starting to get to Pastor Gene. He was hearing rumours of the poor being preyed upon by the Ponzi scheme of the Church of the Lord's Abundance and he needed to make sure his little flock was well guarded and not likely to be deceived by the prosperity gospel. That Sunday morning he decided to preach upon the very popular verse in Jeremiah 29:11 loved by prosperity teachers.

For I know the plans I have for you, declares the Lord, plans to prosper you and not to harm you, plans to give you hope and a future.

"Wow, what could be plainer than that? God wants to prosper you. This is what the prosperity deceivers are doing. They take a verse like the one I've just quoted, take it out of context, twist it and then use it for their own ends.

"Before we go further let me quote from Randy Alcorn who you may have heard of and read some of his books. In his book *Happiness* he says:

I don't want to be uncharitable but I will be blunt. I believe prosperity theology is straight from the pit of hell. Centred on giving people what they want, this worldview treats God as a genie or a cosmic slot machine, insert a positive confession, pull the lever, catch the winnings.

"Now back to Jeremiah. For context, we need to look at the false prophet, Hananiah, who, in the presence of the priests and all the people declared that within two years God was going to release his people from captivity. He even added emphasis to his words by taking the wooden yoke from Jeremiah and breaking it, saying that that was exactly what God would do the king of Babylon.

"So, you see false prophets can be very persuasive telling the people what they want to hear. The Lord gives Jeremiah a word in response, that the wooden yoke would be replaced by an iron yoke and the nations will continue to serve the king of Babylon. He then went on to specifically prophesise the death of Hananiah because he preached rebellion against the Lord."

Pastor Gene then read further from the book of Jeremiah explaining how God wanted the exiles to take root in Babylon, to build houses, settle down, plant gardens, marry, have sons and daughters and give daughters in marriage and to increase in number.

"That doesn't sound like a two-year stay in exile, does it?

"More importantly, and I cannot repeat it enough, Jeremiah hits the nail on the head and reminds the people not to listen to or act on what the false prophets were saying.

"It is only after the 70 years elapse that the Lord will bring the people back to the promised land. Meanwhile, they are to remain in captivity for that period of time but in verse 11, which we love to quote, is now in context.

"I trust you can see the importance of understanding scripture in its context and not letting so-called preachers just take parts of verses they like and use them to deceive and enrich themselves. Let me ask you this question? Who is getting the prosperity and wealth at the Church of the Lord's Abundance? Is it the pastor and his leadership or is it the people?"

Pastor Gene wrapped up his message hoping that new encouragement together with a warning had been sowed into the lives of his people that God had entrusted him to shepherd.

CHAPTER 38

As the Church of the Lord's Abundance continued to grow in number the influence of Pastor Joe was certainly growing his profile in leaps and bounds. It was therefore a natural follow-on to his outward success that he was asked to speak at a major conference to be held in Auckland, "The Rise of the Mega Church."

Although not the keynote speaker he had a 45-minute slot to fill and it was clear this was an opportunity not to be missed. The conference was a superb forum to widen his influence as a 'prophet' of standing. He had to make sure he stood out among the other speakers so he practised his talk until he was quite sure it would be perfect. He spoke up his story, the early anointing prophecy on his life and how God had ordained for him to meet Pastor Carl Quincy Adams who had been his mentor and spiritual advisor. He was also to talk about marketing and preaching topics that people were interested in; namely, prosperity and health. After all who didn't want that?

The conference was for Thursday, Friday and Saturday and was being held in a four star waterfront hotel in the Viaduct Basin in Auckland. Joe wanted to make sure he and his entourage would make a grand entry so he hired a limousine for the drive from Hamilton. He had his glamorous assistants, Lizzie, Rosemary and Moana with him as an entourage.

Fortunately for Joe, Yvette had to remain behind to take care of the car yards.

"Don't get up to any mischief," were her parting words as the limousine pulled out of Kotahi Avenue.

"No chance, my love. I have three women to keep an eye on me and each other. See you late Saturday afternoon or early evening."

They were soon on their way with Lizzie driving and Rosemary in the front passenger seat leaving Joe and Moana unsupervised in the back. It was a pleasant journey and Joe had the expectation that things would move to a different level once they reached the hotel.

A few of the delegates noticed the white limousine as they stopped outside the lobby and many eyes turned as the delegates from the Hamilton Church of the Lord's Abundance went to the registration desk to pick up their room keys, conference papers and registration tags.

"Well, that's nice and convenient," said Joe.

"They have put us in four separate rooms side by side all on the same level."

As they made their way to their rooms it seemed registration had made a mistake as Moana had the end room with the corner views with the others alongside her. Magnanimously, Moana offered her room to Joe who was next door but in a rare case of humility he declined. After all he had his reasons.

"There is a delegate dinner at 6:00 pm in the ballroom," said Joe, "so, until then, there are several hours of free time. I don't want to be disturbed."

After unpacking and settling in Lizzie decided to have a swim in the pool. Rosemary thought she would grab a coffee in the café downstairs and read through some of the conference materials. Moana declined to join either of the two women saying she didn't want to do either of those things but would just have a shower and a lie down.

After a short time attending to some rather important matters Moana got down to business and got on the phone to Joe.

"Hey, Pastor Joe, I am lonely in my room. The others have gone for a swim and a coffee. How about you come and keep me company for a little while? This room has great views. You won't be disappointed."

Now that was the invitation Joe had been waiting for and he was quick to take it up wasting no time at all to go next door to see what awaited him.

He was suitably encouraged when Moana opened the door. She had applied some make up and her eyes gleamed with anticipation. Her lips were smoothly glossed and inviting.

Joe was a little disappointed that Moana was not dressed in anything overtly sexual but was in her tight jeans and high-buttoned ivory silk blouse. Joe put his arms around her and gave her a hug and Moana whispered in his ear.

"How about we do a role play?" she said.

"I will pretend I don't want it and you will insist. I will pretend to resist and you are to get excited and forceful. It will be a lot of fun."

Moana pulled herself away and turned on the television to a music channel to keep Rosemary two doors away from hearing anything.

Joe was up for the challenge. "Come here you little minx, you know you want it."

"No, no, no, Pastor Joe. You are a minister, you can't do this."

"Oh yes, I can," he replied as he grabbed her quite strongly and began to undo her blouse.

"Please, no," she wailed, trying unsuccessfully to get out of his grip.

"What are you doing? I don't want to," she pleaded.

They struggled briefly and, before long they were both on the bed, with Moana beginning to cry and Joe ignoring her. The deed was done and Moana whispered again in Joe's ear, "That was perfect, I trust you enjoyed it."

"Absolutely. What a great start to the conference. I better go back to my room and freshen up for dinner."

"See you later, Pastor," replied Moana seemingly very satisfied with her performance.

Joe left the room and Moana immediately checked to make sure the very small camera she had placed beside the bed in the lamp had delivered the high-quality video film she had hoped for. She downloaded the content to her laptop and watched it from the start. She was impressed with her own acting, fully deserving of an Oscar, and was pleased that the audio had not picked up any of the initial scene-setting whispered dialogue. The recording was just what she wanted.

Joe happily showered and wondered whether Rosemary or Lizzie would be as easy or as much fun. He suspected not. They would require more time and effort.

CHAPTER 39

In Joe's opinion, Lizzie was a very desirable young woman. At the same time, he recognised that as Yvette's bridesmaid and friend she might take some convincing to sleep with him. She wouldn't be as easy to win over as Moana, who had been surprisingly easy.

He was aware from past studies that pastors could readily get away with extramarital affairs and to be honest he had been inspired by the story of a serial adulterer in a large Auckland church whose affairs came to light some years ago. He would be more careful than that man.

The conference was certainly going to be his best opportunity because he was away from home. There was a degree of privacy and he could create the environment to make it happen.

He had carefully cultivated his relationship with Lizzie, dropping the odd bunch of flowers in her office, complimenting her on her presentation, and also the way she had so easily slipped into her role and the valuable help she was to him.

After having time with Moana, the first part of the conference included a dinner and then opportunity was given for the delegates to wander around one of the reception areas to check out the various offerings of books, DVDs, magazines and product sales at the stands. As this was his first conference in his role as pastor, Joe had not wanted to avail himself of having a stand and staffing it but, rather, he was using the experience to see what was on offer from other pastors and their churches so he could come back next year surpassing all with his supply of wonderful products and superior presentation.

He noted titles of books such as *Declare Freedom and Prosperity over your Life, All it Takes is Seed Faith, Claiming Health and Wealth* and many more of similar ilk.

"Lizzie, we need to talk about this stuff and how we can leverage our position to become the largest church in New Zealand. Let's go. It's too noisy here. How about we go up to my room? It will be a bit quieter there."

Lizzie perceived no threat as she was often alone at work with Joe and while there had been the odd pat on the backside, flirting and innuendo, she took her job seriously and was happy to strategize any new opportunity. They rode the elevator without incident and Joe ushered Lizzie to the seat beside the writing desk being the only chair available while he sat on the bed.

His first job was to follow up on the pretence and discuss what Lizzie thought of the products on offer.

"For a start most of the books were way over-priced and there didn't seem to be anything new in them to attract interested readers. I would not spend $40 on a paperback. It would probably be worthwhile having Rosemary get a set of inspirational DVDs from Pastor Lloyd Longhurst as he is pretty well known and there might be some inspiration that could be gleaned from his ministry."

"Yes, maybe. I guess I thought the same as you," Joe replied. "Over-priced trash."

Suddenly Lizzie had a brainwave.

"How about a book about yourself? You could call it 'From Car Yard to Mega Church.'"

"Mm, not a bad idea," reflected Joe, thinking about how many of those he could sell and what the margins would be.

"I don't think we have fully seen what God is doing in our midst so we should put that idea on the back burner for a year or two and see what else happens. The church is only going to get bigger and bigger. I still think we could add branches around the country and I am still working out the best plan to achieve that."

"Lizzie, there is something important I want to share with you. Stand up please."

Lizzie stood up beside the chair and Joe took her by the hand. She was nervous but complied, curious to find out what was going on.

"Lizzie, God spoke to me in a very vivid dream. You know the story how it was prophesied over me at birth that great things would happen and I was to be a prophet of his choosing in these latter days."

She had heard various versions of the story from Joe and Yvette but she would hear him out again.

"Well, I tell you I was shocked when I saw in the dream what God had shown and commanded me to obey. It just seemed unusual but afterwards when I thought about it, it made perfect sense. Lizzie, God wants me to take you and have you as my 'spirit bride'. It is a holy and special role that very few are fortunate to receive. Let me remind you Abraham had Sarah and Hagar. Jacob had Rachel, Leah, Bilhah and Zilpah and he was blessed with 12 sons through those women. God has shown me you are very special in his sight and you have been faithful in the ministry and he wants to give you this blessing. He showed me a picture of a young and beautiful woman with fiery red hair. The red hair represented the fire of God. I knew in my dream God had given me a vision of you. By taking on the role of 'Spirit bride' together the ministry of the church will be strengthened and we will be a power to be reckoned with in the spiritual realm. Prosperity and healing will be released with a 10-fold increase in the lives of our community. You want this to happen, don't you Lizzie. We must obey God."

Naively, Lizzie who was feeling stunned, replied, "What does it involve being a 'spirit Bride'?"

"It is just like a marriage really but in the spirit. We will have to consummate the marriage in the usual physical way, but after that you will live your life knowing God's favour rests upon you in a special way. While you continue to love and serve him and provide the assistance I need to run the church you, yourself, will see the amazing benefits such a relationship can bring."

It was overwhelming but Lizzie really wanted to serve God and she could see that Joe was really genuine in this unusual set of circumstances. Surely if God had revealed this to the anointed prophet who was she to disobey? She didn't want to miss out on this new and unexpected blessing. She felt very special although a little hesitant despite knowing Joe to be a handsome and desirable man.

Joe knew that he had accomplished what he had set out to do and without the slightest guilt or shame led the gullible Lizzie to his bed.

CHAPTER 40

Rosemary was sitting by herself in a quiet spot in the café enjoying a mochaccino when a young man in his 30s approached her. He had a short-back-and-sides haircut, tidy but unimpressive clothing and nicely polished brown shoes, which did not go with his blue trousers.

"Sorry Miss, to butt in on your coffee, but I would very much like to introduce myself to you and have a chat. Do you mind?"

The man seemed harmless enough and as he was polite Rosemary invited him to sit down. After the waitress had approached and he had ordered a long black, he introduced himself.

"My name is Detective Robert Hayden. I am with the financial crime group of the New Zealand Police. Part of my role is to analyse and collect financial intelligence and investigate money laundering."

He showed her some ID to back up his introduction.

Rosemary was shocked.

"What has this got to do with me? You don't even know who I am?"

"I'm sorry Miss but at this stage our investigation is at its start and we have some suspicions that we are checking on. You are Rosemary Plimmer and you work at the Church of the Lord's Abundance, don't you?"

"Yes, to both. but I still don't understand what either has to do with the police?"

Detective Hayden responded, "Look, can I be frank with you? You seem a trustworthy person. I am here registered for the conference just like you. There are many churches registered at this conference and if I may be so bold to say so, the majority of these churches are collecting a great deal of funds from their congregations. The commissioner believes that some of the churches may have links to gang activities and money laundering. This is really just the start of an investigation and, it is not as if the Church of the Lord's Abundance is the only place, we have our eyes on."

"Good grief, that is preposterous," exclaimed Rosemary. "What planet are you guys on? Churches don't do those kinds of things. They preach the gospel and give to the poor and do other good works."

"Yes, I agree with you, Rosemary, the majority of churches are faithful to the gospel and are doing a great job. For instance, in your own city Mercy Fellowship is a stand-out congregation with a faithful minister who preaches a Christ-centred message and the need for repentance of sins and faith in the Lord Jesus Christ."

"Oh, you know about that church?"

"Yes, my brother attends and I also listen to some of Pastor Gene's online sermons."

Rosemary asked, "Is your brother Stanley Hayden? I know of him because I attended that church for a while."

"Yes, that's him," the detective responded. "Anyway, can I get back to the point of what the police are doing?"

Without waiting for a reply Detective Hayden set out roughly without going into detail how difficult it was to get into workings of various churches without getting a warrant from the High Court. He needed eyes and ears in the various churches to discretely gather intelligence.

Rather than ask for Rosemary to assist, the magic moment opened up when Rosemary volunteered her cooperation. What she proposed might suit her own agenda as well, as she certainly had misgivings about Pastor Joe's attitude to women and money although in itself this was nothing that the police would find interesting.

Detective Hayden expanded on some of her misgivings and suggested that Rosemary might be able to assist by bugging Pastor Joe's office with a miniature recording device.

"Look, from our point of view, it will probably be a complete waste of time but from what you have told me you might be doing yourself a favour by protecting yourself in the event of anything unpleasant happening. It may be that any evidence collected would not be available in any criminal investigation but it might assist you if there was ever a need to make a complaint to the Employment Tribunal. You can't be too careful. Would you be willing to plant a listening device somewhere suitable in his office? Even if we find some information that is inadmissible it will at least indicate that further resources should be used to scope things out further."

Rosemary thought it over for a minute. She certainly had been thinking she needed to do something because Joe was always coming on to her friend Lizzie and she knew Moana was being 'hit on' regularly. She thought in some ways this was her own fault as she sometimes dressed provocatively and deliberately leaned over Pastor Joe when she applied the makeup for the filming. This behaviour was totally unprofessional and quite scandalous in a church environment, so Rosemary thought it best for everyone's sake that some covert listening device be agreed to.

"Okay, I will do it. Can you get me the equipment and I will install it? I do appreciate your help. At least as you say, it could be helpful in an employment dispute but I'm sure you are barking up the wrong tree when it comes to money laundering. You know I have nothing to do with the finances. The only two involved in that department are Pastor Joe and Walter, the accountant."

Keeping what he knew close to his chest, Detective Hayden replied, "Let's hope you're right that nothing is going on. But, here is my card and please phone me any time day or night if you have any concerns. Thank you for your assistance, we'll stay in touch. I will have the equipment delivered to you by the end of the conference. What room are you in?"

Rosemary answered, then Detective Hayden said his farewells and wandered off.

Rosemary was left somewhat anxious and perplexed. Should she tell anyone? Had she done the right thing? What would Jesus do?

CHAPTER 41

After the conference Joe was anxious to continue increasing the revenue stream and there seemed to be no end of ways the 'prophet' could make money.

He decided to set up an exclusive group of keen young men whom he would take under his wing, to be known as 'the sons of the prophet'. There would be a sign-on fee of $200 and for that each young man would receive a cheap signet ring, which would set them apart as an elite group in the life of the church.

Their obligation was to swear an oath of submission to the prophet. To enhance the exclusivity, each 'son' would swear a binding, enduring and unbreakable oath to the anointed prophet, promising obedience, honour, loyalty and a public role of serving in whatever way or need the prophet had. There was also the mandatory tithe of an additional $20 per week. He would require this as proof of their commitment to God but more importantly their commitment to him.

He had the gall to say to them, "Just as Jesus said come follow me as his anointed prophet I now say come follow me. This is biblical because the Apostle Paul said, 'Follow me as I follow Christ'."

He was quick to grease the wheels by informing them they were the up-and-coming next generation of God's leaders and they had a special call over their lives. They were to serve an apprenticeship just as Elisha served Elijah.

Looking to the future, he could envisage selecting suitable talent to set up branch churches throughout the country using thc similar franchise system that he was under. He told them they were 'God's generation' raised up for such a time as this. He shared with them that after a year of faithful service the opportunity would come for them to set up their own satellite church but they would have to prove themselves to be disciplined, obedient and submissive to authority. In return for the commitment from the chosen sons the prophet would spend one hour per week with them and provide motivational talks and encouragement. Of course, the weekly tuition would come at an additional cost of $20 per person per week and the group was limited to 25 'sons'. That in itself would create $500 per week in addition to the $200 up-front fee (minus $50 per person for the cost of the ring).

To further promote exclusivity to this new club Joe organised special neckties to be given to each member so they would stand out more in the church as the signet ring would not be immediately obvious. The exclusive group would also be something other young men could aspire to join.

He made a particular impact at a Sunday service when he brought the young men forward introducing them to the church and prophesying blessing and prosperity over their lives. They would truly be 'anointed' just as he was if they followed after him and modelled themselves after him.

In fact, after a few weeks the scheme proved so popular and successful that a woman's scheme seemed a natural follow-on. Joe talked matters over with Lizzie and together they decided to set up 'the daughters of the prophet'. Joe was keen to keep it exclusive and 25 daughters aged between 18 and 25 were chosen as the lucky few. The plan followed similar lines to the 'sons' but, avoiding the cheaper signet rings Joe went for simple gold rings with a small diamond in the centre and, because he was purchasing 25, he managed to get a good deal from a local jeweller.

Joe naturally ensured that the selected 25 were all good looking and attractive young women who were keen to be promoted in the life of the church. Who knows, some might even be ready after a suitable time of instruction to serve as additional 'spirit brides' to the prophet. In fact, this was Joe's primary plan, with the secondary plan to generate an additional income stream.

Like the young men, the women also had to promise allegiance to the prophet and submit to both his and Lizzie's leadership. Lizzie was quite encouraged to be given this additional responsibility and Joe impressed upon her that as his 'spirit bride' this was a job she was well suited for and indeed God had called her to this role. She had to be an example to the girls particularly with her role of displaying submission to the prophet.

In fact, in Joe's eyes this scheme would almost certainly be a fail-safe way of obtaining the services of more spirit brides. It was all falling into place. Joe could have it all, power, money and women. He didn't think his mother saw this happening all those years ago and it made the taunts of his sisters fade to insignificance when he compared his extremely successful lives to theirs. He could see an even more prosperous future as in due course he could open up churches across the country and readily duplicate what he was doing in Hamilton. In a year's time some of the sons would graduate and even if they fell flat his share of their income from their newly planted churches would be better than nothing.

As a test of the faithfulness and loyalty of the sons and daughters of the prophet Joe's next step was the introduction of his blessing circle. A sure-fire way of making money was a pyramid scheme, and being at the top of the pyramid was the best place to be. Joe had heard of blessing looms, but decided as a small point of difference to call his scheme a blessing circle.

He encouraged eight of the young people to give $1000 each in five steps of $200 per fortnight so it wouldn't seem insurmountable, particularly to those who had not been as financially blessed as he had. He promised them that as they sowed such a seed they would move a step closer to the centre of the circle. Joe would receive the initial $8000. At the same time, he promised those joining that this was a sure-fire way for them to bless someone else by recruiting them to join an outside rim of the circle. Eventually, the person giving the money will move into the centre of the circle and collect $8000 for themselves. Of course, the circle requires more and more people to join in and pay their $1000 to keep money flowing into the enterprise.

It started with a hiss and a roar but once members begin to experience trouble recruiting new members the circle ended up by not being such a blessing after all and the money began to dry up. People waiting to get to the middle of the circle would never quite make it.

Joe was ready for any such consequence, berating the people for failing to recruit people and also berating them for their lack of faith. In due course, the scheme fell apart.

There were several favourite 'daughters of the prophet' who became somewhat aggrieved but Joe managed to smooth their losses by buying some expensive gifts and sympathised with them concerning their lack of faith, saying the faith journey was sometimes a hard and rocky path. This also had the benefit, as Joe explained, that he was not doing this for everyone. They were the chosen few whom God had told him to favour and in return he would encourage each of them on their journey to become a 'spirit bride'.

CHAPTER 42

Back from a successful conference, Pastor Joe was in his office when Lizzie knocked on his door, opened it and said, "Pastor Joe, I have a very urgent call for you. It is Zeke and he wants to come and see you immediately. What shall I tell him?"

"Oh, what does he want now?" muttered Joe.

"Put him through and I will talk to him."

Lizzie put the call through, and Zeke after minimal small talk, came to the point.

"I have a rather delicate matter I wish to talk to you about. It is very important and serious. We need to talk in person rather than over the phone. I'll leave it at that. When can I see you?"

"Well, if it's that important you better come and see me now. Church office or somewhere else?"

"I think the church office will be the best option for this meeting," replied Zeke.

"I'll be around in ten minutes."

True to his word Zeke appeared and strode into Joe's office barely acknowledging Lizzie as he went past her.

"Okay," said Joe, "I'm a busy man so what is so important that you have to come barging in so urgently."

"Let's just say, I'm not a happy man after hearing from my sister about the conference she's just been to."

Surely, Moana wouldn't have said anything to Zeke about their little rendezvous. I mean, why should she? Joe wondered as he turned a little pale.

"I don't know what you mean," said Joe, starting to sweat a little.

"Perhaps it would be better to let pictures rather than words speak for themselves. Here, put this USB drive into your laptop and press play on the video."

Joe did as he was bid, then turned ghostly white as he watched the clear evidence of rape happening before his eyes.

"That's not what happened. It was consensual. Moana asked me to role play. She said she would have more fun that way."

"Come on," said Zeke, "Do you think a jury is going to believe you with evidence like this?"

Joe was too panicked to think of anything, too panicked to think there would be reasonable doubt particularly as the so-called 'victim' had gone to the trouble of secretly setting up the filming and entrapment. He was beside himself and could only see he was in a deep hole that he had dug himself. Most of all he didn't want either Yvette seeing this film or it coming to the attention of anyone in the church.

"What do you want Zeke?" he asked.

"Look, I think things can be settled amicably between us. After all we have got a good working relationship. I'm a reasonable guy. How about we reduce our fee and instead of paying you $500 a week we will just pay you $50. That way the relationship keeps going and we have a win-win on our hands.

"In return, I hold on to this thumb drive and promise you not to release it to either your wife, your church elders or the police. How does that sound? I think I'm being more than generous in still giving you $50 per week. After all you don't really deserve any money now do you?"

After a short pause and the enormity of what was happening to him Joe could see no win for himself but to agree.

"Okay, Zeke, that sounds pretty reasonable to me," he said, seething inwardly but trying to grasp some sense of calm, which had already eluded him.

"Good, we have our arrangement, which will start next week. Always a pleasure to do business with you. And, by the way, much as she liked working with you don't expect to see Moana back at work any time soon. She needs time to recover from the horrible experience you put her through."

"Zeke, cut me some slack. It will look very odd if Moana leaves. The other staff are fond of her and too many questions will be asked. How do I explain why she left? How about I just pay her some more money and she can come back?"

"Okay I will talk to her and let you know. Will be in touch." Zeke walked out grinning ear to ear satisfied at the rebalancing of his finances.

Joe was pleased to see the thug depart and immediately reached into his drawer found the key to the filing cabinet, unlocked it, took out the whisky bottle and poured himself a stiff drink. He had to calm down and think things through.

His first thought was how could he, a successful car dealer, now a successful con man, rather an 'anointed' pastor, be so easily duped. His next thought was, "Don't get mad but get even." This might take some planning.

Having realised what a predicament he was in he decided to give Pastor Carl a call. Hoping it was untraceable, he was using WhatsApp, which he had heard was encrypted end-to-end.

Although the relationship was not 100%, and a bit soured after the one-year anniversary performance, Joe had no other option but to place his cards on the table.

"Carl, it's me Pastor Joe. I am in a heap of trouble. I'm going to have to disappear and the church will inevitably fold. I've been found out having sex with a staff member."

"Oh, for goodness' sake, is that all? Happens all the time. We are fallible but God loves us and forgives us. Just move on and be a bit more careful next time."

"But you don't understand it was a set-up. The young woman had secretly filmed us and she asked me to play a little rough and the film makes it look like rape. I could get 10 years for that and now her brother is blackmailing me."

"I guess that makes it a bit more serious. You know I value this relationship and despite some troubles I like the way you have built the revenue stream. Let me think of some options and get back to you in a few days."

"What did Zeke want?" said the nosey Lizzie whose job was to really keep an eye on things as Joe's right-hand lady. She was even more attentive and committed now that she was the 'spirit bride' of Pastor Joe.

"Oh, nothing much," said Joe trying to put on a brave face and bluff his way through the conversation.

"It's just you don't look your normal happy self," said Lizzie. "In fact, you look a little pale. Are you sure everything is okay?"

"Yes, yes, all good, just dealing with something that has come up."

"Can I help you with that?" Lizzie inquired.

"No, it's a bit personal but I assure you I will be fine. Thanks for your concern," as he faked his best smile to Lizzie.

"I do appreciate your help and support and the way you look after me."

Feeling pleased and valued Lizzie let it go and returned to her work.

For Joe some sleepless nights followed and he was stressing badly. Yvette wanted to know what was going on but of course he remained tight-lipped.

"I think I'm just tired, and coming down off the high of that Auckland conference," was his rather weak excuse.

"Perhaps a holiday will cheer you up," replied Yvette.

"We've both been working pretty hard and a holiday would do us good. Why not take a few days off next week and head to Chateau Tongariro for some fresh mountain air? We could do some of the walks and enjoy some us time."

"Good idea," replied Joe, wanting to keep things as normal as possible.

"Just give me a few days to sort things out with church and we will take off say next Wednesday for a couple of nights."

It was agreed and now Joe just needed Carl to come up with a clever solution so he could get some peace.

The next day Carl called with a proposal.

"There is only one thing to do with a blackmailer. You have to stop paying him."

Stating the obvious Joe responded, "But he will release the film."

"Not if we get it off him."

"How do we know he hasn't made a dozen copies?"

"We don't, but we will just have to ask him, won't we?"

Joe was not sure where this was going so naively followed up, "He's not just going to volunteer that information to us, is he?"

"Well, he just might under the right circumstances. Let's just say I think I can solve your problem and at a discounted rate. For US$15,000 and $5000 expenses I will fix things for you. Don't ask any questions, just email me all the information you have on this guy and I'll sort things out for you."

Now with the pennies finally dropping down the slot Joe figured out what was going on.

"I can't pay this in a lump sum, if there is ever an investigation a lump sum payment may be suspect."

"Understood. No worries, I will send an amendment to the franchise agreement and we will just increase the percentage you are paying for one year and then revise again after that. There should be no suspicions with that kind of arrangement."

"Okay, send it through as soon as you can and I will sign it. I'll go to an internet shop and send you through the details you want."

"Maybe, but it would be better if you just get a burner phone and send it via that, then bin it," replied Carl.

Relieved that his problems might soon be over Joe got busy buying a phone with some internet minutes. Then he assembled a detailed email with Zeke's picture, his address, his cell phone number and as much other information about who he lived with and as much as he knew about his hangouts, which was not much.

Now the waiting would begin.

CHAPTER 43

Rosemary was feeling used and abused and was no longer comfortable in her role. She had rebuffed Pastor Joe's advances at the conference and didn't relish ever being alone with him again. She was glad she had Moana with her during the weekly filming.

She had pondered long and hard about Detective Hayden's request, and her opportunity, to install the very small recording equipment in Joe's office. This could easily be accomplished when she found out that he and Yvette were going out of a town for a few days. While not a spiteful person she justified installing the equipment herself on the basis it was not just best to protect herself but it could also be helpful to protect Lizzie and Moana. However, she was too afraid to share her plan with them.

The week after the conference Moana didn't show up for work so, fortunately for Rosemary, Joe decided to cancel the show for that week. He explained he was not feeling well.

Rosemary was glad, but she didn't trust Joe's explanation and wondered if Moana was okay. She would call her after work and check up on her.

Later that evening she touched base. "Hey bud, how you feeling? Missed you at work today. Joe said you weren't well. Can we catch up?"

"Sure, hon, why don't we meet at Wonder Horse in Victoria Street in thirty minutes and I'll tell you all about it?"

"Okay, see you shortly."

Arriving at the bar on time, Rosemary found Moana had ordered herself a large gin and tonic. Rosemary made do with a lemonade, lime and bitters and they found a quiet spot for what Rosemary hoped was some honest girl talk.

Rosemary kicked things off. "I don't know what happened at the conference but Joe has definitely been edgy and worried since then. He said you weren't well and were not coming into work this week so he cancelled the filming. He's quite vain as he didn't want to film without some makeup to make him look more young and handsome. So, what's going on?"

"Well, it's like this, hon. I will tell you straight up. We had only just got to our rooms on Thursday afternoon. You know when you went down to get a coffee and Lizzie went for a swim, Pastor Joe made some lame excuse that he needed to see me. He came to my room and came on to me really strongly. I wanted none of that. Even though I am not the most virtuous person you would know. In fact, I am not even a Christian. But I didn't want to be the woman who broke up Joe's marriage. I mean you've seen us. I flirt a lot with him and he definitely reciprocates. I thought it was just a fun thing to do. Anyway, he must have misread things because he really wanted to have sex with me right there and then in my hotel room."

"What happened next?" interrupted Rosemary, shocked but nevertheless keen to hear the rest of her story.

"He grabbed me and started mauling me with his hands everywhere and with you guys out of your rooms there was no point screaming so I did the only thing my brother Zeke has trained me to do, and that was give him a hard slap on the face and a knee in the groin. He got the message and was spitting tacks as he left my room, his ego and his balls severely battered."

Rosemary couldn't help stifle a giggle and she placed her arm around her friend.

"That's amazing. You're such a strong woman. Well done you. I don't think I would have had a clue what to do."

Moana grinned and thanked her friend for standing by her.

"What's next, work-wise?" inquired Rosemary.

"You surely can't be expected to work at church any longer. In fact, you have a great opportunity for a personal grievance in the Employment Tribunal."

"You are absolutely right, but, hon, I've been in tough situations in my life and I think I can work this to my advantage. I reckon it is safe working with Joe while you are around so I will ask for a good size pay rise and take advantage of the fact that if I ever need to, I have the goods on good ole Pastor Joe. It might not work out but, like you say, at any time I can quit and threaten to take the church to the Employment Tribunal so at least, if I leave, I will get a good payout. I mean, it is not a good look for a church to go before the Employment Tribunal, is it?"

"Wow, that's very gutsy of you. I wish I could stand up for myself as well as you."

"Let me say this Rosemary, you're a dear friend and if ever Joe comes on to you then call for me and I'll be there in a flash."

Well, what a strange turn of events this was. Rosemary certainly felt even more justified about installing her secret device in Joe's office.

CHAPTER 44

True to his word Carl was on to it. He wanted to keep his investment going and one of his colleagues knew someone who knew someone who thought it might be quite nice to take a short holiday in New Zealand.

A tall solid built man in his early forties arrived at Auckland International Airport a few days later and was warmly welcomed into New Zealand as a tourist here for a two-week holiday. Anyone who was particularly observant would have picked him as possibly ex-special services, which he was, having done several tours in Afghanistan. He was now an extremely discreet private gun for hire. He was doing a favour for a friend at a discounted rate and quite happy to come to New Zealand, where he had not previously visited.

Clint Kowalski passed through immigration and customs without difficulty. No unexpected red flags popped up on the screens and he quickly walked out of the terminal building.

He wasted no time picking up a Ford Falcon from Avis Car Rentals and as per his instructions set off on his journey to Hamilton. He had no need of a map as his phone would suffice for that purpose. He drove cautiously out of the airport being the first time he had driven in a right-hand drive car and, after a few anxious moments at the first roundabout, he was soon on the motorway heading south. The journey was uneventful and he made no stops along the way. He checked into the 4-star River Motel in central Hamilton. This would do nicely for his stay. It was quiet and discreet.

After a good meal and an early night, Clint woke early before dawn, put on his running gear, then he was off to check out the immediate environment. It was not a long run to the target's address and, as he ran past, he carefully scoped all points of interest in the neighbourhood, the house itself, the immediate neighbours, the number and location of barking dogs, location of street lights, the absence of CCTV on the street and other information he thought would be useful.

Although Zeke's house was in a good area, it was secured by a solid brick fence but the former sergeant could see no surveillance cameras and no dogs. The wall was easily climbable. This seemed to be a place where confidence reigned and there was certainly no expectation that trouble would ever come calling. The house looked large from what the hit man could see through the gated fence. It had a basement garage, which might prove handy.

His employer had sent him the plans of the house, which had been readily obtained from the Hamilton Council website.

Not wanting to loiter, after stooping down to retie his Nike footwear, he set off running, being particularly interested in the rear of the building, which was adjoining an older house down a right-of-way from the block behind.

He decided to risk running down the drive to get a better view, observing that the grass was overgrown. He was in luck. It looked like the house was deserted. He risked flashing the beam of his powerful flashlight through several windows to look for signs of life. Maybe an older person had died and nothing had been done in the last month or so. Perhaps the occupant was simply away on holiday. There were a number of possibilities. He decided that, although early, he would give a quiet knock on the door and see if there was any response. As anticipated, there was none, so he edged around the house and peered over the back fence. Access through the back was straightforward and there were plenty of trees and shrubs to give an element of surprise to a forced entry.

Satisfied with his preliminary reconnaissance Kowalski returned to his run and made his way back to the motel to plan his next steps. From the intel that had been provided it was likely there could be four people in residence, possibly more – the target, two male associates (could be brothers) and a sister who was the star of the video.

That day he assembled the various supplies and equipment needed and preparation was underway for the early morning raid the next day.

Four in the morning was a good time to go. The fog would be rising over the Waikato River and it was the time when most people had settled into deep sleep. He assembled his gear in a backpack, not really concerned that it had been too risky to bring his silenced Glock with him. Another alternative would have to suffice. He was more than confident in his ability and particularly so as surprise would be his advantage.

With a degree of nervousness he set his alarm and, although sleep evaded him for a few hours, he still had a solid four hours' sleep before his alarm buzzed. His kit had been assembled in his backpack. He had a Fairbairn-Sykes knife, a powerful penlight, a Swiss army knife, disposable overalls and plastic ties in one of his deep pockets, something to pick a lock as well as other tools of the trade.

He was dressed in robust dark clothing suitable for the kind of work he had anticipated.

True to the weather forecast the fog was starting to rise and, although early, he felt sure he could run and, if stopped by cops, he could just say he was jet lagged and needed to get some exercise. He didn't want to take his car as the make, colour, and registration could be noted by any insomniac when he came to park it.

The city was deserted as he jogged slowly to the target address. Being a residential area there was no one about. Arriving at the house all was quiet so he slipped carefully down the right-of-way to approach the dwelling from the rear. Satisfied the rear house was still vacant he easily scaled the brick wall and carefully went from tree to bush anxious not to make any sound. Stopping for a short time, he checked that no lights were on and then donned disposable hospital style overalls to protect the clothing he wore underneath.

Kowalski had a strong beamed penlight, which he used to help find the back door. While the darkness and fog were his friend, finding the lock, without some artificial light was not easy. To his surprise the door was not locked. Fortunately, it didn't squeak as he opened it and he moved forward cautiously into what was a laundry area with random clothes scattered around on the floor. The house was quiet. He edged forward carefully and checked the first room where he saw a young woman sleeping soundly. It was an easy matter for him to make the several paces to her bed where he placed a handkerchief soaked in chloroform over her face and kept it there for about five minutes. With barely a struggle and no noise, she continued to sleep, although this time somewhat deeper.

He made his way to the next room where a young man was out to it with some drug paraphernalia on a bedside table. Making sure this man slept a little longer was straightforward as he was already stoned. Not concerned with the reaction from the administration of chloroform with the drugs the man had been taking he moved on to the next room.

Zeke was asleep but, unfortunately for Kowalski, he was a light sleeper and sensing movement he seemed to wake up almost instantly, sitting bolt upright.

"Who the hell are you?" he demanded before a heavy blow to his throat followed by an equally effective punch to the stomach keeled him over. He was rendered speechless, and it was a simple task to put the plastic unbreakable ties around his hands and feet. Kowalski followed this procedure up with a gag around his mouth. He then placed the subject in a convenient chair that was by the desk.

Kowalski left him there to check on any other occupants in the house and was fortunate to find none.

Returning to Zeke, he pulled the gag from his mouth, unsheathed his knife, put it to Zeke's throat and said, "We can do this the hard way or the easy way? First, you make one squeak and you and your family are dead. Secondly, I've come for the USB drive and the copies you made. Where are they?"

"I don't know what you're talking about," said Zeke trying to be the big man.

The fear on his face indicated to Kowalski that he could readily be broken and he decided he would give him one more chance.

"Last chance before this knife goes into your eye," he said, as he put the knife three millimetres away from Zeke's right eye.

Completely terrified Zeke immediately caved, "Okay, okay, don't hurt me. The USB drive is in the top drawer of my desk," he said, gesticulating to the corner of the room.

Kowalski moved over to the desk and finding three drives he pocketed them. He saw a handgun in the drawer and picked it up. He expertly removed the ammunition. He made no comment.

He moved to the laptop and turned it on. Half a minute later he asked for the password and the screen came to life.

"Okay, what have you called the video?"

This time Zeke was quick to respond and Clint soon found the video clip on the hard drive. Methodically, he inserted each of the other drives and found what he needed. He was certain Zeke had been too terrified not to tell the truth.

He then took out his Swiss army knife, removed the back from the laptop computer and extracted its hard drive.

"Where are the other USB drives?" he demanded.

"I swear to you, there are none. I made no copies except for the ones you have. I didn't need to, just what is on the computer and the three USB drives you have in your pocket."

"My friend, I don't believe you."

Kowalski applied the knife to the Zeke's wrist, severing an artery. Blood began to gush out over the floor and splatter on the overalls Kowalski was wearing, which was not unexpected.

"Look what you've done. You're messing up my clothes man.

Now listen carefully, not long to go until you bleed out so if you want me to stop the bleeding you better tell me what you have done with the other drives."

"There are none. You have them all. For God's sake stop the bleeding," screamed the desperate man.

Satisfied that he had the truth Kowalski efficiently and without another moment's thought plunged the knife into Zeke's heart and he was soon dead in the chair. Calmly, he carefully wiped the knife clean on one of the bed sheets before sheathing it and returning it to his backpack.

Kowalski wiped any potential prints off the desk, the laptop, Zeke's gun and the door handles of the house before checking to see whether the other two residents were still fast asleep.

The young man was barely breathing and to be on the safe side he quickly broke his neck.

The woman was sleeping peacefully and looked quite beautiful as she slumbered. It was a shame that she too would have to die as his briefing had made it clear that she was a key party and her evidence could easily sink Carl's associate (whose name Kowalski had not been given). In a callous and clinical manner he quickly broke her neck as if she was merely some kind of animal to be dispatched.

Kowalski left her room without a second thought and went to the bathroom, saw that he had a good quantity of blood on his overalls and his shoe coverings were also leaving blood stains wherever he walked.

As he exited the house, he paused to quickly change into spare clothes which he had in his backpack and then placed the blood-stained overalls and shoes into the backpack. He then replaced his shoes and walked briskly through the backyard and down the right-of-way, confident that no one had seen him either enter or exit the house.

He arrived safely back at his motel and the first thing he did when the hour was reasonable was to use the laundry facilities, throwing in all the clothes, including his socks and underwear. He made sure he used plenty of detergent to remove any stains. He hadn't seen stains on the clothes but he knew from experience that sometimes blood could sneak its way past disposable overalls.

Satisfied with his work he got in his car and drove downtown. Spotting a construction site he threw the laptop, which he had taken along with its drive having placed them in a council rubbish bag, into the skip. Finding another construction site out of town he dumped the backpack with the bloody overalls and shoes into a council rubbish bag and then into the bin. He observed no CCTV or any workers arriving so was safe in the knowledge that evidence wouldn't be found that could link him to any foul play. Mission accomplished and just in time for breakfast.

He'd worked up an appetite and sat down in a nearby café to enjoy a nice hot coffee, bacon, eggs, sausages and hash browns. He did not interact with anyone. He ate with gusto, tipped the pleasant waitress then departed back to his motel.

This was an easy job. He departed the next morning after bringing his flight forward and returned home confident in the knowledge that this had been a quick and profitable job. He was a ghost and this mission had been much easier than other missions undertaken with the military. In and out with no trace of any evidence left behind. No drama, no unexpected difficulties, just what he liked. His employer would be pleased.

CHAPTER 45

One day when Pastor Gene Jacobson was in his study he came to the realisation that it was not the best approach to simply react and hit back at the nonsense being spouted from the Church of the Lord's Abundance.

He discussed this with his small group of elders who talked through the issues.

They decided the best way to deal with the counterfeit was to teach the truth. One of the elders, Norman Beasley, had been a bank teller in his earlier working life and he reminded the team how they were taught to look for counterfeit notes. It was not by looking and feeling the quality of paper or carefully examining the design flaws but rather it was in the day-in-day-out handling of thousands of real notes so the feel of a counterfeit would readily be noticed as money was being counted. Study the truth and preach it and the counterfeit would be exposed was his summary.

The next Sunday morning Gene announced from the pulpit they would be spending quite a few months exploring and learning from the book of Romans written by the Apostle Paul to the church in Rome. He explained it was perhaps the most important book in the Bible and contained a powerful outline of God's plan of salvation. He encouraged his congregation to get a head start and to read it fully.

He drily mentioned that the book of Romans lacked holy soap, gold dust or lemon-scented holy fragrance. However, it was a letter written by a man who had been a strict orthodox Jew before a blinding light hit him when he was travelling from Jerusalem to Damascus and he had been converted. The Apostle Paul had encountered God, and was spoken to by Jesus himself, while travelling on the road. As a result, he was changed from being a persecutor of Christians to the most effective evangelist and teacher in the early church. He reminded the congregation that they could read his story in the book of the Acts of the Apostles.

"In the first three chapters of the letter to the Romans Paul is highlighting the problem of sin. Paul outlines the sin of the gentiles and highlights various different sins and then goes on to say to the Jews that they are equally guilty. In fact, the Jews are even more to blame because they have had the advantage of knowing the promises of God, the law and the covenants. They had the prophets and also the word of God in the Old Testament.

"I dare say you could attend the Church of the Lord's Abundance for a year and not hear even a single mention of the word 'sin'.

"Moving on with our summary, Paul then starts to introduce God's solution to the problem of sin, which is God's gift of salvation accomplished on the cross through his Son, Jesus Christ.

"Now that he has outlined to us the problem of sin and how we are powerless in ourselves to change this state, he then explains there was nothing a person could do – no sacrifices, no obedience to the law, no tithing, no giving of seeds of faith, no buying holy soap or handkerchiefs, or anything else you might do that would make you right with God. Paul says that salvation is a gift of God through faith alone.

"He contrasts Adam and Christ. The first one brings sin into the world and the other brings salvation. He talks about having freedom from the power of sin in our lives.

"Later in the book of Romans Paul reaffirms that God still has a plan for his chosen people, the Jews. For a season the Gentiles are the recipients of God's grace but the Jews who were pursuing God by law and not by faith have not yet come into the kingdom. This will all change, as God has not abandoned the Jewish people. He is using the Gentiles now to preach the kingdom of God. Paul doesn't want the Gentiles to get boastful about their salvation.

"Paul talks about the need for love to one another, submission to government authorities, loving and building up the weaker brothers and sisters in the faith by deeds and not putting stumbling blocks before them. Accept one another even though you may have some differences.

"So, my friends, I trust as we study the book of Romans in depth the word of God may dwell richly in our hearts and bring us to a closer knowledge of Jesus Christ. Amen."

CHAPTER 46

Rosemary had been anxious and wanted to get the equipment installed as quickly as possible so rather than wait until Joe went on holiday, she stayed late one night after both Joe and Lizzie had gone, and got to work.

She found a suitable spot in the office, tested the equipment and was satisfied she had an element of protection for herself and, at the same time, should there be any money laundering evidence that too could be picked up.

Rosemary felt somewhat alone in the office now that Moana was taking time off. She thought she wouldn't be back. After all, given the trauma that she had disclosed and confided in her, why on earth would Joe have her back? Why would she even want to come back? She would be mad.

Then there was Lizzie, who since the conference had seemed to have distanced herself from Rosemary. She seemed very much in Joe's camp and it appeared as if Joe had some kind of hold over her. It was almost as though some wicked person had cast a spell on her. Rosemary was not sure what to do. Talk to Lizzie or just let her maintain her new distance. It all just seemed so odd.

Fortunately, she had secured the recording apparatus in place just in time as not long after Joe returned from his short holiday she managed to record a very strange conversation. She couldn't hear the caller, only the response from Joe.

"That is great news Carl."

"When do I get the tapes?"

"Don't screw me over Carl. I have just as much on you as you have on me."

"Okay, I guess I could live with that."

The conversation ended. Rosemary didn't know what to make of it.

CHAPTER 47

That evening Rosemary watched the 6 o'clock news and the lead story was of a triple homicide in Hamilton. The police were not releasing names because the family had not been notified. All they said was it could have been gang related. The next day names were released and the church staff were in shock to hear that Moana Haunui was identified as one of the deceased, together with her brothers, Zeke Haunui and Carlos Haunui.

Lizzie and Rosemary cried bitterly over the loss of their friend. Joe went white and he too shed a tear in sympathy. He had been really fond of Moana despite her treachery. He had not expected the hit on her, naively thinking that only Zeke would be dealt with. Even then he couldn't believe it. In his mind he thought that some hoodlums would just grab Zeke, take the recordings from him, threaten him and perhaps put him in hospital, to show they were serious.

On reflection Joe came to realise that it made sense to tie up those loose ends. Had he now gone from the frying pan into the fire?

In a few days church would be back to normal but, in the meantime, he sent his staff home to grieve personally.

Rosemary got home and was just settling down in her lazy boy chair when her phone rang.

"Rosemary, are you okay? It is Detective Robert Hayden here and I just heard the news concerning your colleague, Moana Haunui."

Careful not to say anything untoward he said, "You have heard the news I suspect?"

"Yes, I heard today."

"Well, just a heads-up, as Miss Haunui worked part-time at the church, detectives will be conducting interviews with her work colleagues to see if they can find anything that might be relevant. I will be with my colleague. I am not primarily involved in the case but am coming along just as back-up and to see if there is anything that might be revealed that may be of interest to the Financial Crime Group."

"I don't know what you expect to find, as Moana was well liked and her role at the church was very much part-time as a makeup artist."

"Why does the church need a makeup artist?" the bemused detective asked.

"The church uploads a video to its YouTube channel once a week and the pastor likes to present well. It's quite professional really."

"Oh, okay, I'll see you and your colleagues tomorrow. Goodbye for now."

CHAPTER 48

The whanau of the Haunui Hapu had the mission of taking care of the funeral of all the deceased.

The Tangihanga was, as Maori custom dictated, a minimum three day affair and was scheduled to take place at Taupiri marae, the home marae of the whanau.

Of the staff, Lizzie and Rosemary were the only ones who wanted to attend. Joe couldn't bring himself to go and shied off home with a sudden overpowering headache. He felt sick and Moana's funeral would be the last place he would want to be.

On the last day of the three day period of mourning Lizzie and Rosemary were formally welcomed on to the marae. The women were met by karanga (calls) of the women who were adorned with kawakawa wreaths worn around their heads.

The bodies of the deceased were laid out in open caskets in a separate house to the side of the Wharenui (the main communal house) and the women paid their respects.

"Moana, looks so peaceful," remarked Rosemary to her friend.

"Zeke and Carlos not so much."

A minister presided over the service which was very moving. There were many tears. Some lovely tributes were given. In death the gang members were such gentle and beautiful souls and it was beyond understanding how their young and innocent lives could be snatched from them in such a callous and brutal manner. Many whanau spoke of the young men and Moana growing up on the marae and what great kids they were, the troubles they got into and the fun they had playing on the banks of the Waikato river. Tribute after tribute followed. One was different.

"This was a gang slaying and if I ever get my hands on the scum who did this he's a dead man," said one of the cousins who was close to and regularly worked with the brothers.

"We are making our own inquiries and whoever did it will wish he hadn't been born."

Not wanting the service to get out of order the minister took control and suggested a hymn. The assembled crowd sang with gusto.

At the conclusion of the service the large contingent drove to Taupiri Mountain where the caskets were slowly carried up the winding path to their grave sites.

Rosemary and Lizzie waited at the base of the mountain and just watched. Dark and foreboding clouds blew in from the south and it started raining. This did not deter the young men as they laboured to carry the caskets up the steep path. Traffic was stalled at the base as the funeral procession and the great number of vehicles had slowed progress on one of the main roads south.

Moved with emotion, the women could not contain their tears. Rosemary in particular was closest to Moana and could not understand why she had to die. Did God not care? Life was so fragile. One minute a lively beautiful person and next minute taken.

They stayed in the car until the end then slowly made their way back to Hamilton.

CHAPTER 49

The following morning the police arrived to begin the interviews. They started with Joseph Smith.

After introducing themselves as Christopher Douglas and Robert Hayden, the detectives got down to business with Detective Douglas taking the lead.

"So, Pastor, I understand you employed Moana Haunui?"

"Not quite correct. She was an independent contractor in a role of makeup artist usually for three to four hours per week depending on what was needed."

"Why does the church need a makeup artist?" asked the detective.

"We do a weekly upload to our YouTube channel and she makes me look good."

Satisfied, the detective moved on asking general questions about length of time she had been employed, how they met and what sort of relationship existed between them.

"She was a delightful and effervescent young woman. Why would anyone kill her? I can't imagine her having any enemies."

"That is what we are trying to find out. Did she attend church on Sundays? Did she have any close friends, people she hung out with, recent disputes or even enemies? You were, of course, aware her brother is one of the local gang leaders?"

"What? Of course not. Why would I know her brother is a gang leader? It is not something she mentioned. And no, I wasn't aware of any of her friends, disputes or enemies and I'm pretty sure the staff will tell you the same thing. She got on well with me and all the staff. Yes, she did come to church on Sundays. After completing her makeup routine sometimes she stayed around but other times she went off."

"Okay, moving along, what can you tell me about Carlos Haunui?"

Pastor Joe was confident in his reply, "Nothing, I've never met him."

The detectives asked a few more questions probing a little more and then moved on to Zeke.

"Yes, I know Zeke Haunui. I had no idea he was a gang leader. He seemed to be a good bloke. Moana had introduced him to me, and it turned out I had met him a few years ago when he bought a Z28 Camaro from me when I owned a car yard."

Detective Hayden was interested in this answer so jumped in. "That seems an interesting background. Why did you leave the car industry to start a church?"

"It's a long story but I had a very strong impression from God that it was the right thing to do and, growing up my mother had always said I was destined for the church."

Back on track detective Douglas steered the question back to Zeke.

"What was your relationship with Zeke?"

"Strictly business. I understand he ran a security consultancy firm and, after having some trouble at our soup kitchen, we contracted his firm and paid him a good sum to provide security to the soup kitchen. These places are notorious for undesirables so he and his crew kept an eye on our people. He also provided security for us at church on Sundays. You know, it is a shame but necessary. In a relatively small community like Hamilton there are sometimes nutters who will come to a church to disturb the proceedings and Zeke and his crew would quietly escort them from the building."

"Again, were you aware of any enemies he might have?"

"Absolutely not. He was a valuable member of our team. I suggest that if he were a gang leader, you should probably look at his relationship with other gangs rather than waste your time here," said Joe, becoming more confident and less intimidated by the two detectives as the interview progressed.

"Well, if anything comes to your attention that you think will assist us in our inquiries, here's my card. Don't hesitate to give me a call."

The two detectives finished up the interview and moved on, interviewing Lizzie next, then Rosemary.

Lizzie was not much help and kept to the party line because she had been kept in the dark. Payments to Zeke had been made without her knowledge by Walter, the accountant, who the detectives would interview shortly.

Rosemary, on the other hand, did have something interesting to pass on.

"For the record your name is Rosemary Plimmer?"

"Yes."

"How long have you been employed here?"

"Just six months," she replied.

"Do you enjoy your work?" was the next innocuous question by detective Douglas.

"Mostly, there are some days it can be difficult."

"What do you mean by that?"

"Sometimes Pastor Joe can be too flirty. He will sometimes make innuendos, not just at me but to all the women. I find it uncomfortable but, to be fair, both Lizzie and Moana seemed to enjoy that attention."

"So, Pastor Joe flirted with Moana?"

"Yes, despite being a pastor, he seemed to flirt with a lot of women and Moana was quite a beauty."

"You, said she enjoyed the attention? Do you think it went further than a bit of flirting?"

"Absolutely not. I don't think Moana would have let him take matters further."

"Okay, thanks. Moving along now, what was your relationship with Moana?"

"We had a very close working relationship. She did Joe's makeup while I was in charge of the filming, editing and uploading to our YouTube channel. Socially and outside of work times we never connected except for this one time fairly recently."

"And was there anything out of the usual that made you catch up with her socially on that occasion?" said the detective encouraged, hoping perhaps a breakthrough was coming his way.

"Well just a week ago after we came back from 'The Rise of the Mega Church' conference in Auckland Moana failed to turn up to work. Pastor Joe said she was not feeling well. I went to see her after work. We met at Wonder Horse in Victoria Street and had a drink together."

"Did you find out why she didn't come to work and what the problem was?"

"Yes, she told me that at the conference Pastor Joe had come on real strongly towards her and wanted to have sex with her. She declined and, in her words, he got angry about that and she resolved the situation by slapping him in the face and kneeing him in the genitals."

"Okay, how did you react?"

"Well, I told her she was gutsy and brave to do a thing like that. I mean, she was probably going to get fired but I think she sent a very strong message that she was not the type of girl who would tolerate unwelcome sexual advances."

"Thanks Rosemary, that is very helpful. I would appreciate it if you don't tell Pastor Joe what you just told us. It might muddy the waters a bit. If you think of anything else that could help us just let us know."

Detective Hayden asked his colleague for a few minutes alone with the witness as he said it was a private matter because Rosemary knew his brother.

After leaving them alone Detective Hayden asked the question, "Did you manage to bug Joe's office?"

"Yes, I did, some days ago. However, I noticed the other night when I stayed a bit later the bug had been removed."

"Blast, so you have found out nothing?"

"Not exactly. I did hear one side of a conversation some nights ago where Joe was speaking to Carl, who I am thinking was Pastor Carl Adams, Joe's mentor from Memphis in America. As I say, I could only hear one side of the conversation, which was pretty short. It went something like this; 'Great news Carl. When do I get the tapes? Don't muck me about and I have just as much on you as you have on me.'

"I didn't know what to make of it except to say I think Joe was ordering more sermon material. He gets most of his material from Carl, and he must have been in a hurry to get some stuff. Not sure what the last thing was about."

"Okay, thanks, Rosemary. You have been super helpful so let me know if you think of anything else. Given that the bug was discovered, I don't think it wise to put in another one at this stage. Stay safe."

The detectives moved on to interview Walter and found out that, yes, the church did contract Zeke to provide security services. Yes, Carlos had never been contracted to do anything and Moana was contracted to provide makeup services. They also found that the church paid a regular amount to Carl Adams, which Walter confirmed was for mentoring support, provision of sermon material and other information. As far as Walter was concerned Joe and Carl had a good relationship.

Back in the car the two detectives shared notes and basically came to the conclusion that although Joe might be a bit of a rogue with an eye for the women, they were probably barking up the wrong tree and needed to put the pressure on the local gangs around town to see what they knew.

A few days later Detective Hayden was still bothered by the comment "I have as much on you as you have on me."

He was stuck and would have to stew on that to figure out what it might mean.

CHAPTER 50

About a week after the interviews Joe was with Lizzie in a coffee shop when he was bumped into by a middle aged man whom he hardly noticed. As the man left the shop a note had been dropped on the table, which Joe immediately pocketed, then made an excuse to go to the bathroom where he read it.

"Business as usual. You will be contacted shortly by a Mr Jones who is effectively Zeke's replacement."

Mr Jones? That seemed a bit cute. A Smith and Jones show? With the unsolved triple murders still current and fresh this was not what Joe wanted, despite the easy money to be made. He was hoping this would just go away.

He was also concerned about whether Zeke's mob were bugging his office to get more material and he was fortunate that by a strange bit of luck – perhaps a word of knowledge from God – that he had broken an ornament on a shelf overlooking his desk and had found a very small recording device. Becoming a bit paranoid he had called all the staff together and announced that he had found the bug. He looked around the faces gathered and they all looked concerned.

"Anyone know what this is?" he asked, holding out the small device.

He was met with blank stares except from Rosemary who taking the bull by the horns said, "Yes, I know what it is. It is a small recording device. We learned about miniature devices like this at 'tech' as part of our course."

"Where did it come from and who put it in my office?"

Silence.

Joe continued, "You know, we are now the largest church in Hamilton and it wouldn't surprise me if someone from another church bugged me to see what the secret of our success is. I think its jealousy from someone when they see me driving around town in my Porsche. Anyone seen any strange visitors lately?"

Lizzie ventured a reply. "It wouldn't be the police would it?"

Joe's head started to buzz in dread. Surely, they were not on to him already. Wouldn't they need some kind of warrant?

"I don't know, but I want each of us to be on our guard and watchful of people coming and going. None of the office doors have internal locks and we are always in and out so any number of people could slip in. In the meantime, I will have a security person sweep every office to see if there is anything else".

Rosemary sighed with relief as the meeting was closed and she had remained undetected.

The next day Lizzie put a call through from a Mr Jones.

"Hello Pastor, how about we meet? Coffee Culture at 5 Crossroads in 30 minutes," and he hung up not waiting for a reply.

Informing Lizzie that he had an urgent meeting come up, he left.

Joe was there early and shortly afterwards a white middle aged man in a fashionable suit sat down beside him and said "Pastor Smith, Mr Jones, happy to meet you."

"What's your real name Jones?"

"That is my real name."

"How convenient. What can I do for you?" inquired Joe getting straight to the point.

"I know about the arrangement you had with Zeke and I want to offer the same deal?"

Being wary that Mr Jones could be an undercover cop, Joe asked, "And what deal is that we are we talking about?"

"Don't play the smart arse with me, Pastor. I will tell you what I know so you will know I'm straight-up. You have had a long-standing arrangement where Zeke would donate $4000 to the church and you would employ him doing security work and return $3500 per week back to him. Ring any bells? I can tell you more. The arrangement was changed recently and your cut dropped from $500 to $50. So, you see I know all about you and your dodgy church scam."

Realising that only a contemporary of Zeke would be aware of this information Joe was confident that, indeed, Mr Jones was fully cognisant of the arrangement and was probably higher up the food chain than Zeke. As he was already in over his head and he could readily be convicted on the past transactions there was no need to decline. In fact, it might be suspicious if the books were to be thoroughly audited. Joe was, if nothing else, pleased that the original amount was to be reinstated.

Jones then dropped a bombshell, "Quite convenient, wouldn't you say that Zeke and Moana suddenly have an untimely 'accident' around about the time your cut is reduced?"

"I don't know what you are insinuating and, if you think I had anything to do with those lovely people passing away, you're looking in the wrong place. From what the cops told me it was obviously a professional hit from another gang."

Joe was seething but saw the best form of defence as a full-frontal attack.

"Yeah okay, settle down, Smith," said Jones, just wanting to get a reaction to a very vexing puzzle.

"Forget it. My assistant, Hannah, will meet with you and drop the money off in the offering each week. She will be in touch."

The meeting was over and both parties went their separate ways.

CHAPTER 51

A few days later another visitor arrived without warning at the church office. His name was Hika Haunui, a cousin of the three deceased.

He barged into the office and brusquely demanded of Lizzie, "Is the boss in?"

"Yes, he is but he is on the phone. Would you like to take a seat and I will see when he will be free?"

Lizzie was concerned as the man appeared strong and fearsome. She had noted the five tattooed dots above an eye and having recently read an expose on the gang problem in Hamilton she understood this was a man who had served a sentence of five years in prison.

He scowled at her. "I'm not waiting," and he barged into Joe's office. Lizzie thought it best to say nothing.

Luckily for Lizzie Joe was behind his desk standing up and talking on the phone so she would not cop any flak from this stranger for telling lies.

Taking two strides, he moved to the desk, ripped the phone from Joe's hand and then grabbed Joe's shirt at his neck with his other hand. He practically picked Joe up with one hand before shoving him roughly down to his seat.

"Sit down Pastor, we're going to have a little chat."

He shut the door and as he did so warned Lizzie that they were not to be disturbed.

He produced a knife from his belt. He waved it in Joe's face.

"Not nice to have your wrist slashed and then to have a knife thrust into your heart and bleed out, is it?"

Joe remained silent.

"Hey mate, I asked you a question," sneered Hika.

The adrenaline was rushing and Joe responded, "I don't know about that. Who are you and what do you want?"

"Let's just say Zeke, Carlos and Moana were my whanau and I'm looking to get some information."

"I know nothing about their murders. Moana worked here and was well liked by everyone. Zeke did some security work for us. It was a terrible tragedy and I wish I knew what was going on. The Police said it was a professional hit. Probably a turf war from another gang. Look I want to find out who did it as much as you."

It was at this point that Joe was hoping Zeke had not shared the film around his gang or things would take a decidedly bad turn for the worse. He had no weapon and no way to defend himself against this hulk of a man.

He was one lucky man.

"I'll be watching you. You find out anything you call me first. Don't go to the cops. You can get me at this number."

Joe wrote the number down and Hika repeated himself and said, "You know what to do? Any information comes to me. I want the son of a bitch who did this. Understand?"

Joe was by this stage quite red in the face and stressed.

He didn't know what to do.

"Yeah sure, I'll keep my ear to the ground and let you know if I hear anything."

"Yeah, you do that," and Hika gave Joe a shove and calmly walked out of the office.

Joe sat down and a few seconds later Lizzie walked in.

"Are you okay? I heard all that. Should I call the Police?"

"No, don't do that Lizzie, he was just a grieving jerk and different people grieve in different ways. Can you just get me a strong black coffee please?"

Lizzie gave Joe a long warm embrace then left to get the coffee. While she was out Joe took a slug from his whisky bottle that he had in one of his filing cabinets.

Lizzie soon returned with the coffee and they sat together talking things through.

"Why would he think you would know who did it?" she asked.

"No idea. I guess because Moana worked here and had not been here all that long he thought he would throw his weight around and check all avenues. Like I said I don't know what gangs are doing in this town but it's obvious this was a gang killing. Some kind of reprisal for who knows what."

After a few minutes Joe had his heart rate back to normal but he had been quite shaken by the intrusion.

He was pleased Lizzie was such a comfort and he thanked her for that.

That afternoon Joe made an appointment with his Doctor, complaining about lack of sleep and stress and she prescribed some sleeping tablets.

That night Joe enjoyed the sleep of the innocent and felt much better as he arose to face another day.

CHAPTER 52

A strong earthquake hit Wellington three weeks after the murders and Joe used his pulpit to take advantage of the situation.

"There is no doubt in my mind that this disaster should serve as a wake- up call to the nation's politicians. They have passed many anti-God laws and now they reap God's judgment. In particular, I refer to the killing of God's innocent children. I have no sympathy for those who lead our country down the paths of recklessness.

"The land is fighting back and is heaving under the weight of sin brought about in Wellington by these politicians. This is not a sermon. This is God speaking. Sometimes you're going to hear something from me but most of the time it's going to be from God. I tell you if you are not a God-loving, tithing Christian then you need to think carefully where you are at."

Joe carried on moderating his stance. The bad news must precede the good news with which he wanted to finish on.

"As a church we love to see the blessing of God and this latest news is no surprise. Politicians deserve the judgment of God but, as you know, we major on preaching love and acceptance. Now there are many unfortunate people in Wellington, some of them very good living people who need our help. I want you to dig deep this morning as we take up a freewill offering to help those in need. The money will go to the Church of Life in Wellington who will distribute to those in need. Come on people don't be stingy. Let's open our wallets and contribute to the needs of the saints. Let me be an example to all of you."

Joe took a $100 bill from his wallet, held it up for people to see and dropped it in the collection basket. The sons and daughters of the prophet were expected to follow his lead and, although many were unprepared, they would be reminded again next week that sacrificial giving was important.

After the service when Joe and Walter were counting the money, they recorded a very generous offering of $17,000. There was, in fact, closer to $25,000 that had been given but because it was in cash there was no difficulty skimming off $8000, which Joe and Walter split $6000 and $2000, respectively. Walter needed the kickback because he was an important party and, as the accountant, he knew about all the rorts being used to fleece the congregation.

The following Sunday there was much applause and spontaneous praise to God when Joe announced they had taken in such a large offering of $17,000. Once again, he encouraged those who were not there the previous week to dig deep and assist the poor people of Wellington.

He also read out a press report that he had insisted that the pastor of the Church of Life had released to all the newspapers.

"Money pours in from the Hamilton Church of the Lord's Abundance," screamed the headline. "The donor church is true to its name and we are overjoyed to be able to distribute emergency funds to families in need following the recent earthquake. We received a massive $17,000 from this one church and more has been promised. We praise God for their generosity and may God bless them as he has indeed blessed us."

Joe milked the earthquake for two more weeks and then let it go, looking forward to the next opportunity. Needless to say, Joe had informed Carl that as there was no benefit to the church with money coming in and going straight out, he would receive no cut.

Carl was furious and, in an email, practically screamed at him.

"You ignorant coot, don't you know that any offerings for such things always have at least a 10% administrative cost deduction? You just don't get it do you? I saw online that the church in Wellington got $17,000. So, my cut is coming out of your own stupidity."

Carl was being such a greedy overlord that Joe (who, of course, couldn't see his own greed in the situation) decided that something had to be done. So far, he had managed to avoid giving any share of the additional income from things, such as handkerchief sales, oil sales and income from the sons and daughters of the prophet, but all this would surely be picked up in the next audit. But what could he do? He needed more untraceable cash rather than too much giving coming into the coffers online.

He decided to ask Yvette if she could revisit Postow, Mitchell, Crews and Cheeseman-Skinner and see if there was any way the church could extricate itself from the clutches of Carl Adams.

CHAPTER 53

Yvette arrived early for her appointment and was served a cappuccino with cinnamon on top just how she liked it. There was something to be said about the care taken by a law firm who remembered the coffee preferences of their clients. They kept an up to date database that was for sure.

She was soon ushered in to the plush meeting room where she sat down with Mrs Postow and her assistant, a young graduate learning the skills. Without having to be asked, Mrs Postow explained, "I am not charging extra for Stephen who is learning the ropes. I trust you don't mind that he sits in with us."

"Not at all," replied Yvette.

Mrs Postow came straight to the point.

"What can I do for you? Is it about your franchise agreement?"

"It certainly is. Is there any way we can get out of it?"

"Well, you will recall our advice that it was certainly a novel and trend- breaking innovative agreement. We provided comprehensive advice at the time and the United States firm that put it together are a major player in the industry. What is the real issue?"

"It seems to Joe and me that our relationship with Carl Adams at the church in Memphis is fundamentally breaking down. We just don't seem to be able to continue to work with him."

Before replying Mrs Postow paused and considered matters, "There are the usual conflict resolution clauses so you will probably be required to go to mediation and if that fails, to arbitration in the United States. There is also a clause that says the State Law of Tennessee applies. Who knows what strange laws they have over there? So, for a start, we would have to find a reputable law firm in Memphis who could provide us with advice. That would likely be quite expensive. You have no doubt heard about the reputation of American Law firms for charging astronomical sums of money.

"Another option but a long shot to would be to allege the contract was contrary to public policy."

Yvette remembered something vaguely about the topic from her year in contract law but invited Mrs Postow to elaborate.

"Let me enlighten you for what it's worth. A contract is thought to be contrary to public policy if it results in a breach of law, harms citizens or causes injury to the state."

Starting now to show off her superior intellect she continued. "It originated with the Latin phrase 'contra bonos mores,' that means contrary to public morals.

"So, we have to ask is the franchise agreement injurious to the community?"

Yvette had to think about that.

"I can't see it. Like you say, we entered the contract freely and after receiving advice. We were neither forced nor coerced in any way and there were no misrepresentations. If I can be blunt with you, knowing that whatever I say is protected by legal privilege, it seems to us that Carl Adams is just too greedy and with all our costs of running the church we are paying him too much. What happens if we just stop paying?"

"I expect he will get judgment in the courts of Tennessee and then seek to enforce the judgment here in Hamilton. All of that will take some time. At the end of the day judgment can be enforced by taking church assets. From what I recall Joe was the only personal guarantor required. You will recall I warned you in my written advice to avoid giving personal guarantees. However, we should be able to manoeuvre around that if we are lucky and have enough time.

"Next step, if we can spin things out for a while is to get all the assets out of the church charity and into another entity. That new entity could lease the assets to the church and any more assets purchased can be owned by the new entity. That could get the church off the hook but it might be a bit trickier to get Joe out of it."

"What about the publicity?" Yvette asked.

"You might be okay if we can put some positive spin on it. You know, a young couple starting a church face law suit from a large American church who supplied mentoring skills, sermons and the like, and we will delve into Carl Adams to see what he owns. I heard when he was in town last, he came by private jet. Not a good look for a pastor. We might even go to the cost of hiring a private investigator in the United States to see what he can find."

"Oh, that's an encouraging angle. I'll talk it over with Joe and see what we should do next. Thanks for your help. I will get back to you."

Yvette was escorted out and Stephen was quick to ask his boss,

"Do all your franchising clients have such interesting work?"

He was too careful not to add "and are they all as good looking?" as Mrs Postow wouldn't stand for such sexist talk.

CHAPTER 54

Despite Carl having removed the blackmail problem Joe was not sufficiently thankful to Carl to want to stay in the franchise system. Getting out was going to be a problem.

Joe and Yvette talked it over but Yvette was of course still in the dark concerning the recent murders. Joe decided best to keep it that way, yet he wondered what Carl might do if he suddenly broke the franchising agreement.

Having given it some more thought he suggested to Yvette that while the decision made sense, they should give it a few more months, as Joe still needed to rely on Carl's sermon material and other assistance. He wouldn't put it past Carl to send an anonymous tip-off to the police about how Joe was being blackmailed and had every motive to arrange the murders. While neither Joe nor the police had any idea who the killer was any blame thrown on Carl would get nowhere.

The following Sunday Hannah turned up at church and introduced herself to Joe. Another potential honey trap but Joe was determined to stay out of that scenario. So, was it business as usual?

CHAPTER 55

The large investigating team of detectives continued to work on the angles.

Despite shaking the local gang trees there was no ripe fruit falling and when push came to shove the other gangs were getting worried about whether a newcomer was moving into Hamilton. They had no idea who or where such a gang could come from – Australia, Hong Kong, Russia, Albania – the list of possibilities was endless.

The police suspected the same. Most of the initial attention was focussed on the recent 501 returnees from Australia who seemed the most likely group to be involved. They professed ignorance and, at the same time, were very reluctant to talk to the police about anything.

The trade in meth was a growing problem in Hamilton and the police were aware that the smaller towns based around Hamilton were being supplied from the larger city. The motive had to be drugs.

The murders were certainly professional. Chloroform had been detected but there had been no recent local source of supply having been made. Kowalski had taken a chance and had got away with bringing the chemical in from the United States.

The scene investigation had revealed plenty of blood from Zeke and a footprint analysis identified a common Nike running shoe print. Thousands, if not millions, of that shoe had been sold worldwide. A careful and thorough examination had not picked up any sign of a struggle where loose hair from an unknown party may have been found. Any hair samples had all been linked to the deceased. No unknown DNA samples were found. The police had no useful clues about the killer from the crime scene. It was very unfortunate and, again, it smacked of a professional hit.

The pathologist indicated a possible clue. The knife thrust into the heart, which caused death, could have been a military-type knife as he had previously seen a similar type of wound in an earlier high profile murder. However, he would not swear to it. It was impossible to identify the myriad of military knives or their civilian counterparts any one of which could have made the wound.

The slashed wrist on Zeke looked like a request for information but what sort? Drug suppliers? Had it simply been a payback for missed payments? Clearly Zeke had seriously given the finger to someone. It must have been bad, whatever he did for the South American cartels or the Asian suppliers to ruthlessly take out a whole family as a reprisal.

The police were determined to test their theory about the case that the killer had come into the country from overseas and then returned. This led to the time-consuming analysis of thousands of people leaving the country within several days of the murders. Surely the killer would not have been so confident to stay a week or two longer just as a decoy? They started with departures on the day the pathologist had identified as the day of death, the next day and the day after. In the initial sweep they ruled out old people on their own and families with children. They ruled out women. The search was narrowed down to men aged between twenty and fifty as a start, with the focus on travellers to Honk Kong, Bangkok, Melbourne, Sydney, Los Angeles and, particularly, those on the Los Angeles flights who were then transferring to South America. The initial inquiry was on men travelling alone. Even with the search narrowed down there were still many potential people to check out.

The police appealed to the public via news bulletins to come forward if they could provide any information that might result in an arrest being made. Rewards for good information were also offered but after a week there was nothing from the public. It was as if a ghost had come in then left. Again, the likely assumption was a professional hit. The police didn't strike lucky with the evidence thrown into skips. The skips had gone to landfill shortly after the murders so there was still a long road ahead in the investigation. Having no physical evidence they saw no gain to be had by putting a team through all the Hamilton rubbish dump sites.

Detective Hayden remained concerned at Rosemary Plimmer's remark, "I have just as much on you as you have on me."

Pastor Joe was not squeaky clean and he had been rejected by Moana Haunui. He had to figure out who he'd been talking to. Would being slapped and kneed in the balls get him sufficiently angry that he would take out the whole family? This was surely in the realm of impossibility and his motive must just be coincidental to the real inquiry.

His next step was to get a warrant to check Pastor Joe's phone records but he would need to get lucky with the right judge because he was certainly flying a kite with no real evidence of any involvement.

A further avenue in which they might get lucky with was to check every place in Hamilton for overseas visitors and especially those who checked out within a day or two of the murders.

After a number of officers were assigned to this task there were still a number of people of interest, and these were routinely followed up with information as to their point of origin and their final destination.

A spreadsheet was provided and names and places were displayed and showed to detectives Douglas and Hayden.

Detective Hayden saw one place that stood out. He was very interested to see a visitor from Memphis had arrived, stayed in a motel in Hamilton, returned to Auckland, then departed to Memphis via LAX the day after the murders.

Was there a connection somehow or was it just coincidental a man in the possible search pattern had come from a city that had close ties to Hamilton, via two pastors? Detective Hayden had a hunch and he would follow the lead himself by contacting Interpol who would obtain information from the FBI.

A few days later information came back on a Clint Kowalski. He was ex- Delta Force, a unit as highly regarded as the Navy Seals. He had no criminal convictions and, the information available showed that he was a security consultant. No information from his service record could be obtained as it was highly classified. Nevertheless he was clearly a man with skills.

A team was dispatched to the motel. It was discovered that he had kept to himself as there had been no noise from his unit. It was left in a tidy state and on the morning of the murders it was discovered that he had used the washing machine made available for guests. That in itself was unremarkable. No trace of any bloodstains had been left in the motel so there was no way to link the murders with Mr Clint Kowalski and, therefore, no way to pin them on either Pastor Joseph Smith or Pastor Carl Adams.

The police would need a break before they could bust the case open. Nevertheless, Kowalski would remain a person of interest until further evidence would rule him out.

Despite asking the FBI to interview Kowalski Detective Hayden thought this would either never happen or be a dead end. The only outcome was the guy would explain he wanted a quick holiday and then he was interrupted with an offer of work or some other excuse to cut the holiday short.

CHAPTER 56

Joe was certainly not himself. He was suspicious that the police knew more than they were letting on. He was worried about the hidden recording device he'd found in his office. He was not sure whether Moana or Zeke had planted this some while ago as part of their blackmail scheme or had the police somehow obtained a secret warrant to do this. He was feeling guilty and stressed.

He was still anxious about his visit from Hika Haunui.

The church was in an excellent financial state but it could all go pear-shaped if he was busted. Time to get a little desperate. Through one of his church members, he had discussed the possibility of setting up a branch church in Rarotonga, which he hoped might be sufficiently removed from the heat that was happening in Hamilton and safely away from the prying eyes of the police. He broached his idea with Yvette, forgetting for the moment he was dealing with his wife.

"The Lord has spoken to me clearly telling me I am to set up a branch church in Rarotonga. Brother Sione Tavioni has some land we can build a meeting hall on. What do you think?"

Yvette sharply responded, "Enough of the Lord told me bullshit. What is going on?"

"Okay, okay. I have a problem. I don't know why but I'm pretty sure the police reckon I have something to do with Moana's death."

"Don't be so paranoid. That is clearly ridiculous. Look you must have found her death pretty hard to deal with but don't link your idea of going to the islands with her death. They are clearly not connected. Just admit it might be good to duplicate what you are doing in Hamilton with something similar in Rarotonga and be done with it. You might actually be on to a good thing as I am sure the people of Rarotonga will be just as gullible, if not more so than the people of Hamilton. In fact, I know ministers are very respected in their culture and often own the best house in the village, so having a prosperous minister is not frowned upon like it can be here."

"Sorry, yes, I have been hit pretty hard with Moana's death. In the meantime, Brother Tavioni and I will head over to Rarotonga and stay for a week to investigate the situation with a view to a future setup. I will leave Lizzie and Walter to run the place for a couple of weeks and we can get a guest preacher for next week. My mind is made up. I'll get on and book the flights."

With his devious mind still weighing the angles, Joe explained to Yvette that because he was going to be busy with business it would be better to go on his own. After some persuasion he got away with it and the next day promptly made the arrangements to leave as soon as he could. There was a flight on Wednesday, which he promptly booked paying for his ticket and that of Brother Tavioni, while leaving the return date open. He had, of course, used church funds since it was church business.

On Wednesday, with a sigh of relief, he went through departure without problems and safely boarded, keen to distance himself from the long arm of the law, not realising and not checking that there was an extradition treaty in place between the Cook Islands and New Zealand.

The flight, taking off on time early at 8:55am, was uneventful and they touched down on a balmy Rarotongan afternoon at 2:50pm on Tuesday afternoon. Crossing the date line always left Joe feeling a bit confused. Exiting the plane Joe was engulfed in the heat and aviation smell as he walked towards the terminal noting the words of greeting "Kia Orana" Rarotonga. They were welcomed at the airport by a ukulele-strumming man singing about the beautiful frangipani. It was a pleasant start to a new adventure that he thought he could easily get used to.

He had booked himself and Brother Tavioni into a nice up-market resort. As part of his plan he thought it useful for Brother Tavioni to enjoy a week of luxury rather than staying with family. By the time the taxi arrived they were quite tired and went straight to their rooms. They enjoyed a sumptuous buffet beside the pool that evening before taking an early night.

Waking up the next morning Joe felt refreshed with the warm weather, and the cool ocean breeze blowing in. A quick and refreshing swim in the pool followed by breakfast of fruit and bread rolls washed down with strong black coffee was all Joe needed and then it was down to business.

A car had been hired by Brother Sione Tavioni. He seemed to like being called Brother Tavioni rather than being referred to by his first name. Perhaps it was more respectful and part of his Cook Islands culture.

On the way to Brother Tavioni's land and on the way back to the resort a complete tour of the island was called for. The trip circling the ocean road around Rarotonga was only 32 kilometres. Joe was gobsmacked over the number of churches already present. There was the traditional Cook Islands Christian Church (CICC), Catholic, Mormon, 7th day Adventist, Assemblies of God, Jehovah Witness and various independent churches.

The land Brother Tavioni owned was idyllic. It comprised several hectares in banana trees, coconut trees and a taro plantation. It had access to the ocean so it would be an ideal location for a church. There was a small building on site that was not currently being used but could be tidied up and used as a home for the pastor or the church office. Brother Tavioni was effusive in his recommendations saying how quick and cheap it would be to get a church up and running on his family land. He even had a cousin who was a builder.

The idea of quietly remaining in the Cook Islands was very tempting to Joe but, after a few days of talks, including with government officials, building people and the like, he began to think that much would be promised but delivery might not be as readily accomplished. Driving back from the site he asked Brother Tavioni to pull in at an abandoned complex of buildings. It looked derelict and half finished.

He asked, "What happened here?"

Brother Tavioni explained that it was the site of what was to be the Sheraton Hotel thought to have been funded by mafia money and then at 80% complete, the developer suddenly went bust and abandoned the project. All the skilled workers up and left, heading for jobs in New Zealand. However, if Pastor Joe wanted a closer look they need only sign up for a game of paintball with the operator who was running that business in the ruins. They could run around the complex checking it out.

"Pastor Joe, this is a cursed project," he intoned. "Nothing good would ever come from this site."

Was this going to be symptomatic of his attempts to get a branch established? Pondering his situation, he went to the government's administrative centre and to the attorney general's chambers.

Having introduced himself as a tourist he inquired whether the Cook Islands had an extradition treaty with New Zealand.

"Oh, yes," was the reply, "and you would be surprised how many scoundrels come up here that we have to send back to New Zealand."

He asked for more information about the Sheraton site and whether it could be purchased. Others had tried and the young assistant to the attorney general informed him that no-one local would be interested in buying it. A local family who were involved with a dispute over the ownership had cursed the site and it would definitely not be a good place for a church.

Well, that answered his questions and it seemed the long-term prospects of enjoying a good life in these particular islands would go no further. If he could get used to a slow pace of life and then the door was still somewhat open to use Brother Tavioni's land in the future.

His next stop was at a local bank to open an account, mentioning he might be transferring a large sum of money there as a temporary measure before sending it off to a yet unidentified country.

Away from New Zealand and enjoying a quiet evening Joe looked at his situation trying to work out where he stood. At the end of the day, he decided his position was sound but still shake-able. He thought through the current issues:

The police had no direct evidence of who the killer was and; therefore, no link to him.

Carl was in it deeper than he was as he had arranged the hitman so could this be exploited by cancelling the franchise payments?

He was not so sure about the money laundering. He could plead ignorant on the amount of the donations but could simply say he thought the security payments were reasonable.

Setting up in the Cook Islands at this time was problematic. Too much was on his plate and the fact that there was an extradition treaty in force was significant in his decision to postpone the new church for at least a year, telling Brother Tavioni that he needed to set aside this period to raise funds and gain further support for the project.

To get a better understanding and flavour of the local culture and its church going practice Joe and Brother Tavioni attended a traditional service at the CICC on the Sunday. Whilst not under-standing the sermon, Brother Tavioni was able to provide a quick summary as it was preached. The singing was enthusiastic but Joe could see young people playing on their phones and quite bored with the proceedings. Yes, there was definitely room for a shake up and for a new vibrant church to be planted.

Joe noticed nothing was open after church so he figured most of the 17,000 population were probably attendees at church. This had to be a good thing. His mind was made up and he would return home in much better spirits.

In the meantime, he tried to enjoy a few days' break, soaking up the sun, and watching the guests flirting with the beautiful young women who brought them drinks by the pool.

Conscious of his role as a pastor he did not want Brother Tavioni to see him in any bad light so was on his best behaviour.

The flight back was uneventful but as soon as the plane touched down at Mangere Joe began to feel stressed again. The memory of the last week faded all too quickly as he found himself back in reality.

The following Sunday Pastor Joe reported to the good folk at the Church of the Lord's Abundance. He preached a fiery message misquoting the prophet Isaiah and stating that their tent had to be extended and strengthened.

"My friends God spoke to me again through this word. Let us not have a small vision. Brother Tavioni and I have seen the promised land. The land is good and the people of Rarotonga need to see the Church of the Lord's Abundance planted there. Brother Tavioni has family land we could build on but there is even land with an abandoned hotel that I believe the Lord will give us. It is 80% finished and would make a superb base for our ministry to the whole island of Rarotonga. No-one wants it and, although it is a cursed property, I have no doubt I could lift the curse and speak blessing over it. God has anointed me for this task and it cannot fail. We will not be put to shame.

"As I hand out small flax bags to remind us of the plight of these poor islanders let us dig deep again for the sake of the gospel. I believe within a year and a day we will take the land. I see a thriving church. I speak it into being. Believe God for an abundance in the offering this morning. As the word says, 'Do not hold back.'"

As Walter and Joe counted up the offering, they were pleased to see many thousands given for this work. He would lay it on them for a month, promising that if the people would give generously then the work could readily be established once the money was in.

Joe was back to his positive self, forgetting the past for the moment as he counted the money. Surely as the Lord's anointed prophet he was untouchable.

CHAPTER 57

About six weeks after the murder Rosemary received a letter with a USB drive stuck to the page. It had been on quite a journey around the country as Moana had omitted to put the name of the town on the envelope and had only put Rosemary's street address.

It was a shock to read something from Moana after her death.

Dear Rosemary

You have been a good friend and one of the few people I can trust. I did not tell you of my gang connections and my seedy past but I want you to believe me in what I am about to say next.

I am sorry I lied to you about the sexual encounter I had with Pastor Joe. Please forgive me. I initiated it and did it as a favour for my brother, Zeke. I used to be a street worker so it was not difficult for me. Our purpose was to blackmail Pastor Joe. You will see that when you play the video it was a set up. I knew Joe could not keep his pants done up, so arranged to privately film our sexual encounter at the Mega Church Conference. It was easier than I thought. Talk about a lamb to the slaughter.

After the conference Zeke showed Pastor Joe the recording to get some money from him. I didn't trust Joe as he might know some bad people in the church who he could use to come after me and get the film. I recorded an additional copy and have sent it with this letter.

Zeke doesn't know anything about it.

Please don't think anything bad about me after watching this film.

I also ask, knowing you are trustworthy, not to watch it unless you hear of something bad happening to me. I am concerned and I think I may even leave Hamilton and go to the South Island and start a new life down there. I cried out to God the other night repenting of my sins and asked for his forgiveness. I asked him to be my Lord. It was amazing, I felt washed clean. It was not something I could have ever done in my own strength but God has done a great work in my life. I am determined to start attending a proper church. I feel sick as I consider Pastor Joe is a complete hypocrite and just scamming people for their money.

Much aroha
Moana

Rosemary was in shock and had to sit down. She started to shake and sob. This drew the attention of Lizzie who got up from her desk and came and put her arm around Rosemary and asked what was going on. She showed her the letter and Lizzie too reacted but in a more cold-hearted manner as she understood all too quickly that the evening before she had been inducted as a 'spirit bride' that the whoring pastor had been having sex with Moana.

They watched the recording together and both felt sick. It was just as Moana had said.

Lizzie reread the letter, dwelling on the last sentence. The light came on. Yes, Moana was not a fool. She had seen Joe for what he was.

Time to get even.

Rosemary asked, "What do we do? We have to take this to the police."

Lizzie replied, "Not yet. We have to think things through. It is clear now that Joe was being blackmailed but is this letter enough for the cops to arrest him for murder?"

"You're not saying …?"

"Yes, I am," said Lizzie emphatically.

"How else do you explain Moana's death and the death of her two brothers? Joe must have arranged the murders to get out of paying the money. He has the motive but we don't have the connection at this stage. Before we go to the police we need to set a trap."

"What sort of trap?" asked Rosemary.

"I don't know at this stage but it is important we don't let on to Joe that we have this recording. Let me make a copy for each of us that we can take home and keep safe."

"Okay, but are you sure we shouldn't go to the police?"

"We will, but not just yet. It is a good job Joe is not in today. We don't have much time to consider what to do next."

CHAPTER 58

A very angry Lizzie schemed and plotted, each time rejecting what she had planned. One idea was to simply play the tape at church on Sunday and watch what would happen. No doubt Joe would blame the devil and deny it was him, blaming someone with one of those 'mission impossible' masks who was masquerading as him just to discredit him. She was also not sure what, if anything, to say to Yvette.

She was not even sure if Joe had told her she was his special 'spirit bride'. Maybe she could use that angle.

She conferred with Rosemary and asked her about bugging the office. Lizzie was of course aware that Joe had found the last bug but Rosemary had not admitted planting it. As a technical expert she volunteered to Lizzie she would be happy to look for something with which to bug the office.

"I am not sure whether it is worthwhile bugging the office again as he found the last one and he has security people sweeping the office regularly. It might only last a week and would only increase his paranoia."

"So, you were the one who bugged the office the first time?"

"Yes, I was just being careful and I wanted to record any untoward sexual advances. Joe has wandering eyes."

"I have underestimated you Rosemary. That was a very smart move. Are we open to bugging his office again and even his home as well?"

"You would have to ask Yvette out to lunch while I go in," she volunteered.

"Can't do any harm," admitted Lizzie, "the more bugs, the better. Even one in his car."

"What we really need is good audio. There is no real need for video. The audio devices are quite small and easy to conceal but we will have to see how smart we can be and how good the security consultants are," Rosemary confirmed.

"I think we are wasting our time with the office," Lizzie acknowledged. "Joe will be very aware of that after finding the last bug."

"Yes, I suppose you're right. I don't really feel comfortable bugging his house or car either," said Rosemary.

After further discussions the plans were put on ice. They would have to think of something else.

What they were hoping to achieve was remote but Lizzie was gradually formulating another plan. She had a friend who worked as a pharmacist and would ask if she could get hold of some sodium thiopental for her. This was a so-called 'truth drug' but it had only sketchy reliability. Although it was originally developed as an anaesthetic, it was soon noticed that when the patient was in the twilight zone, halfway between consciousness and unconsciousness, they became chattier and uninhibited. After the drug wore off, the patient had usually forgotten what they had been talking about. It might just work if the circumstances were suitable. On the other hand, it could be just a big waste of time.

CHAPTER 59

Despite the lack of expectations because Joe would be super careful after the discovery of the first bug, the office was bugged again in what was hopefully a more secure location. Rosemary got anxious and pulled out of bugging the family home but was happy enough at Lizzie's request to bug her place for her. Lizzie had no access to Joe's car so no bug was placed there. But they did manage to put a magnetic GPS tracker under the car so they could at least watch his moves and see if anything came of that. They were certainly not confident but would wait a little before going to the police. The more evidence they could find and then present the better.

After Joe's return from Rarotonga and the successful offering, Lizzie seized her chance the next Monday.

"Joe, I missed you so much. This 'spirit bride' wants reminding of how fortunate she is to be in such a role. Have you some time for me?" She smiled sweetly although feeling a distinct knot starting to form in her stomach.

"Sure, babe, what do you have in mind?" he replied.

"I wondered if we could both knock off early and have a 'business meeting' at my house and perhaps you could bring me up to speed with the operation in Rarotonga."

"I'll even supply the drinks," said Lizzie hoping the hook was sufficiently baited.

Joe had no reason to be suspicious of Lizzie and was quite keen to knock off early and head to her place. Lizzie could readily see how easy it had been for Moana to set the trap and hoped this would be just the same.

Sure enough, after arriving at her flat Lizzie wasted no time drugging Joe's whisky. She had earlier arranged a supply of different drinks that she knew Joe favoured. Joe, of course, came on to Lizzie and, when his eyes started to look as though the drug was working, Lizzie put the brakes on and began to ask some questions, which she hoped Joe was amenable to answer.

"Joe, am I your favourite spirit bride?" she asked.

"Yes, of course you are," was the positive reply said without hesitation.

"How many other spirit brides do you have?"

"Only three."

"And have you slept with all of them?"

"Yes of course," answering in such a manner that he thought the question entirely stupid.

Joe was starting to feel drowsy but Lizzie pressed on.

"What are the names of your other spirit brides?"

"Naomi, Jilly and Stephanie," he replied with certainty.

Lizzie was starting to fume. Yes, they certainly were the best looking of the daughters of the prophet, but time now for serious questions.

"What is your computer password?"

"Money4me"

"Who killed Moana?"

"Don't know."

"Why was she killed?"

"She was blackmailing me."

"So, you arranged it?

"No. I liked Moana. I didn't do anything," and with that Joe promptly passed out.

Well, that didn't help in finding a link between Joe and Moana's death but at least she confirmed what she knew already and that Joe was a serial adulterer.

From what Lizzie and Rosemary had been able to research on

the internet it certainly seemed that none of what they had was reliable evidence and admissible in court. Time for other options.

As expected, Joe woke up with no memory of what had happened but after some positive promptings from Lizzie he returned home confident that he and Lizzie had had a mutually enjoyable time.

CHAPTER 60

Joe spent one day a week at home and often used that time away from the office to prepare his Sunday messages and the mid-week YouTube video. Sometimes he would pop down to the yard and have lunch with Yvette.

It was on one scheduled day off that Lizzie went down town after having had a good look through Joe's computer. She'd found nothing that would be good evidence. No private notes or diary that would sink him. 'The Lord's Anointed' indeed did seem untouchable.

In her hand she held an authority to pick up and peruse the church legal files at Postow, Mitchell, Crews and Cheeseman-Skinner. She explained to the receptionist the church was very pleased with the work the firm had done to date and reassuringly said she was just here as the church CEO (that was what the particular business card she held said she was) to get up to date on the various legal matters.

Not being a lawyer and seeing no issue with the written authority, the firm was not concerned and sat her down in a conference room with the various files. She didn't read everything but did read and take copies on her phone of all the advice from the firm about the franchising arrangement believing this to be important in the general scheme of things. She also took a copy of the amended franchise agreement that was on file and had been signed around about the time of Moana's death. She didn't link anything of significance to this. Other documents were copied, including Charity

Commission filings and the like. She didn't see any accounts as Joe probably had no reason to send them through to his lawyer. Again, in Lizzie's mind, it seemed to be a dead end.

CHAPTER 61

In a lucky break, the police intercepted a large drug importation operation and one of the men caught up in the sweep was one 'Mr Jones' who turned out to be William Stephenson. The police now had a significant party in their custody who was facing long jail time for importation of class A drugs. Unbeknown to Mr Stephenson, he had been observed at the Crossroads Café talking to one Pastor Joseph Smith.

Stephenson didn't want money laundering added to his rap sheet so made up the usual lies.

"I met the good pastor at church. This was just a follow-up meeting at his suggestion so we could get to know each other and talk about God."

The detective could barely stop himself laughing and of course immediately knew there was something fishy going on between Stephenson and the church.

Stephenson was not confident that the security consultation fee for services provided by his underlings would pass the 'sniff' test so after further questioning and cajoling he agreed to assist the police. After handing over his passport, and knowing he would be under constant surveillance as a police informer, he was set free, with the task of nailing pastor Joseph Smith.

The next day he wasted no time and arranged another meeting with Pastor Joe back at Crossroads Café.

"Pastor Smith, I have to tell you that I am being squeezed a bit more from my bosses and can no longer give more to the church. I have been offered a better return on my money. You will agree that at the moment I am depositing $4000 per week in the church coffers, providing security for you and then you are giving me $3500 per week back?"

"Yes, yes, so what's your point?" asked Joe not wanting to spend any more time than he needed with Zeke's replacement who was not nearly as friendly as Zeke had been.

"Well, the situation is this: we drop the security as my boys are kept busy on other duties. Instead we continue to drop $4000 per week into the offering plate but then you give back to me $3950, you pocket the $50 per week and no security is needed."

"Not a chance," said Joe.

"Why would I do that? I need those security services. I am not going back to what your predecessor wanted. You are just too greedy and besides you've got nothing on me. The money stays the same or you get none of your $4000 back. You choose."

Joe added for emphasis, "Don't mess with me all right? Look what happened to your predecessor when he tried to screw me over."

"You threatening me?" said Stephenson, leaning over into Joe's face, and grabbing Joe's shirt at the neck. "If you are, then I suggest you watch your back."

"Look" Joe replied, "Let's not get unpleasant here. We each have friends, okay? We can continue to do business on the same terms or you call it quits and look for some other way to launder your funds?"

There it was, in black and white and not even prompted. Evidentiary gold unless one could successfully argue entrapment.

Stephenson replied, "Look mate, it was good while the ride lasted but unless you agree to the changed terms the deal is off completely and no more cash is coming your way."

"Suit yourself," said Joe, "plenty of other ways I can get money."

The meeting concluded and both parties exited the café and back to work.

Stephenson met with his handler who was immediately distraught when he realised the wire had not worked, whether through battery failure or some other cause was not sure. The bird had slipped the net. Stephenson had honestly reported the conversation but there was no way this guy could ever be used as a credible witness. He just said whatever he was told to say just to get a reduced sentence for his own crimes. There had to be another way to get the pastor.

Fortunately, a further piece of the puzzle turned up when Rosemary Plimmer and Lizzie Harris, having run out of ideas, turned up at the police station for a meeting with Detective Robert Hayden.

"We received a letter with a USB drive just a little while ago from Moana. It had been poorly addressed so we only just got it. We want you to see it," said Rosemary.

They watched as Detective Hayden read the letter and then played through the recording.

"Yes, there is clear evidence of motive, for the murder of Zeke and Moana. Carlos was probably just in the wrong place at the wrong time. However, in our view we have no evidence at all linking Pastor Smith with these murders. We need more than motive."

Much as she felt sick about Pastor Joe being involved in her friend's death Rosemary remembered the bit of the conversation she had recorded.

"What about the bit where he says to Carl in Memphis, 'I've got just as much on you as you have on me, or something similar'?"

"It's good but the crown prosecutor will want more," the detective responded with a grim look on his face.

"I might be able to help," said Lizzie. "I went to the church's law firm in town and got a copy of the amended franchise agreement for the church."

"Sorry? Before you talk about an amended franchise agreement, tell me about the original? What exactly is the church doing in a franchise? I've never heard of it before. And, besides, what has a franchise agreement got to do with three murders?"

"Well, Joe was not always forthcoming about his relationship with Carl Adams in Memphis. I always thought there was a connection of mentor/mentee and Carl sends regular sermons and talks about leveraging money out of the congregation in new and dynamic ways. I didn't know the extent of it until I saw the franchise agreement at the office of the lawyer. I read it and saw that the Church of the Lord's Abundance pays Carl Adams (or an entity associated with him) a monthly percentage of the offerings taken."

Stunned by this unusual revelation Detective Hayden, said, "You mean the church is nothing but a franchising scam?"

Lizzie interjected, "I hadn't thought about it like that before, but now that you put it like that, then yes, it sounds like it to me."

"Me too," said Rosemary.

"I had been considering giving my notice in for a while now but have been too fearful. The money has been good and I might not find a job in the same field. I liked my work, except for Joe's attempts to get me into bed."

"I understand," replied the detective trying to sound as empathetic as he could but still gobsmacked at the whole scam.

Wanting more, he followed on, "So, what was the amended franchise agreement?"

"About the time of Moana's murder there is a new amendment to the franchise agreement and the fees suddenly increased."

"Interesting. Was there any noticeable increase in services rendered for the increase?"

"No, I don't think so," said Lizzie,"

As a smart woman Rosemary connected the dots, "You don't think Pastor Joe arranged the murders to escape the blackmail and Carl paid a guy and now he wants pay back by amending the franchise agreement?"

"Exactly."

"Oh dear, what happens next?" Rosemary inquired.

"Detective Douglas and I will put a brief together, take it upstairs and they will then refer it to Crown Law to see if we have enough for an arrest warrant for a charge of conspiracy to commit murder.

We believe we have evidence of money laundering but murder is the one we are after. Can you women still work after what we have discussed? We don't want the 'prophet' being aware of what we know. We may now be in a better position to get a legal bug on his phone and at his home. Are you two happy to keep all this tight and head back to work tomorrow as if you know nothing?"

"Yeah, we will be okay," replied Lizzie resolutely, adding as a departing comment, "Just nail the murderous bastard."

Lizzie and Rosemary returned to work but it was obvious to many that their hearts were not in it. Anxious not to spill the beans, they avoided confrontation and basically became clock watchers waiting to see what would happen.

A week went by. Joe was suspicious. He had not seen Lizzie like this so inquired, "Lizzie, what's the matter? You've lost your spark."

"No, I'm fine, just feeling a bit run down. Maybe a bit of flu or a cold coming on," she lied.

"Well, take a day or two off if you need to. It's not a good look to have people moping about a church like ours that sells visitors a positive outlook," Joe responded.

He then added, "Do you want me to speak and declare health, prosperity and freedom over your life?"

"Why not?" responded Lizzie, not for a moment thinking it would make the slightest bit of difference. He should be speaking freedom over his own life before the axe fell.

Lizzie smiled, pleased she was able to get away from the office for a few days.

CHAPTER 62

Funds were reduced with the money laundering having come to an end. This provided Joe with the opportunity he had been putting off. He had decided enough was enough and, as he had the goods on Carl, he would stop paying the franchise fee, which was due that week, for a three-month period. It would have been the first with the increased payment.

He instructed Walter not to pay it and any emails or phone calls on the subject were to go straight to him. Lizzie, when she returned from her sick leave, was given the same instruction.

As circumstances would have it, Pastor Carl had a fairly large payment due on the Gulfstream as he hadn't been able to raise the full amount needed for it. He was also due to pay a large bill to his workers for the swimming pool at his Florida beach house. He was relying on the cream from Hamilton New Zealand to keep everyone happy. A few days later he was on the phone.

"Joe, It's me, Carl. What's going on? Didn't see any payment come through. Any problems?"

"No," said Joe. "No problems, must be a bank issue your side as money was wired two days ago." Joe wasn't looking for an argument so he thought he could gain a couple of days.

Of course, this was futile because two days later Carl phoned again.

"Joe, still no money. Tell me straight."

"Well, the offerings have taken a dive lately and to be frank we can't afford to pay you."

"What? We have an iron clad deal. You can't just bail and say you 'ain't gonna pay'. It don't work like that, man."

"I'm sorry Carl, but the fees are too high and unless we can negotiate them down considerably we are paying nothing more. It's a rip-off. Your church can afford it. Where's the love?"

This was the wrong thing to say as Carl went ballistic.

"You bastard. I want my money and I want it now. I did you a big favour sending a friend over to sort out your issues and this is how you repay me? You owe me more than just a franchise fee buddy. I saved your bacon."

"I don't know what you're talking about," replied Joe and, not wanting to wait around, for the first time he hung up on the great man.

This didn't go down well with Carl who phoned straight back but, at Joe's chickenhearted request, Lizzie was instructed that he had left the building and could take no more calls.

Carl demanded of her, "You tell that cheat of a pastor you work for that he has 24 hours to get the payment to me or there will be trouble."

Knowing the police phone tap was probably now in place Lizzie bravely continued,

"What sort of trouble shall I tell him is coming? Will the church be sued?"

"Sued. He would be so lucky. Tell him I'll have my same friend who he knows about on the next flight to come and speak to him personally and that's not something he or his pretty young wife may want. You got me, sugar? You tell him straight, ya hear?"

"Yes sir, I'll see he gets the message as soon as he is back in the office."

She passed the message on to Joe.

As he understood the picture, he had a number of options that he could act on:

1. Immediately grab some cash and leave town in a hurry and

hide out in some country that had no extradition treaty.
Perhaps Brazil? He would love to get lost in the vast Pantanal
region.
2. Hand himself in to the police and tell them the whole sordid
    story making sure to spin it so he could escape the conspiracy
    to murder charges.
3. Eat humble pie and Pay Carl.

Reluctantly, he understood his plan to quit the franchise had
failed and logically he had no option other than to pay Carl. He
was an idiot. He had acted impulsively and he should have thought
things through more thoroughly. He was clearly under stress and
not thinking. Carl's threat came as a shock. He transferred the
money that afternoon.

At the same time, he wondered about making an anonymous
tip-off to the police about the murder investigation so they would
set their sights on Carl Adams. However, after thinking about it, he
couldn't because of the implications for himself. Was he just pan-
icking or were the police on to him? He felt like a cornered rat and
something had to be done quickly.

He concluded then that he was at the point he needed to plan a
getaway to a non-extradition country. He would just go and, when
he had established himself in a few weeks' time with an apartment.
he would ask Yvette to join him. As he considered she was not
aware of even the half of his problems he'd better not spill the beans
at this stage. Again, he decided to act impulsively and quickly.

The following day he had a local travel agent book him a return
flight to Brazil with an open-ended return. He opened an account
with an international bank that he was aware was operating in Rio
de Janeiro. He explained to Walter that he needed some funds
urgently and, after giving Walter a bonus and, in a moment of
weakness, leaving sufficient funds to cover two weeks wages plus
holiday pay for the staff, he not only took the balance of the cheque
account, but also the building funds for Hamilton and Rarotonga.

With the money safely in the new bank account he was free to go.

The next day, after making sure Yvette had gone to her car yard, he drove up to Auckland, dropped his beloved Porsche 911 that he had only owned for six months off at Turner's Auctions Manukau. He gave them his bank account details and instructed them it would gain more money if he sold it with a $1 reserve auction. He then called a taxi and headed to the airport.

The flight was an Air Aerolineas Argentinas direct to Buenos Aires and then from there to Rio de Janeiro. It was due to leave Auckland at 10:50 pm so he had a few hours to kill. He ate a good meal, watched some rugby in a bar and then decided to head through departure and customs to start his new life.

At emigration he scanned his passport but the machine malfunctioned and a message came up that he should see an officer. An efficient young woman approached and he explained his predicament that the machine didn't seem to like his passport.

"Just a small problem, sir," she smiled. "Come with me to the office and we will straighten things out."

They walked about 40 metres to a plain looking standard government office and Joe was invited to take a seat. He was no sooner seated than there was a knock on the door and Detectives Hayden and Douglas walked in. It was all over.

Detective Hayden read Joe his rights. "I am arresting you on suspicion of money laundering, running a pyramid scheme, conspiracy to commit murder and murder. You do not have to say anything, but it may harm your defence if you do not mention when questioned something you later rely on in court. Anything you do say may be given in evidence."

Joe replied, "I think I will say nothing. I will discuss this with my lawyer as soon as I have opportunity to do so."

At least he was spared the ignominy of handcuffs as he was led through the back of the airport and out to a waiting police car. He was taken to Auckland Central where he spent the night in the cells before being formally charged and brought before the Auckland Court the next day. He would then be transferred to the Hamilton Court for the trial that would take place at a later time.

CHAPTER 63

Rosemary and Lizzie found out the next business day, when the police arrived with search warrants, that all had fallen apart at the Church of the Lord's Abundance.

At least Walter had had the decency to pay the staff their wages and holiday pay. His arrest for theft as a servant would follow later.

Rosemary and Lizzie remained friends and, at Rosemary's request both decided to attend a 'real' church, choosing the Bible-believing, Bible-teaching church of Mercy Fellowship where they were warmly welcomed by Pastor Gene Jacobson.

Rosemary remarked after the conclusion of their first service there together, "Isn't it good to be in a place where there is sound teaching, no constant demands for money, no fake miracles, no people laughing insanely, no-one rolling around the floor, no abuse and no hype or manipulation? I feel so free."

"I agree," said Lizzie, satisfied she had left the circus behind. For the first time in her life, she set foot in a church with genuine God-fearing people. They were happy to encourage her in her steps to finding out who the real Jesus Christ is and not the fake one she had imbibed at that 'other' church.

"I didn't hear a single 'God told me, God showed me in a dream, I am the anointed prophet, blah, blah, blah'," she said laughing.

"It was so good to hear a clear gospel message that we are all sinners, that we cannot save ourselves whether by good deeds, infant baptism or some other method. I really appreciate that I can come into God's family and have my sins forgiven. Not through anything

I do but by accepting that Jesus has paid the price for my sins by his death on the cross and resurrection from the dead."

Attending church became a real blessing to both women and they soon felt the Church of the Lord's Abundance was just a bad dream.

Unfortunately, it all came back when nine months later they gave evidence at Joe's trial. This was a huge newspaper and television spectacle the likes of which Hamilton had never seen before. It was on everyone's mind and was the only discussion in lunch rooms and offices throughout Hamilton.

The trial took three weeks and, despite Joe having the best criminal trial lawyer in town, it was impossible for the jury of twelve ordinary men and women not to sock it back to the greedy pastor and find him guilty on all charges.

As expected Joe was then remanded in custody for a pre-sentencing report and was to appear again in six weeks.

CHAPTER 64

The Hamilton underworld wasted no time. Joe had barely been in remand for twenty four hours before he suffered an 'accident'. A gang prospect, also on remand for sentencing, had been tipped off a week or so earlier that an important prisoner was likely to be arriving. The prisoners were in the exercise yard when Joe was randomly approached by a young man and before he knew it, a sharpened and lethal plastic knife manufactured from a toothbrush was thrust into him.

Fortunately for Joe the ignorant prospect did not know what side of the body the heart was on so Joe got lucky. He was also lucky in that a prison guard quickly got to him and administered first aid.

Joe spent a week in hospital under guard and sentencing was adjourned for a further six weeks to give him more time to recover.

Now twelve weeks after the jury had brought down its unanimous verdict Yvette sat at the rear of the High Court in Hamilton having watched the sentencing that had just concluded. She looked at her husband of just a few years as he was escorted by two burly prison guards through the door that led to the cells. He was no longer a free man and would serve many years behind bars before he would be eligible for parole.

Joseph Smith was a dejected and broken man. The Lord's 'anointed prophet' had been taken down. The rise to riches, the lust for women and power had been meteoric and now the fall was equally as quick and devastating for Joe as he contemplated the bleak and hopeless future that lay before him. He had lost weight from his time in hospital and prison and his handsome erect bearing was missing as he stood stooped in the dock. He had recovered from his stabbing. The only thing he had to look forward to might be a trip to Memphis to give evidence in a case against Carl Quincy Adams but knowing the tightness of the prison system he might have to do it via video link, so even that opportunity was a pipe dream. He would be a lonely man as he was positive the only way to survive in prison was to be in isolation. He was sure the Haunui whanau was large and he was not beyond the reach of any of them who wanted their 'utu'.

If he had looked back at just the right time as he was led out through the side of the courtroom to the cells, he might have noticed a smile, even a smirk, that crossed the face of his young and beautiful wife. Her plan had succeeded beyond expectations. Trap and marry an ambitious entrepreneur and make sure she manipulated and encouraged actions that would benefit her financial future.

Having been raised in a middle class family but having to wear her sisters' hand-me-down clothes and having been deprived of the overseas holidays that their neighbours had enjoyed, Yvette had always wanted more. She had one strong attribute if nothing else on her side. She was a meticulous planner, happy to patiently wait out her scheme, which had now come to fruition today in the courtroom. Initially, she had not expected the 'church' scam but, once it started, she could see how quickly money could be made. She was always aware that the whole thing would implode at some future point. She had just not expected the implosion to be so quick.

This happened at a pace greater than she had anticipated and now her wealth was beyond the grasp of any creditors or the government. Through a careful and well thought through relationship property agreement, which Joe had willingly signed, Yvette had come to the position she was now in. Initially thinking she was mad to let him have the church assets and income stream while she only received two car yards with their long-term lease liability and a nearly unencumbered house in the best part of town, what would Joe be thinking now.

It was a rag to riches story but, as she reflected, Yvette acknowledged there had been a cost. She, of course, had been aware of her husband's moral failures, aware he had a weakness for a 'skirt' and aware that being in a business relationship with Carl Adams would only lead to disaster. She had loved Joe on one level but he was just a cog in a bigger wheel and it was his own fault that he had fallen so quickly. Yes, she had been shocked by the revelation of Moana's video, but in retrospect this was not unexpected, as she considered that everyone had their own agenda to get ahead and make money. She neither judged Moana nor the other women Joe had fallen for.

Yvette sat in court a little longer wondering what was next. She would, of course, file for a dissolution of marriage after two years living apart.

Yvette marvelled at how easy it had been for Joe to make money out of such a gullible group of people. She didn't feel any emotion of pity towards those people who had attended church regularly and given so sacrificially. She chose to believe they had also been led astray through their own greed for a quick fix of prosperity and health. In a way she felt they were not victims. They were culprits and guilty because what they wanted was exactly what Joe had wanted and it was not God.

The world was not a kind place and she had to find her own way in it. As Joe would surely say, "God helps those who help themselves."

She did wonder whether if there were a God, would he find her just as guilty as Joe? No, she had not murdered anyone. She was innocent in her eyes.

As she stood to leave the courtroom, she thought about whether she would immediately search for another target. In the meantime, though she had to put on the face of the poor and innocent wife of a philandering mega church pastor as she left to face a barrage of television and news reporters. She exited the building and observed the young land agent who for some reason had taken time off to attend the sentencing. During the sentencing he had stared at her and she had coyly turned her eyes away but it seemed every time she had looked up 'puppy dog' eyes were looking at her.

She recognised potential when she saw it.

She thought of her tattoo. 'Seize the day.'

AUTHOR'S NOTE

Before I get flooded with emails, for the sake of the story, I have ignored the covid travel ban.

I have also ignored the fact that shops for many years have not given children money back on empty bottles.

The prosperity churches are large and take in millions of dollars. Like Pastor Joe their leaders teach a false gospel.

Of course, there is other fiction for the sake of a good story but some of the antics of Pastor Joe may have been experienced by many readers.

I was one of them.

OTHER BOOKS

A Dangerous Legacy: Search for the wakazashi (2014)
ISBN 978-0-473-27886-1 (epub)
ISBN 978-0-473-27887-8 (kindle)

Greed (2019)
ISBN 978-0-473-46692-3 (softcover)
ISBN 978-0-473-46693-0 (epub)
ISBN 978-0-473-46694-7 (kindle)

The author can be contacted at neilevansauthor@gmail.com